THE QUEEN OF THE NIGHT

THE QUEEN OF THE NIGHT

Paul Doherty

headline

First published in 2006 by
HEADLINE BOOK PUBLISHING

1

Cataloguing in Publication Data is available from the British Library

ISBN 10 (hardback) 0 7553 2879 5
ISBN 13 (hardback) 978 0 7553 2879 6
ISBN 10 (trade paperback) 0 7553 2880 9
ISBN 13 (trade paperback) 978 0 7553 2880 2

Typeset in Trump Mediaeval by Palimpsest Book Production Limited,
Grangemouth, Stirlingshire

Printed and bound in Great Britain by
Clays Ltd, St Ives Plc

Headline's policy is to use papers that are natural, renewable and
recyclable products and made from wood grown in sustainable forests.
The logging and manufacturing processes are expected to conform
to the environmental regulations of the country of origin.

HEADLINE BOOK PUBLISHING
A division of Hodder Headline
338 Euston Road
London NW1 3BH

www.headline.co.uk
www.hodderheadline.com

This book is dedicated to
Sarah, Sean and Tom Christie

PRINCIPAL CHARACTERS

THE EMPERORS

Diocletian	the old Emperor
Maxentius	formerly Emperor of the West, defeated and killed by Constantine at the Milvian Bridge
Constantine	new Emperor of the West
Helena	Constantine's mother, Empress and Augusta
Licinius	Emperor in the East

IMPERIAL OFFICIALS

Anastasius	Christian priest and scribe, secretary to Helena
Burrus	German mercenary, Captain of Helena's bodyguard
Chrysis	chamberlain
Ophelion	imperial spy
Cassius Chaerea	imperial spy

THE TEMPLE OF HATHOR

Sesothenes	high priest

VILLA CARINA

Carinus	senator and merchant
Antonia	his daughter
Theodore	an actor

VILLA AURELIAN

General Aurelian	
Urbana	Aurelian's second wife
Cassia	former courtesan, close friend of Urbana
Alexander	Aurelian's only son by his first wife
Casca	a physician
Leartus	a eunuch

THE FRETENSES ('THE WILD BOARS')

Postulus	centurion
Stathylus	decurion
Crispus \	
Secundus |	
Petilius /	cavalrymen
Lucius /	

THE CHRISTIAN CHURCH

Militiades	Pope, Bishop of Rome
Sylvester	Militiades' assistant, principal priest in the Christian community in Rome

AT THE SHE ASSES

Polybius	the owner
Poppaoe	his common-law wife
Oceanus	former gladiator
Januaria	serving maid
Claudia	Polybius' niece
Murranus	a gladiator
Simon	the Stoic
Petronius	the Pimp
Sallust	the Searcher
Sorry	tavern boy
Caligua	tavern cat
Apuleius	the Apothecary
Callista	his wife
Venutus	the Vine-dresser
Torquatus	the Tonsor
Narcissus the Neat	former embalmer
Mercury the Messenger	tavern herald

Introduction

During the trial of Christ, Pilate, according to the gospels, wanted to free the prisoner. He was stopped by a cry that if he did so he would be no friend of Caesar's. According to commentators, Pilate recognised the threat. Every Roman governor and official was closely scrutinised by secret agents of the Emperor, 'the Agentes in Rebus', literally 'the Doers of Things'! The Roman Empire had a police force, both military and civil, though these differed from region to region, but it would be inaccurate to claim the Empire had anything akin to detectives or our own CID. Instead, the Emperor and his leading politicians paid vast sums to informers and spies. These were often difficult to control; as Walsingham, Elizabeth I's master spy, once wryly remarked, 'He wasn't too sure who his own men were working for, himself or the opposition.'

The Agentes in Rebus were a class apart amongst this horde of gossip-collectors, tale-bearers and, sometimes, very dangerous informers. The emperors used them, and their testimony could mean the end of a promising career. This certainly applied to the bloody and byzantine period at the beginning of the fourth century AD.

The Emperor Diocletian had divided the Empire into East and West. Each division had its own emperor, and a lieutenant, who took the title of Caesar. The Empire was facing economic problems and barbarian incursions. Its state religion was threatened by the thriving Christian Church, which was making its presence felt in all provinces at every level of society.

In AD 312 a young general, Constantine, supported by his mother Helena, a British-born woman who was already flirting with the Christian Church, decided to make his bid for the Empire of the West. He marched down Italy and met his rival Maxentius at the Milvian Bridge. According to Eusebius, Constantine's biographer, the would-be Emperor saw a vision of the cross underneath the words *'In hoc signo vinces'* ('In this sign you will conquer'). Constantine, the story goes, told his troops to adopt the Christian symbol and won an outstanding victory. He defeated and killed Maxentius and marched into Rome. Constantine was now Emperor of the West, his only rival Licinius, who ruled the eastern empire. Constantine, heavily influenced by his mother, grasped the reins of government and began to negotiate with the Christian Church to end centuries of persecution. Nevertheless, intrigue and murder still held sway. There was unfinished business in Rome and the Agentes in Rebus had their hands full . . . Helena favoured the Christian Church but soon realised that intrigue, robbery and murder were no respectors of emperor or priest.

Prologue

Northern Britain: AD *296*

Iacta alea est.
The die is cast.
  Suetonius, *Lives of the Caesars*

The tribesmen, the Picti, slipped through the summer darkness to gather in the pitch-black copse of trees. They had already visited the sacred stones on the summit of the Hill of Sacrifice a few miles further north, where their priest had made the blood offering, the heart of the Roman scout caught earlier in the day. They had watched the man, eyes drugged, face slack, being stripped, bound and laid on the altar stone. The high priest's obsidian knife had flashed in the setting sun and fell just as their chanting reached its climax. Afterwards the chieftain had massed the entire war band and they had swarmed here to recover what was theirs – or rather his – by right: the Golden Maid, taken by the Men of Iron, the Crested Ones, who hid behind their wall of stone. The chieftain, so determined on vengeance, had even brought his only son, a mere boy, the sacred insignia etched on his thigh, to his first blooding. The boy was now a member of the war band, hair plaited, face and body daubed in war paint.

The Picti stared out at the brooding, crenellated wall of the fortress, the house of the Crested Ones, the Romani, with their body armour and eagle standards. The war band had attacked two days previously, bringing up specially prepared ladders, but had been beaten back, so they'd watched and waited. The chieftain had begun to wonder about the stories that had come whispering like the wind across the heather. How the Crested Ones were fighting amongst themselves, weakening their defences along the Great Wall, an abrupt change from a month ago when the Romani had launched their own raid and captured the Golden Maid. Since then, nothing but silence except for that solitary scout. The Picti had tortured him and forced the sacred drink down his throat, and the scout had confessed how his companions in the mile fort were few, divided and unsupported. They were weak, ripe for the scything.

The tribesmen now squatted, all eyes on their chieftain. He sat a little forward of them in the fringe of trees as if studying every step of the open heather stretching between the copse and the Great Wall. The chieftain was feathered and painted for war. Full of fury against an enemy who'd taken what was his, he sat sniffing the air like a wolf, then raised a hand. The war band stiffened; their leader had decided to attack, brave the open ground, defying the possibility that the Crested Ones might dispatch a charging line of cavalry through the great double gates of their fort. The Picti feared this above all, being caught out in the open by the fiercesome Catephracti Cavalry, armoured men on fast-moving horses, wheeling and turning, spears jabbing in a hail of iron, swords cutting like sickles at harvest time.

The moon slipped between the clouds. The night air was still. An owl hooted. The faint sound of other animals and birds echoed. The chieftain edged forward. He paused for a few heartbeats, rose to a crouch and charged silently into the night, his war band surging behind him. They streamed across the moorland, dark, sinister figures armed with club, axe, stabbing dirk and shield. The wall reared above them, silent and forbidding. The double gates of the mile fort were closed fast. The Picti glimpsed the glow of an oil lamp through a window, and the flicker of orange flame from the beacon on top of the tower licked the night sky, yet no horn or trumpet blew the alarm. Makeshift ladders, poles with pegs along each side, were placed hurriedly against the stone. The Picti clambered up, jumping through the crenellations on to the desolate fighting platform at the top. The beacon fire glowed hot in its iron brazier but there were no guards, no Romani. The Picti pulled back the heavy wooden trapdoor and poured down the steps into the narrow rooms below: empty, nothing but sconce torches glowing.

The chieftain raced through a recess into the room beyond, his comrades clustering behind. A solitary Roman struggled to his feet from a cot bed. He was unarmed, heavy-eyed with sleep. He was reaching for the tamarisk twig broom, the only weapon at hand, but war club and axe fell, smashing his skull, splashing the walls with his brains and blood. The Roman, dressed only in his tunic, slumped to the ground, drenched in gore, eyes dulling, as the Picti swept through the rest of the fort chambers. A shout of victory brought the chieftain to the steps leading down into a cellar; his followers had found the pay chest, a small coffer full of silver. He gestured at them to reseal it; it was a great find, but the chieftain ground his teeth in anger for the Golden Maid was not here! He stood in the square courtyard, heart thumping, blood seething. He had a choice. He could retreat through the narrow alleyway, force the wooden gates at the far end and escape back on to the moorland, or he could breach the south-facing gates leading out beyond the wall and sweep down to plunder and pillage the isolated settlements and villas beyond.

The chieftain glared up at the sky. He was a fearsome, war-like figure, his thick hair and beard caked with the blood of his enemies, his swarthy skin festooned with sacred war paint, magical roundels etched all over his body. He ran a finger around the rim of his war belt, then stared down at his feet and rejoiced at how they were smeared with the blood of his enemy. He gripped his long shield and, with the other hand, raised his axe club, howling like a wolf. His war band responded. They had found jars of posca, the coarse legionary wine, and were eagerly ladling it into their mouths, making themselves ripe for more mischief. True, they had not discovered the Golden Maid, but they had taken a mile fort, a fortress along the hated wall. No sooner had he given his war cry than the chieftain began to regret his impetuousness. His flesh tingled as the sweat cooled, the fury ebbed and his mind grew clearer, sharper, more cunning. He pushed back his lime-stained hair and stared at the double wooden gates facing south. Should he open them or retreat back to his settlement, to the women with their weaving and the minstrels with their silver-noted harps? There'd be feasting and dancing; perhaps he'd done enough to boast about before the camp fires? All around him milled his men. One, already drunk from the posca, had fixed the severed head of the Roman on the end of a pole, the jagged neck still wet with blood, the eyes half closed, the mouth red and gaping. Another had castrated the man, displaying the severed testicles on the point of a spear.

The chieftain remained still. He was confused. He'd expected to find the Golden Maid but there was nothing except that solitary Roman. Was he an officer? A sick soldier left by his comrades? Had the Romani left because of their own dissensions? But why were the torches, oil lamps and beacon glowing? He hesitated too long; his warriors were already moving, swinging open the gates facing south. Like a turbulent river eager to break free from an obstacle, the Picti streamed across the heathland south of the wall. The chieftain, beckoning his son to join him, had no choice but to follow. The cold night air swirled around them, chilling their sweat. They could already glimpse pinpricks of light beckoning them on to villas and farmsteads where they might find women, plunder, horses and other riches.

The war party fanned out across gorse, the long grass bending under the strong night breeze. The moon had broken free of the clouds; the sky was star-lit and clear. They hurried forward like a wolf pack eager for the kill. Their chieftain was moving to the front when he heard the clink of chain, the creak of harness, the neigh of a horse. He froze stock-still like a hunting dog, eyes peering through the darkness. Shapes were approaching, horsemen spreading out into an arc; a number carried flaring torches. The chieftain narrowed his eyes, wiping away the lime-mingled sweat. He tried to count. Eight, maybe nine horsemen, perhaps even more, were moving slowly towards his war party of about thirty men.

The Picti was a veteran. He might outnumber the enemy, but these were Catephracti, mailed, mounted troopers, highly disciplined and dangerous on such terrain. He screamed a warning, pointing back to the gates, and broke into a run, gesturing at his men to follow. Those quick-witted amongst his warriors had already sensed or seen the danger. Others were too drunk or confused. They only realised the ambush they had walked into when the formidable line of horsemen moved into a trot, then a full charge, the air riven by a hideous rumble of hoofs, the sounds of the night drowned by the clatter of weapons and the heart-chilling war cry of the Roman cavalry. The horsemen swept in, cloaks billowing, swords rising and falling. The tribesmen scattered. Out in the open they were doomed. If they fled towards the wall the riders would pin them against it and cut them down. They had to break free of the wall, retreat into their own territory.

The chieftain raced back to the fort, in through the yawning gate, down the hard-paved gully to the north-facing gate, but when he and his companions reached it, they found it fastened shut, the bar nailed down. Outside echoed the screams of their dying comrades. The riders had fired the heathland by emptying small sacks of oil and throwing in torches to start a blaze. The flames roared up, illuminating the night. The Picti had little defence against such armoured men on their heavy mounts who now loosed powerful shafts from their reinforced Scythian bows. The chieftain turned away from the north gate, desperately searching for his son. He looked towards the ladder leading to the roof, but the Crested Ones were too swift. Some were already dismounting and crowding in through the other gate, bows at the ready. A few of his men tried to reach the ladder, only to be brought down by the long feathered shafts. The chieftain raised his shield and gripped his war club tighter. He recognised that his life-web had been spun to its full. The gods were ready to cut the thread. The Catephracti, hideous figures, faces almost hidden behind their mail coifs, were already pressing forward, bows pulled back. The chieftain smiled. He'd take the swan-path of glory. At least he'd possessed, if only for a short while, the Golden Maid . . .

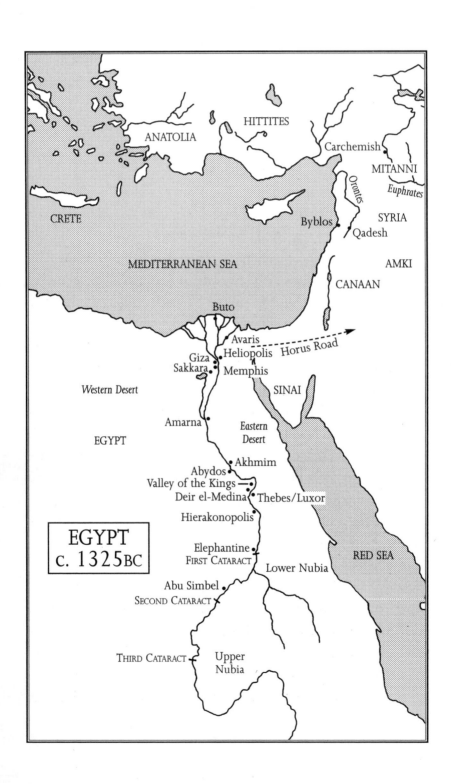

CRETE

ANATOLIA

HITTITES

Carchemish

MITANNI

Euphrates

Orontes

SYRIA

Byblos

Qadesh

AMKI

MEDITERRANEAN SEA

CANAAN

Buto

Avaris

Horus Road

Heliopolis

Giza

Sakkara

Memphis

Western Desert

SINAI

Amarna

Eastern
Desert

EGYPT

Akhmim

Abydos

Valley of the Kings

Deir el-Medina

Thebes/Luxor

Hierakonopolis

Elephantine

FIRST CATARACT

Lower Nubia

RED SEA

EGYPT
c. 1325 BC

Abu Simbel

SECOND CATARACT

THIRD CATARACT

Upper
Nubia

Chapter 1

Rome: August 314

Justitia est constans et perpetua voluntas ius suum cuique tribunes.
Justice is the constant and perpetual wish to give everyone their due.

Justinian, Institutes

Most people agreed that the Villa Carina, nestling in the Alban Hills above Rome, was a veritable paradise. 'Most handsome' was the worst sneering jealous critics might descend to, although that made little difference to Senator Valerius Carinus, descendant of a former emperor. Valerius Carinus had amassed a fortune as the owner of an extensive range of quarries throughout Italy. If the Severan Walls of the city needed new stone, the Temple of Serapis fresh glazed tiles, or the Portico of Octavian to be refurbished,

Valerius Carinus was your man. His motto was *Salve Lucrum* – 'Hail Profit' – and he stayed true to this. His critics claimed he washed his hands with wine, bathed in milk and would only allow the rarest silk to rest against his skin. Most of the criticisms were untrue. Carinus owned the most fruitful vineyards in Campania and hired the best chefs, yet he was on most occasions frugal in his eating, breaking his fast every morning only on bread and boiled Attic honey as recommended by the great physician Galen. However, when it came to others, he was always generous, especially to his beloved only daughter Antonia, whose coming of age was being celebrated with the most magnificent party in the sumptuous gardens of the villa. The house itself was grand enough. Many of its chambers were self-contained suites with serving quarters, baths and other amenities. Nevertheless, the fragrant late summer evenings had convinced Carinus that the terraces overlooking the garden with its fountains, ornamental pools and shady nooks would be the best place for Antonia's party. He believed that the cool shade offered by the surrounding ivy-clad plane trees, the greenery of the box hedges and shrubs, the sweetness of the fruit orchards and the perfumed water leaping from the marble fountains were far better than anything else.

Senator Carinus was now congratulating himself on this decision. He sat slightly drunk in his white marble bedroom, separated from the garden terrace by elegant folding doors, cradling his precious ivory goblet and staring down at the mosaic on his bedroom floor celebrating the glories of Pomona, Goddess of Autumn. He half listened to the music from the gardens and heartily wished autumn would soon come: when it did, the insidious heat of the day would break and they could all bask in a refreshing coolness. He staggered to his feet, patting the sleeping slave girls on their bottoms, and crossed to the door. He did not trust his stewards, drunken, ungrateful lot! He would visit his aviaries, make sure their doors were closed and that the lights in the elaborately carved pottery masks with their cut-out eyes were still flaring strong. Above all, he must check on his beloved but spoiled daughter. She was pampered, cosseted and very wilful, but there again, since the death of her mother, Carinus had indulged her every whim. The room swayed slightly. Carinus clutched the wall, feeling slightly queasy, and no wonder, since he'd drunk a great deal very quickly.

Carinus sat down on a stool, chewing his lip. If the truth be known, he hadn't really wanted this party, not with those abductions taking place in Rome. Wealthy young men and women snatched from their home or a street in the city, kept bound in the dark and only released for sacks of gold and silver. Who could be responsible for creating such fear? So serious had the crisis become that a delegation of senators had visited the Imperial Palace. They'd bowed low, given tactful speeches, conceded that times were violent but pointed out that this surge in crime involved their precious sons and daughters! Carinus had joined the last delegation. Emperor Constantine, God's Chosen, had sat glaring with bulbous eyes as the representatives of the Great Ones of Rome had demanded that the kidnappings and hostage-takings cease forthwith.

Constantine's wine-purpled face had deepened in colour as he fought to control his seething fury.

However, Carinus and his colleagues were equally wary of Helena, the Emperor's powerful mother, sitting on a high gold-encrusted stool to the right of her beloved son. As usual, Helena had been dressed demurely in a long–sleeved dalmaticus or tunic edged with purple, sandals on her feet, an embroidered stole about her shoulders. The Empress' greying hair was bound up from her face in a thick plait wrapped round her head in the old-fashioned style and pinned with a diamond. No oil moistened, no paint or powder gilded that long, severe face with its sensuous lips, high cheekbones and expressive eyes which had turned agate-hard as Helena listened to their representations. Her only sign of agitation was the constant fiddling with her ivory-handled fan of brilliantly coloured peacock feathers. Every so often she would snap this open to cool herself, or summon forward Burrus, the burly captain of her German mercenaries, so she could sip from a clay beaker of water he held. Burrus was a fearsome figure with his shaggy hair, beard and moustache, light blue eyes glaring from a ruddy face. Despite the heat, he wore a grey fur cape across his motley armour. He reminded Carinus of a great bear from the northern forests which he'd brought to Rome to fight in the arena. In fact the more often he met Burrus, the more the similarity became apparent, both man and beast being highly dangerous and volatile. During the meeting, Burrus' stubby fingers kept caressing the hilt of his broadsword, as if he couldn't understand why his imperial mistress had to listen to these speeches. One word from

Helena and Burrus would have taken all their heads. Behind the Empress stood an innocuous, bland-faced but equally dangerous man, Anastasius, Helena's deaf-mute secretary. He was dressed in a simple white tunic with no jewellery except for the ring on the middle finger of his left hand, which proclaimed he enjoyed the full support of the August Ones.

During that meeting, the sweat had coursed down Carinus' body, due as much to fear as to the heat, especially when Aurelian Saturninus, undoubtedly spurred on by his viper-tongued wife Urbana, had talked about how the lawlessness could be construed as a sign of weakness in Constantine's government. Helena and her son might have emerged victorious after the recent battle at the Milvian Bridge; Constantine might have ended the civil war and destroyed his rival Maxentius, but, as the former General Aurelian trumpeted, power brought responsibility, not only on the borders of Rome, but along the streets and alleyways of the city. Helena's eyes had narrowed at that and Carinus had coughed loudly, a warning to the old general that he'd gone far enough.

Ah well! Carinus rose, opened the folding doors and stared across the exquisite paradise bathed in the light of the full moon. He walked out on to the terrace and picked up the alabaster cup of chilled white wine his valet had placed on the marbled table. For a moment he forgot his fears. This was what he called the 'natural' part of the garden, where his beehives, made out of hollowed bark and plaited osier twigs, stood next to the wild plants his bees preferred: thyme, saffron, crocus, lime, blossom, hyacinths, their fragrance spreading everywhere. Carinus gazed into the darkness broken by pools of light from the lamps and candles. Faint music still sounded but this was almost drowned by the laughter and chatter of Antonia's guests, replete with hare cooked in thyme sauce, spiced pork, dormice stuffed with honey, quail, duck and the best wines from the Senator's cellars. A girl's laugh, followed by a playful scream, echoed from the trees around the Artemis Fountain. As Carinus sipped his wine, he just hoped Antonia was safe and keeping that Greek actor Theodore at more than arm's length.

In fact, the laughter and screaming Carinus heard was that of his daughter, who had taken Theodore, an up-and-coming actor from the island of Cos, deep into the trees to the artificial glade around the cool, splashing waters of the Artemis Fountain. The circle of grass around the fountain, interspersed with coloured stone, was lit by a myriad of oil lamps in translucent jars. Nevertheless, despite the light and the open space, Antonia had assured Theodore they'd be alone, for this was her special place. Now naked except for a coronet of myrtle, orange blossom and verbena, Antonia sprawled on a cold marble bench as Theodore stripped naked to show her the love letters on his body, his present to her on her birthday. Antonia, drunk on the red and white wines of Campania, giggled as Theodore took a pot of ash and rubbed the grey powder into his skin, explaining how with the juice of tithymals he could draw any letters he wished and they would remain invisible until the ash revealed them.

'See,' Theodore walked over to the bench, 'this is the opening line from Seneca's *Oedipus*. Read it.'

Antonia, giggling, pushed her face near the muscle-hard stomach of this gorgeous actor and, in the light of the lamps, slowly read the words.

'Now night has fled. The fitful sun is back to rise.'

She glanced up coyly.

'To rise what?'

Theodore pointed down to the letters just above the hair in his crotch.

Antonia, wetting her lips, moved her face even closer and was about to read when she caught a movement behind Theodore.

'Go away!' she screamed.

Theodore whirled round. Dark shapes, like wraiths from Hades, slipped out of the darkness, a half-circle of cloaked figures, faces hidden behind grotesque masks, in their hands short stabbing swords and clubs.

'What!' Theodore sprang forward.

Antonia heard the hard smack of a fist and Theodore collapsed, lips bubbling on spurting blood. She opened her mouth to scream, but the night-wraiths were swifter. She was seized, a gag pushed into her mouth, a piece of sacking thrown over her head, her wrists and ankles bound. Then she was thrown over a muscular shoulder and a gloved hand smacked her plump bottom. Antonia wriggled; another, harder blow jarred her back and a hoarse voice ordered her to be silent or she'd be killed.

The kidnappers moved swiftly, silent as ghosts. Antonia was carried across the garden. She heard the undergrowth snapping and cracking and the distant sounds of the party. Theodore had yet to raise the alarm. The abductors stopped; Antonia was put down, turned around, made to feel dizzy and then dragged on. She was pushed against a hard wall, roughly hauled over it and the flight began again. This time she wasn't carried but pushed and shoved; now and again a dagger would prick her neck as a sign for her to remain quiet. She felt a deep sense of despair. She was out in the countryside. No one was here to save her!

The abductors knew their way well. Antonia's bare legs and feet were scored by brambles and gorse, but still they pushed her forward. When she complained about the pain in her side, they tied a rope around her hands and dragged her as if she was some captive in a triumphant procession. Now and again she heard the occasional sound, the creak of a cart, but otherwise silence, except for the breathing of her captors. She couldn't believe it! She'd heard of the kidnappings in Rome, but now it had happened to her, so swiftly, so quickly. How had they found their way through her father's gardens to her secret place at the Artemis Fountain? She was jerked on, and tried to make sense of where she was going but eventually gave up. She concentrated only on one thing: obeying her captors. She knew she'd be safe if she did that. At one point they stopped and allowed her to rest, and she was given a sip of water and some dried bread; then the horror continued.

Antonia was aware of orders being whispered, of men fanning out either side of her, but she had no sense of where she was going. She began to cry, pleading about the pain in her feet. A rough pair of sandals was given to her, the thongs tied and she was pulled on. Now she was no longer moving through countryside but stumbling over masonry, and she wondered where she was. She sensed the gang were becoming more vigilant now that the ground had changed. Eventually they stopped and Antonia was thrust down some steps. The air smelled mildewed and dry. She was in some sort of man-made tunnel. The air was cold, and she could feel sharp rocks on either side. Where could this be? What underground tunnels existed in Rome? The sewers? She stumbled and screamed as her hand felt a skull. She was in some sort of cemetery, perhaps the great catacombs which ranged under the Appian Way. Yes, that would make sense; a few miles from her father's villa by a quick, secure route. Would she be imprisoned here? Sobbing and crying, she was pushed into a cavern and left there.

The leader of the abductors, drenched in sweat, the mask still firmly on his face, stared around.

'We have done what we had to.' He looked at his companions. There were twelve in all, and he counted them carefully making sure no one had been forgotten. 'Now we must wait,' he ordered. 'Those who are not of us may go.'

Some of the men left; those remaining squatted down, staring up at their leader.

'You must stay there.' He left the cavern and walked down the long, ill-lit gallery stretching into the darkness. He knew his visitor would be waiting for him there. He saw a torch move and paused. He must go no further. A figure stepped out of the darkness, a woman swathed in robes. He could smell her perfume.

'Did it go well?' The voice was soft but carrying. 'Were there any problems? Was anybody hurt?'

'There were no problems.' The leader felt as if his face was steaming hot beneath his mask; he wished he could take it off, but he knew the rules. 'The girl has been taken,' he continued. 'She is safe. We await the ransom.'

'Good.' The voice echoed. 'But I asked you, was anybody hurt?'

'She was with a man,' the leader replied. 'We heard them talking. He tried to resist but we pushed him to the ground.'

'You did not kill him?'

'No,' the leader replied. 'That was your order, no one was to be hurt.'

'Who was it?' the voice asked.

'An actor,' the leader replied. 'He tried to play the hero.'

'Leave the actor to me,' the voice whispered. 'I shall take care of him.'

On the same night as the attack at the Villa Carina, Lucius Pomosius, former veteran of the *ala*, the wing of cavalry attached to the Second Legion Augusta, left the latrines in the Street of Abundance, which ran off the main thoroughfare stretching down to the Colosseum. He stared drunkenly at the graffiti of crude election slogans painted on the wall of the alleyway, eerily illuminated by spluttering torches. Above these was a picture of Mercury in winged greaves, his helmet similarly winged, in one hand a spear shaped like a penis, in the other a bag of gold. The little god's cloak billowed out whilst his finger pointed to a place further down the street. Lucius tapped the painting, smiled and, one hand trailing the walls, made his way down towards the House of the Golden Cupids with its garish sign of two erect phalluses either side of the doorway.

Lucius paused. He really had drunk too much! He leaned against the wall and glanced back down the alleyway. He was certain he had been followed, and despite the wine had a pricking suspicion that he'd been watched ever since he'd left the upper room of the Lucia Gloriosa tavern where he and the other three surviving members of Vigiles Muri, the Guardians of the Wall, met every month. Tonight they'd gathered specially to discuss the brutal death of old Petilius, found on his bed with his throat slit, his belly cut and his penis slashed off and pushed into his hand. 'Awash in his own blood' was how Decurion Stathylus had described it: 'Floating on a sea of billowing scarlet.' Stathylus always liked to embroider his tales, but then he was a warrior-poet, a bard who liked to sing about his beautiful former mistress and remind them all of their days in Britain. How they'd manned the Wall and stared out over that sea of desolate grassland which stretched and billowed under lowering grey skies. Ah yes, those were the days!

Lucius stared at the graffiti chalked on the far wall: 'He who doesn't invite me to dinner is a barbarian.' He wished he hadn't been invited tonight. He had not wanted to discuss Petilius' gory death. It evoked memories of that night along the Wall when the Picts had been trapped and massacred. The night of their *bona fortuna*, as Stathylus liked to describe it. There had been a dozen of them then, but war, as well as the passage of the years, had depleted their number. Death was to be expected, but not Petilius', not dying like that! Who'd want to butcher a lecherous but harmless old man? Petilius was ugly and mean, and even the common whores haggled hard when they saw that miserable face, yet he'd been killed and castrated in a manner reminiscent of the Picts. Could there be some dark thread winding its way back into the murky past? Lucius secretly conceded there might be, but he didn't want to reflect on it. He didn't want to remember. He didn't want to invoke the ghosts!

He wiped the sweat from his face and stared up at the narrow strip of sky between the overhanging buildings. He wished he was back on the Wall, away from the Vigiles, his comrades, away from the stink and the memories. He looked down the street at the pool of light before the House of the Golden Cupids. Should he take a cubicle downstairs where he could listen to the moans of the girls busy with their customers, or a private room upstairs?

'Sir?'

He turned quickly. The shadowy woman, hair veiled, wrists clinking with bracelets, moved closer.

'Sir, is it custom you want?'

Lucius shook his head, trying to clear the wine fumes. The woman's perfume was fragrantly sweet. She was dressed in gold-edged linen robes. He glimpsed sparkling eyes ringed with kohl, smiling lips parted in a sweet smile. A soft hand caressed his cheek. He grabbed her, and she seemed to melt into him. Lucius started in agony, his hands falling away.

He stared in shock at the woman, who'd stepped back, leaving the dagger deep in his belly. He staggered forward, falling to his knees, and tried to grasp the dagger, but his head was jerked back and a shearing-sharp blade slit his throat.

'They used to call those the Polluted Fields.'

Claudia, sitting on the top of the grassy knoll, moved a little deeper into the shade of the sycamore trees. She munched on a hunk of mushroom bread, took a sip of watered wine and dabbed her mouth with a napkin, then stared again at the desolate heath below her stretching either side of the Via Nomentena leading up to the Colline Gate. The view was almost hidden by the heat haze which had descended on Rome during that late summer's afternoon. The Via was now empty of carts, travellers, journeymen and merchants; even a cohort of infantry which had come plodding out through the city gate had decided to shelter in the shade of some lime trees.

'They still look polluted to me.'

Claudia turned and nipped the arm of her companion, Murranus, Victor Ludorum, Champion of the Games, wearer of the victorious laurel wreath.

'You're not even looking!' she accused.

The gladiator's smooth-shaven face broke into a smile which made him look even more boyish and mischievous.

Oh, Murranus! Claudia reflected. He looked so handsome in his dark blue tunic, long legs sprawled out as he sat with his back to an ancient holm oak. He stared at her, green eyes full of mischief as he scratched his close-cropped red hair and ran a muscular hand over his face, searching for the beads of sweat coursing down over the high cheek-bones. His determined mouth and strong chin were now slack as he relaxed under the influence of the weak wine and the strong sun.

'You've got a square face today,' she teased, using her fingers to demonstrate. 'Your eyes don't look so large and your mouth isn't so fierce, your lips—'

'You enjoyed kissing me.' He stretched forward.

'I always do! Ah no!' Claudia playfully pushed Murranus back against the tree. He stuck his tongue out at her, and she felt her throat constrict and the tears well. For a moment, for the briefest of moments, the playful gesture had reminded her of Felix, her brother, but that was all in the past. Felix was dead and life had gone surging on. The man who had murdered him then raped her, the ghoul who had haunted her dreams with his hard voice, that purple chalice tattooed on his wrist, had paid for his crime. Murranus had seen to that, taking the miscreant's life with his sword in the arena before a roaring crowd. Justice done, vengeance savoured. In the purple-draped imperial box above the arena, Constantine, Helena and all the court had watched whilst the crowd bayed like a pack of savage dogs over that man, her enemy, dying on the sand below.

Claudia glanced away, turning her head as if to catch the breeze. Murranus studied her closely from under heavy-lidded eyes: her black hair, that sweet face, those sharp eyes. Was her skin olive or light ivory? He could never tell, but that was Claudia, she could change so quickly. She'd been an actress, part of a troupe, a very good one, wandering the roads of Italy. Eventually she'd returned to Rome to live with that scoundrel of an uncle Polybius, his pretty plump wife Poppaoe and all the lords and madams of Rome's underworld who made the She Asses tavern near the Flavian Gate their home, the centre of their lives. In a sense it was Murranus' home too.

He picked up the wine flask and sipped the tasty juice. Claudia had brought him to this desolate spot, far away from the tumult of the tavern, so they could talk before the autumn games began. He just wished she wouldn't show that streak of stubbornness when they argued. Claudia could be so obstinate and yet so secretive! Only recently, during the last two weeks, had she grudgingly told him about her work for the Empress, as well as her dealings with the powerful Christian priest Sylvester. Murranus had pointed out that if he was in danger in the amphitheatre, she was exposed to even greater peril in the marbled gardens and stinking alleyways of Rome. They had argued so fiercely, yet all he wanted now was to stretch across and gather her in his arms. He wanted her to relax, to be passionate, not so precise, so organised. There she sat in her sensible dark green tunic with her sensible walking sandals firmly tied, the thongs fastened and secure. She wore little jewellery; only a ring on her finger and a graceful silver chain round her neck. Her thick hair lay neatly clipped at the nape of her neck, a parasol placed close beside her in case it grew too hot. Even the leather satchel in which she carried their meal was precisely positioned, the straps neatly folded, while the food she and Poppaoe had packed was spread in an orderly manner upon a linen cloth: the mushroom bread, the pot of herb and garlic pâté, the sesame biscuits. Oh yes, that was Claudia, so precise! Murranus coughed and, leaning over, tickled the nape of her neck.

'Oh *magistra*!' he teased. 'I'm only a poor Frisian. Why do they call these the Polluted Fields?'

Claudia turned, grinning over her shoulder. She moved further back to sit beside him and pointed down the hill to the round, squat towers jutting up from the earth.

'That's where they were buried alive.'

'Who?'

'The Vestal Virgins, maidens sworn to be chaste and virginal in the service of the Goddess Vesta and the state. Any Vestal charged with unchastity was sentenced to be buried alive. They were, and in fact still can be, brought here and sealed for forty days in one of those underground chambers with a small quantity of food and drink. The Goddess Vesta would decide whether they lived or died; they always died.'

'And?'

'Over two hundred years ago, during the reign of Domitian, the Senior Vestal Virgin was accused of immorality. Three of her sisters were also condemned, their lovers being beaten to death. Anyway,' Claudia brushed at her face, 'the Senior Vestal was paraded through Rome and brought to one of these specially prepared underground chambers. As she was descending the steps, her robes caught on a snag. The executioner offered her his hand, but she drew away in disgust.' Claudia shook her head. 'People are so strange. If everyone in Rome guilty of crimes against chastity was brought here, you wouldn't be able to see a blade of grass for the dense crowds.'

'And?' Murranus asked.

'Even in death,' Claudia laughed, 'people can act the snob. Wealth and privilege are still more important than that final act. It's a strange world we live in.'

'The Empress has sent for you?'

'No she hasn't!' Claudia faced him squarely. 'But I think she will. You've heard about the kidnappings?'

Murranus nodded.

Claudia held up her hand. 'Five cases in the last month; that's what made me think of wealth and privilege and the dangers it brings. The sons and daughters of wealthy Roman senators and generals snatched from their gardens, litters and baths.' Claudia shrugged. 'Mercury the Messenger told me this morning that the most recent kidnapping took place last night. Antonia, the sixteen-year-old daughter of Senator Carinus, was abducted from a party in the gardens of her father's villa in the Alban Hills. Ah well,' she continued briskly, 'that's another reason I brought you here.'

'What, to be kidnapped or buried alive?'

Claudia threw a piece of grass at him. 'The arena! Murranus, you're now the Victor, you have to retire, you cannot—'

'I—'

'You cannot!' Claudia's eyes, like her voice, turned flinty hard. 'Murranus, you'd make an excellent bodyguard for some rich family. You could start your own business, form your own cohort.'

Murranus groaned inwardly, yet at the same time he was deeply flattered by this delightful young woman's affection and concern for him.

'I know what you are going to say, Murranus,' Claudia edged closer, 'but it isn't true. You are not just a killer. You have a soul, you are kind, fair and sometimes very, very funny, especially when you drink. Uncle Polybius regards you as a son; Poppaoe adores you, as does everyone else at the tavern. Even Narcissus the Neat.'

Murranus laughed at the mention of the most recent addition to the company at the She Asses tavern. A Syrian, a former slave, Narcissus now wanted to start his own funeral business with the help and support of Uncle Polybius.

'Are you worried about Polybius?' Murranus asked.

'Don't change the subject. Yes, I am always worried about Polybius and his constant schemes to get rich quickly. He's even thinking of becoming a Christian to win the favour of the priests, not to mention that of Presbyter Sylvester. But Murranus . . .' Claudia began to gather the food together, neatly folding the linen cloth. She glanced up. 'I saw a fresco on sale in the flea market near the She Asses. It depicts a gladiator, a bestiarius, whose enormous penis is a ravening wild animal. The penis, a dog with gaping jaws, is part of the gladiator's own body yet it has turned furiously against him. He is about to slay the beast which is threatening him; in doing so he must castrate himself.'

'And?' Murranus asked.

'It's a parable.' Claudia leaned over and kissed him on the tip of his nose. 'In the arena, Murranus, you entertain, you give pleasure to the mob. But in the end you're not only killing other people, you're killing yourself. If we are to marry,' Claudia breathed in deeply, 'that must stop.'

Murranus got to his feet and placed his hands on her shoulders. 'You mean that?'

'I know that.' She smiled.

'If I don't agree, whom would you marry?'

'Burrus.' Claudia kept her face impassive.

Murranus burst out laughing. He leaned down and kissed her on the brow.

'In which case,' he whispered, 'it's time we talked about this business.'

Claudia looked away across the haunted heathland, the gorse and grass now shifting in the quickening breeze. The heat haze was thinning. She had got what she'd come for.

'It's time,' she murmured, 'it's time we went back.' She held her hand out warningly. 'Remember what I've said and what you have promised.'

Murranus seized her hand and they left; halfway down, Claudia paused and, standing on tiptoe, kissed him swiftly on the check. They continued along the dusty trackway on to the paved via which would lead round to the Flavian Gate. At first Claudia hid her pleasure and excitement by chattering to Murranus, but the day's heat was now dying and the traffic on the thoroughfare had increased, making conversation difficult. Time and again they had to stand aside to allow a cohort or maniple go swinging by under their hoarse-voiced officers. Farmers and peasants, their families bundled into the carts they'd left outside the city gates, were now returning to the countryside. Other wagons heaped with provisions were lumbering towards the city to take advantage of the imperial decree which allowed them in once night had fallen. Claudia watched them go and quoted from Juvenal's *Satires*, the poet's famous diatribe against the noise at night in Rome's busy streets. Murranus nodded in agreement.

Soon Claudia fell silent, doing something she loved: observing and studying what was happening around her. For a while she and Murranus walked with a group of tramping hawkers, each of whom had a tray of cheapjack goods slung around their necks ready to sell. Claudia bought a few hair pins, a comb for Poppaoe, a fine Egyptian knife for Narcissus and a set of bracelets depicting a Thracian facing charging boars for Oceanus, the one-eared former gladiator supposedly in charge of security at the She Asses. The hawkers eventually left the via to shelter under some trees. Claudia then listened to a Numidian muleteer chattering in the lingua franca of the ports as he described the news he'd heard about Licinius, Emperor of the East and Constantine's rival, who was apparently lurking in Nicomedea planning to take Constantine's empire, as Constantine and his mother were plotting in Rome to take his. This flow of news ceased abruptly when the Numidian became involved in an acrimonious dispute with eight Syrian litter-bearers, their hair greased and plaited, all dressed in the same livery, who were carrying a large, plump matron back to her 'dear husband' in Rome. Claudia then decided to follow a cart of actors who were eager to supplement their income by telling their fellow travellers stories from Rome's past. A young man with a bell-like voice was declaiming extracts from the historian Suetonius about Caligula, who had lived almost three hundred years earlier.

'Oh yes,' the actor shouted from the tail of the cart. 'He was so depraved,' the man's hand slipped to his crotch and he made an obscene gesture, 'he used to go into the Imperial Gardens and make love to the moon, whom he regarded as his wife.'

This immediately provoked a shocked denial from a woman in the audience and the declamation was transformed, much to the delight of all, into a fierce slanging match about sexual practices. Claudia half listened as she studied the props piled on the huge cart pulled by serene-looking bullocks. She recognised the grotesque face masks, the imitation jars, the pieces of scenery which could be hastily assembled to fashion a tree, a wall or the door of a house. She recalled her own days with Felix journeying from town to town: such a strange time, always on the move. Since she had settled at the She Asses, her life had been transformed. She was a secret official of the Empress, a confidante of the powerful Presbyter Sylvester and, she concluded wryly, the protector of Uncle Polybius, about whose night-time meetings with shadowy figures in the garden she was growing increasingly suspicious.

Lost in her own thoughts, one hand holding her parasol, the other grasping Murranus', Claudia was startled from her reverie when they reached the Flavian Gate. She glanced up and stared around at the outhouses, barracks and fences, as well as the makeshift market which had grown up there. Guards in half-armour lounged in the shade gambling, whilst their officer, a German clad in tawdry finery, stood surveying the crowd. Claudia wondered idly if the officer was from Burrus' cohort. She knew the real watchers were hidden away. The Ethiopian with his braided hair selling bruised fruit from his wheelbarrow; the scrawny girl offering sulphur matches; the priest of some minor deity clad in dirty saffron robes, chanting over a pot of flame: perhaps they were spies. Or was it the sharp-faced, balding pimp, with three of his ladies, all bewigged, painted and clinking with cheap jewellery, looking for custom, yelling that he had set up an awning in a shady corner just inside the city walls? Any of these could be the 'surveyors' of the Empress Helena, looking for faces, studying those flocking into the city, recalling descriptions and searching for anything untoward.

The entire crowd fell silent as military horns wailed a fanfare. An execution party came marching out, sixteen men under their decurion, divided into squads of four. Each squad guarded a prisoner, a beam across his shoulder, being dragged out to be crucified at the Palace of Bones. Once these had passed, Claudia and Murranus joined the rest of the crowds as they surged through the gateway on to the thoroughfare, which immediately radiated out into narrow runnels, alleyways and side streets.

Claudia heaved a sigh of relief, as she always did whenever she returned to this quarter. It might be stinking, noisy and colourful, but this was her home, a safe place where she could recognise people and knew who they really were, a bustling rabbit warren of narrow lanes cluttered with open-air stalls. The traders set up their makeshift shops in the crumbling loggia and peristyles or at the mouths of alleyways, selling everything from pots to cakes. On the walls around them garishly daubed notices proclaimed the price of certain goods and where these could be bought, as well as the names of candidates for the next election to some municipal office. Claudia and Murranus were well known here and were greeted with good-natured teasing and salutations.

Torquatus the Tonsor, a seller-of-potions-cum-barber-cum-leech, had, as usual, procured the best position under a giant gnarled sycamore tree in the square near the She Asses tavern. Torquatus spent his days shaving people, cutting their hair, listening avidly to their medical ailments and, as he put it, offering his 'best advice', which, he solemnly assured his customers, came from leading imperial physicians. He greeted Claudia and asked if she'd seen the 'Great Miracle' at the She Asses tavern? Claudia stared back in puzzlement. But even before she and Murranus reached the small square fronting the inn, she sensed something was wrong.

The She Asses was one of the most comfortable taverns in the Suburra. It boasted a restaurant, eating hall, small chambers upstairs and a very well-endowed kitchen, as well as Polybius' 'crowning glory', a graceful, spacious garden to the rear. The tavern occupied most of the ground floor and first storey of an insula or apartment block situated between the Flavian Gate and the crumbling Temple of the Crown of Venus. The windows were covered with stiffened papyrus and wooden shutters. It had two main doors, an outer one and, just behind that, a folding door. Above the entrance was a lovely statue of Minerva holding her pet owl. On either side of the doorway, fixed in niches, stood a grinning Hermes or Mercury, whilst the door-knocker was shaped like a huge phallus. The male clientele regarded this as a token of good luck in matters venereal and always asked their girlfriends to stroke it. Petronius the Pimp had boasted how the obscene object was modelled on his own penis, to which Poppaoe had retorted that she personally knew the carver was a very short-sighted man! A large placard to the right of the door advertised the dish of the day, usually sausages and mushrooms grilled in garlic. Little wonder Uncle Polybius was growing increasingly concerned that his menu was beginning to bore his customers! Next to the placard hung another notice listing the prices of drinks and warning wandering warlocks, wizards and pimps to take their business elsewhere, unless they had the 'special permission of the proprietor'.

On this particular afternoon the crowds had gathered and Claudia and Murranus had to climb through one of the tavern's windows, opened specially for them by the barrel-chested, pot-bellied Oceanus. He dragged them through into the long eating hall, also packed to overflowing, and led them around the counter into the kitchen. Claudia immediately conceded that something must be seriously wrong: there were no smells, no odours of piquant sauces, no crackling charcoal in the hearth; the pots remained unwashed whilst the two ovens beside the hearth were stone-cold. She turned on Oceanus.

'What is it?'

The bald-headed ex-gladiator was so agitated he didn't know whether to finger, as he always did when highly nervous, the brass ring in his good ear, or the dried ear hanging on a cord round his neck. In his last great fight this had been bitten off. Oceanus had eventually won the battle and had the severed ear dried and pickled to wear as a trophy.

'Oceanus!' Claudia stood on a stool and seized the man's fat face between her hands. 'Oceanus, tell me the truth or I'll bite your nose!'

'It's a miracle.' Oceanus' eyes widened. 'A Great Miracle. Claudia, you know the cellars beneath the tavern?'

Claudia nodded. The underground rooms and caverns of the insula were also the property of Polybius and he'd always wanted them developed.

'Well,' Oceanus continued, 'what was found has been put down there.'

'What has?'

'What was discovered in the garden this morning.'

'Oceanus!' Claudia gripped the former gladiator's face, pulled it close and winked quickly at the puzzled Murranus.

'Early this morning,' Oceanus gabbled, 'Venutus the Vine-dresser arrived to dig a small oil press in the garden. Well, he didn't listen properly! Hc and his workmen dug deep but they'd chosen the wrong place and they discovered her—'

'Oceanus, it's time for nose-biting!'

'A corpse,' Oceanus whispered, eyes drifting to the kitchen door, which he now wished he hadn't closed.

'A what?'

'A young woman's corpse, wrapped in linen and placed in a long casket. She had the coins of the Emperor Diocletian on her eyes. You know him?'

'I know who he was.'

'She was a Christian martyr,' Oceanus gabbled. 'There were bruises on her neck and along her shoulders, religious symbols around the coffin.'

Claudia got down from the stool and stared in disbelief through the open window above the hearth. It overlooked the garden, its lawn, fountain, orchard, trees and small vineyard. Caligula the tavern cat was basking on one of the benches, being fanned by Sorry, the kitchen boy.

'I really must remember his name,' Claudia murmured.

'Sorry?' Murranus asked.

'Exactly!' Claudia grinned, pointing at the boy. 'That's all he says, hence his name. Oceanus, are you sure? The corpse was that of a young woman?'

'Come and see.' Oceanus took them out of the kitchen and over to a stone building where the insula's hypocaust had once been housed. Oceanus nodded to Mercury the Messenger, the tavern gossip, who was standing on guard outside; he bowed, eyes bright with excitement, lips moving soundlessly as he rehearsed the news he'd later spread through the entire quarter. This self-proclaimed herald opened the door and ushered them into the mildewed darkness now lit by fluttering torches. The place was full of people peering over each other's heads at the open door and stone steps leading down to the cellars. Claudia recognised the usual rogues: Simon the Stoic, Petronius the Pimp, Januaria the tavern wench and others of their coven. These tried to gossip with them but Murranus and Oceanus pushed their way through.

Claudia gingerly followed the two men down the cellar

steps. The brickwork either side was a rough red covered
with cobwebs; the torches fixed into rusting sockets and
niches spluttered noisily, their resin smoke mixing with
the dry mustiness of the cellars. The steps led to a row of
square chambers opening on to each other. In the second
stood Polybius, Poppaoe, Venutus the fat-faced vine-
dresser, and Polybius' friends and neighbours, Apuleius the
Apothecary and his wife Callista. Both husband and wife
were small, grey-haired and anxious-eyed. Claudia had often
met and chatted to them, and liked them both. They originally came from the south, and had the dark, leathery look
of peasants who'd worked for long hours under a broiling
sun. They had moved into the quarter a few years ago, and
since then Apuleius had earned a well-deserved reputation
for being most skilled in the knowledge of herbs and medicine.

All five people were grouped round a casket resting on
a trestle table. Inside the casket, revealed by the light of
the surrounding tapers, lay a young woman swathed in
fresh linen robes, the folds pulled back to reveal her face.
Claudia reckoned she must have been about sixteen or
seventeen years of age, with a thin, rather troubled face,
the lower lip jutting out, the nose snub, a dimple on her
chin. Her eyes were closed and her hands clasped before
her. Her black hair was neatly dressed and parted in the
middle, falling down to her shoulders.

Claudia nodded at her uncle and aunt, picked up an oil
lamp and peered closer. She felt the skin of the face; it was
like touching a wax sponge. In the stronger light she noticed
the reddish-gold dust on the side of the neck, how the

cheeks were sunken, the jaw slightly drooping. She took her hand away. 'What is this?' She felt the powder between her fingers.

'It was on the side of the casket,' Apuleius explained. 'Probably from the wood.'

Claudia nodded and returned to her examination. She leaned down and sniffed the fragrance of wild flowers. She touched the hair; it was slightly dry and brittle. She rearranged the linen folds slightly and noticed the faded dark contusions on the side of the neck and along the shoulders. She went to raise the linen robes but Apuleius tapped her hand.

'I don't think we should,' he whispered. 'I've never seen the like before.' He pointed at the top of the casket and around the rim. Claudia made out the Christian symbols: the *chi* and *rho* as well as crudely etched crosses and fishes.

Polybius handed over two denarii, darkened with age. 'These were found on the eyes.'

'None on the mouth?'

'Of course not,' Apuleius remarked. 'I'm a Christian too. We wouldn't use a coin to pay Charon, the Lord of Hell. We don't believe in such things.'

'What exactly happened?' Claudia asked.

'Not here.' Polybius asserted himself. He picked up the lid of the casket and Claudia glimpsed the small crosses etched along the inside. She helped her uncle position the lid back on, noticing the rusting clamps and how the side of the coffin looked shabby and dirt-streaked, slightly rotting, even though the wood was the finest elm. It had definitely been in the ground for some time. She picked up a lamp and studied the twin denarii. They were mildewed with age but she made out the likeness of the curly-haired and bearded Diocletian, whilst the names and titles of the Emperor were inscribed round the rim.

'Diocletian!' she exclaimed. 'But he abdicated about ten years ago to grow his cabbages. He ruled for how long?' She screwed her eyes slightly. 'About twenty years?'

'Long before my time,' Polybius declared. 'I bought this tavern about four years ago.'

'And who owned it before that?'

'One of Maxentius' men,' Polybius remarked. 'Before the civil war ended he fled or was killed.' His sweat-soaked face puckered in concern. 'Don't let's talk here.' He shrugged. 'Let's drink a little wine.'

Polybius led them out of the cellar, leaving Oceanus and Mercury the Messenger to guard the door, which was locked and bolted. He also promised Simon the Stoic and Petronius the Pimp a free evening meal if they helped to protect what was now commonly being called the 'Great Miracle'. Poppaoe fled up into the kitchen to cut bread and cold sausage while her husband led Venutus, Apuleius and his wife as well as Claudia and Murranus out to a table in the shade of the small orchard. Sorry and Caligula, both sensing this was an important meeting, fled, though not before Polybius had told the boy that Poppaoe should bring out a jug of dry white wine, the best from northern Campania.

Once the wine had been served, Claudia learned what had happened. Venutus and his diggers had arrived just before dawn, and began work on the wrong side of the garden. They had cleared a pit of about six feet when their mattocks hit wood. Polybius, busy in the tavern, hadn't noticed where they were or what they were doing until he was summoned out. He immediately told Venutus and his men to break their fast in the eating hall whilst he, Oceanus and Narcissus lifted the coffin out, opened the clasps and found what Claudia had just seen.

'I was confused,' Polybius took a mouthful of wine, 'and so concerned I sent a messenger to the Captain of the Vigiles: that ugly bugger will be here soon. You know the law, Claudia: if murder is suspected or I am myself accused of secretly burying the corpse . . .' He let his words hang in the air.

Claudia knew the penalty for such crimes: possible confiscation, even crucifixion, or at the very least, slavery in the mines of Syracuse.

'But you're not responsible.'

'Of course he isn't,' Apuleius interrupted. The apothecary sidled on to the bench beside his wife, who sat hunched like a frightened dormouse. 'I'm a healer and physician.' Apuleius smiled. 'Your uncle trusts me, so I immediately hurried here when he sent for me. Callista brought my satchel of instruments and potions.'

'And you examined the corpse?'

'Oh yes, that's why Callista came,' Polybius said. 'The girl was naked.'

'What!'

'True.' Polybius held Claudia's gaze. 'As naked as a newborn baby except for a thin linen drape.'

'It's true,' Callista murmured. 'I asked Poppaoe to fetch some fresh linen; I thought it was decent. I thought—'

'Then I had her moved,' Apuleius intervened, gesturing up at the sky. 'The sun, the heat . . . the coolest place is the cellar. The rest you know.'

'But this is impossible,' Claudia exclaimed. 'That corpse must have been buried at least, what, nine, ten years ago? Yet, judging from the face at least, no decomposition, no corruption has apparently occurred.'

'I can't explain it,' Apuleius confessed. 'I've examined that corpse, and apart from those bruises there's no other mark of violence.'

'So what can explain it?'

Apuleius opened his mouth to reply, then glanced quickly at his wife.

'I'm reluctant to speak,' Callista confessed, blinking quickly. 'I'm glad Polybius summoned us. My husband is a *peritus*, an expert, but we are also Christians. Apuleius recognised those symbols.' She paused and took a deep breath. 'That young woman, according to my husband, probably died a virgin.'

'Excuse me.' Claudia held up her hand and stared round. 'Where's Narcissus the Neat?' she asked. 'He was a professional embalmer; perhaps he could help?'

'Of course he can!' Polybius agreed. 'He too examined the corpse and agreed with Apuleius' conclusion. However, I've sent him out to discover all he can about what happened in this place during Diocletian's reign.'

'Sorry.' Claudia turned back to the apothecary's wife. 'Do continue, you were telling us of a possibility.'

'She may have died a violent death,' Callista declared. 'That bruising to her neck and shoulders . . .' She paused,

31

then her words came out in a rush. 'During the reign of Dicoletian, Christians, as you know, were savagely persecuted. Young maidens were often interrogated and, in return for sexual favours, promised their freedom. Sometimes the questioning took place in private houses. I believe,' Callista stumbled over her words, 'this was the fate of our young woman. She was a Christian, brought into the city close to the Flavian Gate, interrogated and offered her freedom in return for sexual favours. She refused and was beaten or strangled, or maybe her heart gave out.'

'But why bury her?'

'Perhaps she was of good family.' Apuleius spoke up. 'She had not been brought to trial, so her killer may have become very frightened. He stripped the corpse and bought that casket. Being superstitious, he hastily prepared it, etched on the Christian symbols and buried her here.' He paused. 'If Christians had buried her, they'd have returned to reclaim the corpse. Mind you,' he added sharply, 'there's another possibility – our corpse was secretly buried by Christians who themselves died before the persecution ended and so all memory of her was forgotten.'

'It's possible,' Polybius agreed. 'During the Great Persecution and the consequent civil war, many properties out here were left empty. This garden, when I took over the tavern, was uncultivated.'

'But all this doesn't account for the preservation of the corpse,' Claudia insisted.

'Ah well.' Polybius gestured at Apuleius. 'You explain.'

'That young woman,' the apothecary replied, 'was a martyr, a saint. God preserved her body as a sign of her sanctity.'

'I've never heard—'

'Claudia!'

She turned round and groaned. Oceanus stood in the tavern doorway, next to him an imperial messenger, a white wand of office in his right hand, his left hand beckoning her quickly.

'The Empress!' Claudia rose to her feet. 'The dead are not so bothersome as the living.'

Chapter 2

Si natura negat, facit indignation versum.
If nature refuses, indignation will prompt my verse.

Juvenal, Satires

In the Nile Chamber of the Imperial Palace on the Palatine, the Empress Helena sat on a blue quilted stool and forced herself to smile at her visitors. In truth, at that moment in time, she wished she could drown all three of them in the river Nile whose glories decorated the chamber walls. She stared at these marvels in an attempt to calm herself: brilliant frescos glorifying the magnificence of the Great River, the water painted in vivid blue, with light green bullrushes sprouting along its banks in which black hippopotami lurked. Pink flamingos flew overhead shadowing a gloriously decorated barge full of worshippers sailing down to some temple whose gilded cornices peeped welcomingly above luxuriant palm fronds.

Helena shifted her gaze and stared down at her sandalled

feet. She just wished Burrus, standing like the figure of Mars behind her, would stop sniffing. He should blow his nose! She had told him that so many times. Beside her Anastasius, her secretary, sat as if carved out of marble, staring across at Cassia, the former courtesan who was now one of the Magdalena. Helena could understand Anastasius' fascination. Cassia was dressed so simply, so purely in white robes, her only ostentation being the beautiful wild flower nestling behind her ear, its pink petals resting against her resplendent curly golden hair. Cassia's dark eyes smiled. Of medium height, with a voluptuous figure, she reminded Helena of an exquisite statue of Aphrodite she'd once owned when living in Corinth, perfect in every detail. She sighed. Cassia fascinated Anastasius not only with her looks, but also because, like him, she was a deaf mute, something which had happened to her during childhood. Ah well, at least Cassia was pleasant and smiling, unlike the Lady Urbana beside her. Helena glanced quickly at the powerful, beautiful wife of the even more powerful former general Aurelian. Urbana was dressed severely, no paint on her face or jewellery; a simple robe covered her Junoesque figure, whilst her raven-black hair was pulled in a tight knot behind her lovely oval face, making her look much older than she really was.

'Your Excellency Augusta.' Urbana leaned forward. 'We have presented our petition. Senator Carinus is prostrate with grief; the Magdalena are at his villa even now comforting him.'

'I know, I know,' Helena murmured, trying to hide her exasperation. Urbana had already said that! She was relieved when Cassia began to make strange signs with her fingers, the eunuch sitting beside her watching intently. Helena, who communicated with her own secretary in a similar way, couldn't understand the signs, and by his growing restlessness, neither could Anastasius. Cassia's interpreter also intrigued Helena. He was of medium height, olive-skinned, a Parthian who'd served Cassia when she was a leading courtesan in the city long before her conversion to Christianity and the Magdalena. He was good-looking, just past his thirtieth year, his dark eyes bright and intelligent, a snub nose above a smiling mouth, his black hair cropped close; a silver earring in his right lobe, a bracelet on his wrist, and beneath the dark green tunic, a gold chain around his left ankle. He sat watching Cassia, then turned and gently shrugged one shoulder.

'My mistress,' his voice was cultured and soft, the intonation correct, 'wonders why the Augusta, who has so many spies and agents, has not discovered anything about the gangs perpetrating these outrages?'

'Leartus,' Helena smiled at the eunuch, 'who said they were gangs?'

She heard a sound and looked up. The door at the far end of the chamber opened and Chrysis, the fat imperial chamberlain, waddled in. Helena suppressed a sign of relief.

'Ladies,' she turned to the eunuch, 'Leartus.' She spread her hands. 'I do understand your deep concerns. However, I must ask you to withdraw for a while, perhaps have a word with the actor Theodore. I do thank you all.' She played with the ring on her finger, fighting to control her anger. To be lectured here in her own palace about the security of the state, in the presence of a Parthian eunuch! Yet her son had been most insistent.

'Aurelian Saturninus was a great general, a friend of my father.' Constantine had glared at her. 'Mother, you've known him for years and so have I. Don't upset either him or his pious prig of a wife. I want you to smile and keep your voice low.'

Well, she had, but the effort had been great.

Helena wiped the sweat from the palm of her hands on her gown. A servant led her guests out through one door whilst Chrysis, beaming from one protuberant ear to the other, ushered Claudia and Murranus into the chamber. The Empress took a deep breath and relaxed, snapping her fingers at Anastasius to serve light white wine and spiced biscuits. Claudia and Murranus made to genuflect, but Helena quickly gestured at the vacated stools. She grabbed a goblet of wine, sipped quickly and bit into one of the biscuits, examining her visitors out of the corner of her eye.

Murranus, as ever, was a handsome man, lithe and tall, all muscle, no fat, his red hair shorn. His face was smooth, surprisingly unmarked and intelligent, betraying none of the stupid aggression of so many gladiators, or worse, the dandified, slightly effete ways of the great champions. Beside him Claudia looked so small, and for a moment Helena thought of them making love. She swallowed quickly. Presbyter Sylvester had warned her against such sexual curiosity and advised her to rein it in. Helena smiled at Murranus, who had now been brought into what she called the Mundus Secretorum, the World of Secrets. Claudia, his beloved, was one of her agents. He'd been told that and warned that to betray her would mean death. The gladiator had accepted the warning, just a shift in his eyes betraying his annoyance at being threatened.

Claudia sat beside Murranus, nibbling at a biscuit and sipping ever so carefully from her goblet. Helena let her shoulders sag. Claudia the little mouse, she reflected, a mere slip of a girl looking much younger than her years with her mop of black hair and ivory-pale skin. Those eyes, large and expressive, were ever watchful, and behind them was a mind that could twist and turn with the best of them.

'Augusta, Excellency.' Claudia swallowed, hiding her mouth. 'It is good to look upon your face, as it is on yours, Anastasius.'

The secretary stared coolly back, only the brief smile in his eyes betraying his own welcome for this mysterious young woman.

'And of course . . .' Claudia's voice changed, becoming vibrant and voluptuous. She heaved a dramatic sigh and stared in mock adoration at Burrus, captain of the Empress' bodyguard. 'Oh Burrus, I dream of you so often.'

Burrus grinned and bowed.

'And I dream of you too,' he replied, winking quickly at Murranus to show he meant no offence. In truth Burrus was very much in awe of this warrior and certainly smitten by what he called his 'delightful shield maiden'.

'So we are all pleased to see each other.' Helena clapped her hands. 'Chrysis,' she barked at the chamberlain, standing just within the doorway, 'you can go now, and I mean go! Don't stand on the other side and eavesdrop, and there's no need to go looking: you'll find no slit or eyehole in this room.'

Chrysis, still grinning, bowed and withdrew. Helena waited until the door closed, then lifted her head as if listening to the music of the songbirds from the garden. She glanced swiftly at Murranus, now scowling into his cup, then back at Claudia, whose gaze never wavered as she still nibbled that biscuit.

'Now, little mouse,' Helena began, 'listen and listen well.' All propriety forgotten, the Empress got to her feet and moved her stool so close her knees almost touched Claudia's. 'Four weeks ago, the daughter of a wealthy senator was kidnapped as she travelled down the Via Salvana to visit friends in the country. A ransom of twenty-five thousand gold coins was demanded.' Helena held her hand up at Murranus' low whistle of surprise. 'The girl's parents were sent a note which could have been written by any common city scribe, whilst it was delivered by a boy who could provide little description of who had given it to him. The note mentioned where and when the girl would be released, at the great cemetery which borders the Appian Way, close to the mausoleum of some long-dead merchant. Now you know that cemetery, a forest of grass, decayed tombs and undergrowth. A myriad of paths and hiding places wind their way through it.'

'Whilst beneath lie the catacombs,' Claudia added.

'Precisely,' Helena agreed. 'The girl's parents were warned that any attempt to trap their daughter's abductors would mean she'd suffer a slow, lingering death and they would never see her again. On the appointed day, at the appointed hour, the steward of that girl's family left two panniers full of gold coins at the place stipulated. The parents had been advised that once these had been scrutinised, they could return to the cemetery around the ninth hour and find their daughter. They did so with a comitatus of freedmen. The girl was found. She had been released long before the ninth hour. Her hands were still bound; she'd been simply gagged, blindfolded and left to wander!' Helena took a deep breath. 'The parents found her just in time. Some of the Inferni, the rabble who prowl such places . . .' She paused as Claudia flinched. 'You know about these?'

Claudia would not tell the Augusta how, in the catacombs beneath that cemetery, she'd often met Presbyter Sylvester the powerful lieutenant of the Bishop of Rome, as the Christians called their leader. She had always been on her guard when she went there; the Inferni were truly creatures of the dark. For an innocent girl to be found by them . . .

'What happened?' she asked.

'The Inferni had released her gag and were about to rape her,' Helena replied. 'Only the girl's screams alerted her parents. The Inferni fled, and she was found safe and sound. In subsequent weeks three more abductions took place, the same pattern being followed. None of the victims could tell the Vigiles anything.' Helena spat the words out, showing her usual contempt for the corrupt city police. 'They could say little more than that they'd been abducted, blindfolded, chained, kept in a cold place, fed, allowed to use a latrine, and threatened now and again by a voice.

41

They could tell us nothing about that voice, be it Roman or from the provinces, male or female.' Helena paused. 'Then last night, Antonia, the beloved only daughter of Senator Carinus, was kidnapped. The ransom note demanding the same sum arrived this morning. She is to be released in two days' time.'

Helena opened the small casket on the floor beside her and handed Claudia a piece of dingy and grease-marked parchment. The stark message was bluntly inscribed: 'Antonia, 25,000 gold coins on the day after tomorrow near the tomb of the tribune Marcus Sonertus in the cemetery of the Appian Way. She will be released at the ninth hour; failure or trickery will kill her.'

Claudia studied the crude letter and recalled that sprawling, lonely cemetery. She only went there because she had to. Not only did the Inferni roam there, it was also the haunt of warlocks, wizards, sorcerers and outlaws, dark souls who seethed in the shadows of Roman society. The cemetery lay beyond the city gates with many approaches, a dizzying warren of snaking tracks and twisting paths, and beneath it more passageways, tunnels and caverns.

'Claudia? Claudia?' Helena smiled at her. 'I haven't finished.'

'Augusta, I'm sorry.'

'Don't be, just stay attentive. The fate of a few children should not really concern me, but the senators of Rome are agitated, their womenfolk even more so.' Helena licked her lips. 'The peace my son has imposed has engendered a great love for the Christian religion. Groups are forming; the most important of these are the Magdalena. They are

Christians, wives of leading men in Rome who fully accept the Christian way. They believe they are administering to Christ just as the Jewess Mary Magdalene did. Every noble cause attracts their attention, especially,' Helena smiled, 'the conversion of fallen ladies, the women of the night. The Magdalena are led by the Lady Urbana, wife of Aurelian, a former comrade of my husband and son, a general who did great work for us in Britain. Aurelian held the province during our scramble for empire. I have known him since I was . . .'

Helena's voice had turned wistful. It was the closest Claudia had ever seen her come to talking about her early days when, according to snobbish courtiers, Helena had been a great beauty, the daughter of a simple tavern-keeper from some provincial town.

'Ah well.' The Empress smiled softly. 'I have known him since I was a green shoot. Now Urbana,' she added brusquely, 'is British, a refugee from that province. She caught Aurelian's eye and became his second wife, stepmother to the general's beloved only son, Alexander. Yes,' she added as if talking to herself, 'wife to Aurelian, one of the richest men in Rome. Urbana left Britain as a girl and came with her father, a Roman officer, back to this city. Britain was sliding into chaos; the Picti and Scoti came flowing over the wall to the north, whilst pirates were plundering the coast. The roads became swollen with refugees; families were separated. One of these refugees was Cassia, a beautiful child made mute by the horrors she had witnessed. Urbana befriended her, but when they came to Rome they drifted apart. Cassia became a leading courtesan. Urbana, years later, after she had married Aurelian, was baptised a Christian. She met Cassia and converted her, took her from a life of pleasure.' Helena's voice turned cynical. 'Cassia is now Urbana's constant companion, whilst hers is a eunuch, the Parthian Leartus who translates for her. I mention these because soon you will meet them. Treat them carefully, none of your sharp talk.'

'Augusta, why have they come here?'

'Ah, first because they brought the ransom note left at the Villa Carina where the Magdalena are still comforting the good senator. Secondly, they also brought Theodore the actor. He was with Antonia when she was abducted. Theodore claims he tried to defend her. In the struggle he allegedly knocked off the mask of one of the attackers and, perhaps, gained a description of him. Thirdly,' Helena blew her cheeks out, 'Urbana is a very powerful woman. She is, in fact, representing all the senators, merchants, administrators and generals of Rome, and more importantly their wives, who are now protesting at a so-called breakdown of law and order in the city. I need not spell out, Claudia, what is involved here. My son is Emperor of the West; one day he will march east to become emperor of the world. He'll bring that pervert Licinius to battle and annihilate him. We need these powerful people of Rome until . . .' Helena paused, 'until we've marched to the rim of the world, then we'll build a new empire, even a new city.' She glanced at Murranus. 'Is all this beyond you, gladiator?'

'Should it be, Augusta?'

Helena laughed. 'I asked you to come here.' She offered Murranus her goblet of wine. He took it, drank deeply and handed it back. 'Urbana is now very nervous about her stepson Alexander. I want you to be his bodyguard; you'll be paid lavishly.' Helena acknowledged Claudia's wide smile. 'I could have given them Burrus.' The Empress looked warningly over her shoulder at the hulking German still standing to attention behind her. 'But he and his lovely lads have to be kept on a firm leash, otherwise it's wine and women and anything that moves.'

Burrus nodded sharply in acknowledgement.

'Anyway,' Helena continued sweetly, 'the lovely boys would miss me. Every so often they need a good tongue-lashing to keep them in line. Well, Murranus?'

The gladiator shuffled his feet. 'Your Excellency, I . . .'

'Of course he would!' Claudia answered for him.

'Good!' Helena purred. 'You really have no choice. I'll introduce you to Urbana later. You will do it, won't you? You're a freed man, Murranus, a loyal subject of the Emperor. Moreover, it will do you, not to mention Claudia here, the world of good to be away from that disgraceful riff-raff down at the gladiators' school, roaring boys, all of them! Ah yes,' Helena continued in a rush, 'Claudia, for a while you will have a new guest at the She Asses: the actor Theodore, you've heard of him?'

Claudia shook her head.

'Neither have I, but he acts as if the whole world is entranced by him. He is, he was, Antonia's friend. As I said, he was present when she was abducted; he allegedly glimpsed the face of one of the attackers and swears he would certainly recognise him again.'

'Rome is a popular city.'

45

'So it is, Claudia, but Theodore has a description, he can give that to you, you will distribute it, among the gangs which swarm in the Suburra, the poorer quarters. Perhaps Theodore can look around that great midden-heap near the Flavian Gate.'

'You mean the place where I live.'

'I am sorry.' Helena rubbed her eyes. 'I am tired. Well, no, I'm angry!' She took her hands away. 'I don't like being lectured about law and order and its breakdown. Rome has never been an easy city to govern, but to cut to the chase, when you are finished here, take Theodore with you.' Helena rolled the wine goblet between her hands and glanced up sharply. 'One further thing. This may not seem important, but it is to my son. As I have said, Aurelian and Constantine served together in Britain. Twenty years ago that province teetered on dissolution and destruction. The Great Wall to the north, which protected it from the Caledonians and Picts, was breached time and again. It was the Season of the Pretender, the Usurper. The Empire itself was under threat. My husband and son were drawn into the storm. Consequently, for my son, myself and our supporters such as Aurelian, that province and anything associated with it is special! Especially the men who served us. Soldiers who at a time of mutiny defined their allegiance and declared for us.' She clicked her tongue. 'One such group was an *ala*, a much-depleted wing of the Catephracti serving in a mile fort along the Great Wall. They called themselves the Fretenses, the Wild Boars, and did sterling work, not only in holding the fort and supporting my husband and son, but at the time of crisis in trapping and annihilating a powerful Pictish war band. They achieved all this with the loss of only one man, their centurion. Once order had been restored in that province, members of the *ala* received medals, decorations and *praemia*, financial rewards, together with full Roman citizenship. As a group they were given honourable discharge and decided to settle in Rome.' Helena pulled a face and shrugged. 'Some died, five still live, or did until two weeks ago, when one of them, Petilius, was brutally murdered in his chamber; another died last night in the Street of Abundance near the House of the Golden Cupids. Nothing was stolen, but the manner of their murder was truly grisly. A stab wound to the belly, their throats cut, and,' Helena added, 'both victims were castrated, their penises sliced off and placed in their hands.'

'What?' Murranus exclaimed.

Claudia remained silent. Murranus always surprised her. He was shocked, but she wasn't; just mystified, as always, at the sheer cruelty of men.

'There are as many ways of killing a man,' Helena continued, 'as there are dogs in Rome, but this is different. I have spoken to Aurelian. The first victim, Petilius, had been to Aurelian's villa recently. The General had decided, like all soldiers do,' she raised her eyes, 'to have a reunion. Since then, Petilius had returned on a number of occasions, pestering Aurelian's stewards and freedmen for an interview with the General, who was too busy to meet him. Anyway, Aurelian has petitioned my son, the Emperor; he wants these deaths investigated. You, Claudia, will do that. Aurelian now regrets that he did not give Petilius an

47

audience; the castration puzzles him, because that is exactly what the Picts did when they caught a Roman. They always killed him, cut his throat, ripped open his belly, sliced off his testicles and, as a gesture of contempt, left them in the dead man's hand. Three members of the *ala* still live; they meet as a funeral club calling themselves the Vigiles Muri, the Guardians of the Wall, in the Lucia Gloriosa tavern. They'll be there tonight. I think you should meet them. Well,' Helena rose to her feet, 'I'm sure you have questions, but they'll have to wait. Burrus, my furry shadow,' she added, 'bring more stools, some fresh wine and sweet biscuits, then we'll meet our guests.'

Claudia excused herself. She slipped out of the chamber and asked a chamberlain for directions. She found the latrines deserted and momentarily marvelled at the sheer luxury of the tiled floor, the marble walls, the mosaic celebrating Neptune's glories, the paintings of pot-bellied ships with golden sails on light blue seas, their waves gilded with gems under a glowing sun set in an amethyst-studded sky. She relished the coolness afforded by vents high in the walls. She went across to the lavarium, poured cold water into a bowl and washed her hands and face, then sat on a ledge in the corner drawing deep breaths to calm her heart. She was still recovering from the events at the She Asses; now all this! Yet her joy at Murranus' new-found post made it all worth while. At last! Claudia tapped her feet on the floor; she could dance with glee! Murranus would not fight! He would have a secure post, the beginning perhaps of other things.

Claudia recollected herself, hastily checked her gown

and hurried back to the chamber. Helena and her guests sat in a semicircle. The Empress glared at Claudia and gestured around, quickly introducing Urbana, Cassia, Leartus and Theodore. Claudia was immediately aware of the beauty of the two women: Urbana, severe and strict; Cassia soft and mellow like a rare flower blooming under the sun. Murranus sat staring at the latter, mouth gaping. Claudia felt a stab of envy. Urbana was beautiful in a patrician, haughty-faced way, but Cassia was sultry, her eyes full of laughter, lips ripe and voluptuous. Claudia swallowed hard and took her seat. Helena made a sign. Urbana, ignoring Claudia, continued to talk about Murranus' duties in looking after the young Alexander. She acted imperiously, impressing upon the gladiator the need to guard her stepson night and day, how he would sleep in the outer chamber of the boy's bedroom and accompany him everywhere he went. She insisted that he must be armed at all times.

Claudia kept looking at Cassia and the dark-faced eunuch standing a little behind her. Claudia had worked with many eunuchs. Leartus had some of their effete ways but he was not so tense or fidgety. He stood dark-eyed, smiling as if he was enjoying the impression his truly beautiful mistress was making on the company, Helena included. Cassia was now smiling at Claudia, talking with her eyes, glancing quickly at Murranus then back at her. Claudia grinned. Cassia was telling her brazenly that Murranus was handsome but Claudia need not worry. She had to stifle her laughter as Cassia threw a quick glance at Theodore and raised her beautiful eyes heavenwards. Claudia fully understood the reason why. Theodore looked and acted the born actor. He was athletic, of medium height, his smooth-shaven face heavily oiled under a mop of curly black hair, his eyebrows neatly plucked, lips slightly painted. He was a man used to being at the centre of attention. He fidgeted constantly, pursing his lips and playing with the glittering bracelets on his wrists.

Urbana's clipped, precise speech drew to a close, and she turned to Claudia, scrutinising her curiously.

'Claudia enjoys my full confidence,' Helena murmured softly, 'as does Murranus.'

Claudia decided not to wait for Urbana to deliver another speech. 'You have come from the Villa Carina?' she asked. 'Senator Carinus must be distraught and angry. How did his daughter's abductors gain access? Surely there were guards?'

Urbana gestured at Theodore, who was almost jumping up and down on his cushioned stool, eager to speak. 'There were guards,' the actor declared as if delivering the prologue to a play. 'Senator Carinus had hired some bully-boys, but they were quite drunk. It was I who raised the alarm.'

'Tell me,' Claudia interrupted, 'what exactly happened?'

'I was with Antonia in her private part of the garden near the Fountain of Artemis. We were discussing Seneca's *Oedipus*. Suddenly,' Theodore flailed his hands, 'out of the trees slunk these walking shadows, phantasms of Hades.'

'The attackers?' Claudia demanded, trying to keep her face straight.

Cassia had now lowered her beautiful head, that mop of golden hair hiding her face, and her shoulders were shaking.

Leartus was chewing on his lip but his eyes were bright with laughter.

'The attackers?' Claudia repeated.

'They were dressed in leather kilts, bare-chested except for belts and baldrics. Actors' masks covered their faces as if they were characters from one of Terence's comedies. I—'

'Then what happened?' Helena snapped.

Theodore remembered himself and some of his dramatic flourishes ceased.

'They grabbed Antonia. I attacked one and dragged off his mask. I saw his face in the torchlight, bearded and scarred; his nose was broken, his lips puffed out, a former boxer surely?'

'When you join us at the She Asses,' Claudia remarked, 'you must give us that description again. Perhaps there is someone there who might recognise it.'

She paused, studying Theodore intently. She had no evidence, nothing but her own instinct, yet she was sure the actor was lying. She had lived, eaten and worked with the likes of Theodore from Ravenna in the north to Tarentum in the south. They were all the same: good people, but they lived for the performance, the show, whatever that might be. So if Theodore was lying, why? To win the favour of Carinus so that he'd be lavishly rewarded as the saviour of the hour, the great hero, a story he could dine out on in the wine booths of the city? Or was he part of the conspiracy? She recalled those heavy masks actors wore; they were usually strapped very firmly to the face. Had Theodore really pulled one off? If not, and she really believed he hadn't, why did he mention it?

51

'Then what happened?' she asked softly.

Theodore nursed the side of his head. 'I received a blow.' He assumed all the airs of a victim. 'I fell down. I was in great pain, confused. By the time I recovered, Antonia,' his voice broke dramatically, 'Antonia,' he sobbed, 'was gone! Those creatures of the night had taken her!'

'They came and left.' Urbana spoke up. 'I questioned Senator Carinus, his stewards and freedmen. He,' Urbana flicked her fingers at Theodore, 'raised the alarm, but it was too late.'

Claudia rocked backwards and forwards on her stool. Helena glanced swiftly at her. Good little mouse, the Empress thought, sitting in the corner watching and hearing everything. All the time your sharp mind nibbles away at what you observe!

'They must have known.' Claudia raised her head. 'The abductors, they must have known where to go. You said Antonia was in her private part of the garden. Why did they go there? Somebody must have led them to it.'

Theodore, realising he may have placed himself under suspicion, swallowed hard and nodded.

'Someone must have told them,' Claudia insisted.

'Senator Carinus,' Leartus spoke softly as his mistress' lovely fingers made their intricate signs, 'Senator Carinus,' he repeated, 'had hired servants for that night, porters, lamp-lighters, scullions and maids.'

'Ah yes.' Claudia turned so that Cassia could watch her lips. 'That is possible, mistress. I thank you. One or more of those could have been part of the gang and brought them to the fountain, plotting the way both there and back.'

'The grounds of the Villa Carina,' Leartus continued, 'are most spacious. Its curtain wall is screened by a thick line of trees and dense bushes. Further in,' Leartus watched Cassia's hands move quickly, 'there are orchards, vine trellises . . .'

Claudia nodded in agreement. 'Tell me,' she spoke directly to Leartus, 'how long have you known your mistress? Since your arrival in Rome?' She ignored Urbana's quick hiss of disapproval at the abrupt change in conversation. She wanted to shift attention from Theodore, whose lower lip was beginning to tremble; clearly the actor was now terrified of being accused of involvement in Antonia's abduction. Leartus seemed to understand. He glanced quickly at Cassia, who nodded.

'I have known my mistress,' Leartus moved his head from side to side, 'for some fifteen years. We were taught this sign language by one of her . . .' he paused in embarrassment, but Cassia nodded, 'by one of my mistress' former patrons, before she accepted the love of the Lord Christ.'

'Are you a follower of the Way?' Claudia used Presbyter Sylvester's term for his religion.

'Oh yes!' Leartus agreed. 'I have been baptised and received the imposition of hands. I am allowed to participate in the Agape.'

'Ah yes.' Claudia smiled understandingly. The Agape lay at the heart of the Christian faith: their belief that bread and wine could be transformed into the Body of the Risen Christ.

'Theology,' Urbana's voice turned waspish, 'might solve this, but God needs a helping hand. Your Excellency,' she continued brusquely, 'I am most pleased that Murranus can join us, his courage and skill are legendary, but what about the future, the past? These vile creatures who have—'

'They'll be caught,' Helena snapped. 'They will be caught.'

Urbana gestured deprecatingly at Claudia.

'Don't!' Helena drew herself up. 'I am the mother of the Emperor of Rome. My word is law. Those responsible for these heinous deeds will die by crucifixion or in the amphitheatre. Have more trust in Claudia.' She looked at her protégée, who sat, hands in her lap. Claudia was used to such insults and always vowed never to react or allow herself to be drawn in.

'Nothing,' Helena whispered, 'is what it appears in this city.' She leaned over and patted Claudia gently on the shoulder. 'A slingshot is small but it can still bring down a giant!'

Urbana shrugged as if grudgingly accepting this. Helena softly clapped her hands, a sign that the audience was over. Everyone except Claudia was told to withdraw and wait in the antechamber. Urbana glanced haughtily down her nose at Claudia; Cassia winked and fluttered her fingers. They all left, Theodore languidly protesting how his stomach was delicate and how at the She Asses he would have to be most careful what he ate and drank.

Helena waited until the door closed behind them, Burrus standing guard against it. Then she eased off her sandals and went and stood on the balcony overlooking the gardens. She beckoned Claudia to join her and put an arm around her, drawing her close.

'Christians,' she laughed softly, 'I love them dearly but

they can act so superior. They should study their scriptures more closely and exercise humility. Urbana is powerful. Who knows how she got old Aurelian so firmly under her thumb. In two days' time,' she drew Claudia closer, 'Antonia will be released. There will be no soldiers or Vigiles, but I want you, Claudia, like the mouse you are, scurrying around that cemetery to see what you can find.' She hugged Claudia tightly. 'Do that,' she whispered, 'hunt these kidnappers down, and I'll make sure Murranus becomes too fat and wealthy,' she relaxed her grip, 'to bother about the arena.'

They walked arm in arm back into the Nile Chamber. Helena paused before an exquisite mosaic depicting two temple girls in their oiled wigs and linen sheath dresses offering sacrifice to Anubis, the dog-headed God of the Underworld. 'They're certainly not Urbana and Cassia,' she murmured. 'Both those women rank high in the Christian hierarchy, personal friends of the Bishop. Urbana could make a lot of trouble for us. She and Cassia are shrewd. Urbana may have been a dancer in Britain, or so they say, but she apparently controls Aurelian. Cassia may look soft, but she is hard-headed and businesslike. Now listen, Claudia, there's something else. When those two veterans were murdered, a young woman reeking of perfume was glimpsed going down the stairs near Petilius' chamber. When Lucius, the second veteran, was murdered, a similar woman was glimpsed nearby. These are the reports I have culled from my informers. Whether they are true or not, I cannot tell. I've asked Cassia for her help. She still has some connections with the inhabitants of

Rome's underworld; she may be able to help in the many problems we face. I also want to know why Petilius was so eager to speak to Aurelian and why his killer imitated the barbarities of the Picts.'

'And the abductions?' Claudia asked. 'Shall I question the other victims?'

'Little point,' Helena replied. 'Their parents don't want them to be reminded, whilst they know very little except that the room they were imprisoned in was cold and smelly, with a rough floor. What do you think of Theodore?' she abruptly added.

'He could have been involved,' Claudia replied. 'I suspect he is telling lies, whatever the reason. He knows something, but his real game could be that he wants Carinus to reward him as well as being fêted as the hero, the all-conquering Hercules.'

Helena patted Claudia's arm and they walked towards the door.

'He complains about his belly like a child,' the Empress scoffed. 'Oh, by the way, Claudia.' She stopped and drew away. 'What's this I hear about a miracle at the She Asses . . . ?'

Claudia and Murranus, with Theodore walking between them, left the Palatine Palace and made their way down into the busy city streets. Claudia was confused; so much had happened, she really needed to reflect. Theodore was rubbing his stomach and muttering to himself.

'What was that?' Claudia asked, turning.

Theodore stared up at the sky. 'I feel frightened,' he remarked. 'I want to pay my devotions.'

'Now is not the time for religion,' Claudia snapped. 'You are to come with us to the She Asses tavern. Theodore,' she grasped the man by the arm and stared up into his handsome face, 'did you really see an attacker last night?'

'Oh yes.'

Claudia stepped back. 'So what's this about paying devotions?'

'I was saved last night.' The actor now came into his own, lifting his hands so dramatically even passers-by stopped to watch. 'I was saved, I was delivered!'

'Yes, yes, you were,' Claudia intervened, 'but what has that got to do with paying your devotions?'

'Look,' Theodore rubbed his stomach and pointed up at the sky, 'a great danger threatened me. I was there, Claudia! I know what I saw! I was saved by the intervention of the Goddess, so I must give thanks to her.'

'Ye gods,' Murranus whispered. Theodore looked at him sharply.

'It's all right for you, gladiator, you put your trust in your sword arm, but I am different.' He looked pityingly at Claudia, who smiled back. Theodore reminded her so much of the actors she'd worked with, so full of himself, so eager to attract a crowd, he would rise at two in the morning to give a performance.

'What do you truly want?' she asked. 'I mean, to a certain extent you are our prisoner. You heard the Empress; you must come back to the She Asses, but if there is someone you wish to see . . .'

'There is no one,' Theodore declared. 'But I would like to pay devotion to my goddess.'

Claudia stared at Murranus, who shrugged. 'Your goddess,' she asked, 'who is it?'

'The Lady Hathor of the White Walls,' Theodore replied. 'If I could just visit her temple, it's in the Coelian quarter.'

Claudia closed her eyes and groaned. The area of the Coelian Hill was even worse than the slums around the Flavian Gate, but at least it was still daylight.

'I would like to go,' Theodore declared. 'I promise you, I won't be long: sprinkle some incense, make sacrifice.'

Reluctantly Claudia agreed. They left the thoroughfare, threading their way along alleys and runnels into the Coelian Hill quarter. Here Murranus drew his sword. This was the haunt of tricksters, conjurors, sorcerers, warlocks and murderers. Every rogue in Rome thrived here. Claudia followed Theodore as he led her down an alleyway and into a square. On the far side stood a temple much decayed, its pillars crumbling, the steps chipped, the plaster tympanum above the main entrance weathered and decayed. Nevertheless, the number of pilgrims streaming in and out, many of them prosperous, showed how popular the cult was. Claudia recalled how Presbyter Sylvester regarded what he called 'Eastern religions' to be the greatest rival to his own faith.

Theodore led them across, brushing aside the hawkers, traders and tinkers who tried to sell artefacts and objects related to the worship of Hathor, the Lady of Gleefulness. Claudia remembered how Hathor was an Egyptian goddess; in her acting troupe, both Hathor and the Lady Isis were highly popular, often the cause of much drunkenness and joy. They reached the bottom of the steps. Theodore wanted to go in by himself, but Claudia insisted that she and Murranus follow him. A beggar squatted beside the main door with his clacking dish, mouth whining for alms. Two muscular priests stood on guard at the temple door. Theodore whispered to them and they stood aside.

Inside the temple was cool but smelled musty from mildew, age and decay; nevertheless, it possessed a certain grandeur. At the far end, at the top of some steps, stood an altar, a tabernacle or naos in the centre, its doors open to reveal the statue of the Lady Hathor surrounded by oil lamps. Before the altar ranged baskets of flowers and small dishes of burning incense. A priest came forward. He was tall, dressed in the Egyptian fashion, a white linen kilt around his waist, his bare chest and shoulders covered by a thin gauze veil. He had rings on his fingers, bracelets on his wrists, and a sharp, harsh face with pointed nose, pouting lips and piercing black eyes. His hair was not shaved in the Egyptian fashion but oiled and pulled back, fastened in a queue by a clasp at the back of his head. Theodore went up to him and bowed.

'High Priest Sesothenes!'

The man bowed in return.

'These are my companions,' Theodore exclaimed, pointing to Claudia. 'She is a friend of the Empress, and this is Murranus, Champion, Victor of the Games.'

Sesothenes stared at Claudia and then at Murranus. The look wasn't friendly. He licked thin dry lips.

'What do you want, Theodore?' he said. 'Why are you here?'

'I wish to pay sacrifice,' Theodore exclaimed. 'I want to thank the Lady for my escape from great danger.'

'What danger?' Sesothenes asked. 'Oh, I'm sorry.' He turned to Claudia and made a mock bow. 'I am Sesothenes, formerly a member of the infantry in the Third Victrix based at Alexandria, now High Priest of the Lady Hathor. You know she has her main temple at Memphis in Egypt?'

'Yes, yes.' Claudia gestured at Theodore. 'He insisted on visiting her here. He wants to pay sacrifice, give thanks. Can he do that?'

'Of course.' Sesothenes scratched at a bead of sweat running down his smooth-shaven cheek. 'And it is free. Come, my friend.' He nodded at Murranus and Claudia and, one hand on Theodore's shoulder, led him down the temple towards the sanctuary and the opened naos.

Claudia stared around. She'd seen such temples before: the paintings on the walls, the flower baskets, the smell of incense, the hum of conversation. She studied the pilgrims coming in and out. Men and women from all parts of the Empire, eager to pay devotion. She noticed there were no hesets or temple girls here; just four priests. They looked like their high priest. Former soldiers, hard-faced, tough and dressed in white gauffered robes, they moved easily amongst the pilgrims, taking coins and offerings, listening, nodding solemnly as they reassured votaries that sacrifice would be made or prayers offered. Claudia felt tired and impatient. She wanted to get back to the She Asses tavern. She was concerned that Helena knew about the Great Miracle and that Theodore tell the truth about exactly what he had seen the previous night. She looked down the temple. The actor was kneeling on the steps. In one hand he held an incense boat, in the other a posy of flowers. Head back, he was whispering his prayer, Sesothenes standing behind him.

'Why do people believe in all this?' Murranus asked.

Claudia moved aside to allow more pilgrims to drift into the temple.

'Do you believe in it, Claudia?'

She walked across and stared up at the man she loved. 'I don't believe in anything, Murranus, I just believe that we must seize the day and enjoy life. Gods, temples, priests, offerings, what difference do they make?' She gestured towards Theodore, still kneeling on the steps. 'What do you think of him?'

'An actor,' Murranus laughed, 'a man who always plays parts. He's definitely got a delicate stomach.'

'I wonder,' Claudia answered, 'whether it's a delicate stomach or if he's nervous. I don't think our actor is the stuff heroes are made of.'

She noticed how Sesothenes was now leaning over Theodore, listening as the actor whispered something. The priest nodded. A fresh incense boat was pushed on to the altar steps before him and Claudia groaned, but then Theodore bowed, rose to his feet and walked back towards them. He rubbed his stomach and smiled.

'I feel much better now,' he said. 'Shall we go?'

Claudia walked towards the door of the temple, then turned abruptly.

'Theodore,' she said as she walked back, 'you've just given thanks to your lady goddess. Here, in her temple, tell me the truth! Did you see the face of one of those attackers?'

61

'Oh yes!' Theodore's voice rose almost to a yelp. 'I tell you I did!'

Walking out of the temple, Claudia stood on the steps and watched the makeshift stalls coming down. 'The day is nearly done,' she murmured. 'It's time to return to the mischief of the She Asses.'

Chapter 3

Hic vivimus ambitiosa paupertate omnes.
Here we all live in a state of pretentious poverty.

Juvenal, *Satires*

Antonia, daughter of Senator Carinus, squatted in the corner. Despite the blindfold, she'd learned where the cracked water jug stood, the bowl of dried bread and soft fruit as well as the latrine pot. The chain binding her was long enough to reach these, as well as allowing her to stand and walk. She had been blindfolded since she'd been captured, yet she was aware of people coming and going. She'd stretched up and found that the ceiling was high, hence the coolness; the walls were rough. One thing did terrify Antonia – she had regained her wits and desperately recalled what she'd heard about these abductions. All the other victims had survived, so she knew she wasn't going to be killed. What frightened her was not the future but the immediate, a deep suspicion that she was being very closely watched. She quickly realised that her captives owned mastiffs, powerful animals. She had brushed by one of them when she'd been brought here and heard their slobbering when they'd been fed. But there was something else: one of her captors was deeply interested in her. On occasion she'd heard his heavy breathing, then his hard hand had plunged down the loose tunic and roughly felt her breast, followed by a grunt of pleasure.

Antonia backed into the corner and moaned softly. The man was back watching her now. She heard a sound and tried to move but a hard bristly cheek brushed hers; the voice was coarse, the breath reeking of wine.

'Don't shout or scream, Antonia.'

She felt the cords of her tunic being loosened, and it was pulled away.

'Don't scream,' the voice whispered, 'or you die. I'm just here for a little fun. Oh, what lovely breasts, ripe and full. Go on, Antonia, turn round.'

She whimpered, shaking.

'Turn around!'

She felt the tip of a dagger against her throat. She turned round and felt the man press hard against her, gasping with pleasure. Another sound, a slight groan, someone choking; a warm liquid splashed the back of her legs. She whirled round, kicking with her legs, lips parted to scream but she could not. A hand seized her gently by the chin, and this time the voice was soft.

'Antonia, don't be frightened. He shouldn't have done that, but now he is dead. I cut his throat!'

A wet cloth was pushed into her hand.

'Clean yourself, Antonia. Don't worry, *your* throat is safe as long as you do exactly what we say . . .'

Once back at the She Asses tavern, Claudia locked herself in her chamber, took off her tunic and loincloth, washed herself and lay naked on the bed. She felt so tired and harassed she couldn't have cared if half of Rome came trooping through her chamber.

'Ye gods!' she muttered to the ceiling. 'Theodore could talk you to death! He'd win the crown for sheer boredom.'

The actor had chattered incessantly from the moment they'd left the Temple of Hathor until they reached the uproar which still reigned at the She Asses. The crowds, aware of the Great Miracle, had thronged in to view the Sacred Corpse, as Polybius now advertised it. Her uncle was doing a roaring trade charging those who wished to view the corpse, then inviting them to sample the 'fine wines and tasty food' of his establishment. Poppaoe, Januaria, Sorry, Oceanus, Mercury the Messenger, Simon the Stoic, and Petronius the Pimp had all been recruited for the kitchens, the counter or the garden. A hot-faced Poppaoe had whispered how the Vigiles had been and gone, their palms well greased with silver. The police had proudly announced that the Great Miracle was not the result of a murder and, consequently, did not fall within their jurisdiction; their captain had eagerly taken up Polybius' invitation to return after sunset for a 'sumptuous meal' and cups of the best Falernian, all on the house. Apuleius the Apothecary, together with Narcissus the Neat, had also been busy investigating; they had eventually established that the corpse was the mortal remains of one Fulgentia.

'A virgin,' Poppaoe whispered, 'brought in from the countryside by Diocletian's agents. An old porter near the Flavian Gate has identified the corpse. He remembers her being brought to the gatehouse and recalls her name. She later disappeared. No one knows anything about her background. Apuleius believes she was a refugee from the south, fleeing from persecution, being passed from one local Christian community to the next.'

Claudia had only half listened; she'd heard so much of Theodore's chatter about his stomach, his diet, his triumphs, his finest roles, his favourite authors, towns and theatres, then back to his stomach, that she couldn't listen to anyone any more. On their journey back, Murranus had begun to whistle under his breath whilst Claudia had tried to question the actor about what precisely had happened near the Fountain of Artemis in the gardens of the Villa Carina. Theodore could add little to what he had already said, and Claudia's suspicions only deepened that he was being truthful about most things but holding something back. She narrowed her eyes and watched a fly crawling across the ceiling. Theodore was harmless, so full of himself, he had little time for anyone else. She listened to the noise below and sighed. Helena already knew about the Great Miracle. Well, of course she would! Helena's informers swarmed everywhere. Claudia wondered idly who it could be here.

'Simon the Stoic!' she murmured. 'I've always wondered how he came by his paltry coins.' Claudia didn't object. It wasn't that the Empress distrusted her; Helena just wanted to know the truth. Watching Polybius downstairs, Claudia had realised that the uncle she loved so much, for all his roguish ways, was up to something, but what? Polybius, for all his nefarious dealings, would not sink to murder or body-snatching, whilst Apuleius was a man of integrity. Claudia's eyes grew heavy, but she shook herself awake. She had to dress, eat and go out to the Lucia Gloriosa tavern to meet those veterans. Murranus would escort her. She smiled again and stretched. Tomorrow Murranus would report to Aurelian's villa and she would go with him to make sure!

Claudia sat up. She must concentrate on the present. Murranus would have to wait; these abductions had to be investigated. She swung her feet off the bed. One conclusion she had reached was that the kidnappings must have been organised by someone who knew about their victims' movements. Before she left the palace, Claudia had read both the police reports and those of Helena's agents, yet she'd discovered nothing new. All the victims had been seized when they were vulnerable, in a lane, a lonely part of a garden, as they left the house early in the morning or returned from the baths in the evening. The ransom demanded was very substantial but not enough to make the victims' parents hesitate, whilst the place of liberation was well chosen. The great cemetery bordering the Appian Way was a rambling, desolate wasteland with dips and ditches, copses of trees, tangled bushes and thick undergrowth. Miles of decaying tombs, monuments, pillars, many cracked and open to the elements, made that place of death the natural haunt of outlaws, footpads and escaped slaves. The entire area reeked of misery and decay, the meeting place of every undesirable that crawled under the sun. Claudia had heard stories about people getting lost there and, by the time they stumbled out, being almost witless with terror. Others had gone into the cemetery and never returned. The Via Appia bordered one side of the cemetery whilst the rest of it petered out into open countryside, a place easy to slip in and out of. Every so often the city authorities would organise troops, both cavalry and infantry, to make a sweep of what one official called 'the meadows of murder'; even then pitched battles ensued between the inhabitants of that twilight area and trained troops. During the persecution of Diocletian, the Christians not only hid in the cemetery but opened up the gloomy catacombs below, a maze of needle-thin passageways, corridors, galleries and open chambers. The poor used to bury their dead there, but the Christians took it over and transformed it into an underground city.

Claudia had closely studied both the cemetery and the catacombs. The only person to her knowledge who owned a map describing the cemetery and the City of the Dead beneath was the powerful priest Sylvester. He had made a copy and given it to Claudia so she could study and memorise it section by section. He was always pleased to meet her there. She strongly suspected that Sylvester entertained hopes that she'd join his sect. After all, her father had been a Christian, and because of him, Claudia had been drawn into the political intrigue of the Christian community as it fought to escape persecution and gain official recognition. Sylvester had promised Claudia his complete support in hunting down the man who had murdered her brother and raped her.

Claudia lay back on the bed, chewing her lip. She scratched a bead of sweat from her face, half listening to the sounds from the tavern below. Petronius the Pimp was singing a bawdy song about a tavern-keeper who was trying to hire a good cook, another problem facing Polybius. Claudia smiled. Petronius had been drinking all day. She tried to shut out his voice and returned to the question of the catacombs where she used to meet Sylvester. Would they meet again now her enemy had been killed? Would Sylvester use her as a means of strengthening his ties with the Augusta? Or would they use each other and become allies, if not friends, in any crisis which faced them? Claudia quietly promised herself that sometime soon she would meet Sylvester and see what help he might provide. She glanced towards the window. Petronius had stopped singing. She groaned as she heard Theodore's booming voice; the actor was reciting lines about the death of Achilles before the walls of Troy.

'Will that man ever shut up!' Claudia murmured. She swung herself off the bed and walked across to the lavarium. She took a sponge and a tablet of her precious soap and washed herself carefully, cleaning her teeth with the powder Apuleius had recommended. She rubbed oil into her body and tinctured herself with a little of the precious Kiphye perfume, distilled from the blue lotus, which Murranus had bought her. She put on green linen underwear, dressed sensibly in a brown tunic, a belt around her waist with a thin sheath for a knife, and put on what Polybius called her marching boots. She threw a cloak around her shoulders, took her staff with a carved face on its handle from the corner and left the chamber, going down the stairs into the spacious eating hall. The place was still very busy. Daylight was fading so the oil lamps and lanterns had been lit. The kitchen was doing a most profitable trade, although Theodore, refusing the food on the platter before him, sat nursing his stomach. 'You'll have to wait!' Claudia whispered to herself.

Poppaoe went bustling by carrying a dish of steaming food; behind her trotted Sorry, holding a tray of wine cups. The kitchen was also full, people hiring stools so they could sit in a corner and eat from their platters. Claudia escaped into the garden. Murranus, Polybius, Apuleius and Narcissus were gathered in the far corner. Polybius had been drinking heavily and grinned benevolently as she approached. Claudia forced a scowl. She could tell by the almost empty jug that Apuleius and Narcissus had been matching him cup for cup. She quietly muttered a prayer of thanks; at least Murranus was sober. She refused to sit down but gestured back at the tavern.

'Are you sure about what you've found?'

'Certain,' Apuleius slurred. 'The corpse of that young woman is perfectly preserved. I can't find any cause of death.'

'I would agree,' Narcissus quickly intervened. He picked up the wine jug and emptied it into his own goblet. He toasted Claudia, took a generous sip and tried to look sober as he half rose, wagging a finger in Claudia's face. 'I've seen more corpses,' he declared, 'than you have gladiators.' He started to laugh at his joke, then sat down trying to pull his face straight. 'I'm a professional embalmer,' he continued. 'Before I became a slave and the Empress freed me, I prepared the dead, young and old, male and female, rich and poor. I can tell just by looking at a corpse how they died, and that one is a real mystery!'

'What we need,' Polybius slurred, 'is a professional cook to cater for our increased clientele. That pompous actor for one doesn't like our food. Ah well, our Great Miracle has certainly brought increased custom!'

Claudia was tempted to ask more questions, but the sun was setting and a cool breeze was blowing. She had to meet those veterans at the tavern. Murranus was also impatient, tapping his fingers on the table and studying one of the garden statues, a carving of the goddess Diana of the Ephesians, as Polybius liked to describe it. Claudia touched the gladiator on the shoulder, then absent-mindedly kissed Polybius on the brow, patted Narcissus on the head and wished them all good night. She and Murranus left by the side gate. The gladiator paused in the alleyway to tighten the sword belt beneath his cloak. He grasped a heavy cudgel in one hand, Claudia's hand in the other, as they both went down into the busy square.

Claudia always found Rome at twilight a fascinating place, that time between night and day when the Citizens of the Light returned to their garrets, houses or apartments and the Citizens of the Dark came to life! They were all gathering to greet the night. The prostitutes, faces painted, balding heads covered in garish wigs, clustered like a collection of multicoloured butterflies on the corners of alleyways or the entrances to decaying houses and apartment blocks. Sharp-eyed pimps were touting for business. Hawkers and traders were setting up their stalls, most of their goods being the plunder from robberies or what other markets had rejected. Cooks were firing their portable stoves and grills, shouting what they had to sell, most of which was grilled or roasted until it was burned and the putrid taste hidden under cheap sauces and spices. Second-hand clothes-sellers hung their products from the branches of trees, whilst the money-changers, the receivers of stolen goods, lurked deep in the shadows advertising their presence with a tinkling bell. A small boy ran up with a cage of yellow birds; another tried to pester them with purses made out of snakeskin. Claudia just ignored them. She kept thinking of those abductions. Whoever organised the gang would draw their recruits from a place like this, a shifting population of former soldiers, outlaws, tricksters, rejects, slaves on the run, desperate men and women who'd sell their souls for a cup of wine and kill without a qualm for a silver coin.

The deeper into the city they walked, the busier the crowds became. Here and there a squad of auxiliaries or a group of Vigiles squatted outside the door of some tavern keeping an eye on what was happening, though they were more prepared to take a bribe and look the other way than do anything. Of course people recognised Murranus and greeted him with good-natured abuse and catcalls, which the gladiator just ignored.

'I wish . . .' Claudia paused at the corner of the alleyway leading down to the Lucia Gloriosa tavern.

'What do you wish?' Murranus bent down to hear above the sound of a line of clattering carts.

'I wish I'd questioned Theodore more closely.'

Murranus just squeezed her hand. 'Oh, don't worry about him,' he reassured. 'Theodore will make himself at home. He'll relax and tomorrow it will be all the easier to question him.'

Claudia agreed and walked on towards the Lucia Gloriosa, a fine, spacious eating-house and wine shop, in many ways very similar to the She Asses tavern. The owner, a former soldier, explained that there were no chambers upstairs, only a long, high-ceilinged room into which he ushered them. The chamber's pink plaster walls were unadorned except for hanging baskets of woven reeds and the occasional coloured cloth. The veterans were already assembled, grouped at one end of a trestle table in the middle of which stood a small portable Lares, its doors open to display a statue of some god, a figure on a rearing horse. The statue looked old. Fashioned out of bronze, it had already turned slightly green, the metal starting to flake. Before the statue glowed two small oil lamps placed either side of a loaf of bread, a bunch of grapes and a jug of wine. The three men were busy, heads together, talking amongst themselves. At first they ignored the new arrivals, then Murranus coughed and the three men drew apart.

'What do you want?' The large, burly-faced man sitting at the end of the table spread out his hands and stared at them aggressively. 'Who do you think you are coming up here? Don't you know?' He glared at the tavern-keeper, who was still standing in the doorway.

'I think you'd better explain,' Murranus whispered.

Claudia undid her cloak, laid it on the end of the table and came forward, hands extended. 'My name is Claudia,' she declared. 'I have been sent by the Empress Helena; she wishes me to investigate the deaths of your two comrades.'

'You? Investigate?' One of the men sniggered and turned away.

'You had better listen to me,' Claudia retorted. 'Two of your comrades have been killed: a cut to the belly, their throats sliced and then castrated.' She paused. 'I am Claudia, agent of the Empress. I carry her *bulla*, her seal. Shall I call up a squad of Vigiles or those mercenaries lounging in the nearby market, then we can go to the palace so all this can be verified? Oh, by the way.' Claudia noticed how the veterans had shifted their attention to her escort. 'This is Murranus, Victor Ludorum – Champion of the Games, but also a freedman.'

The veterans relaxed. They waved the newcomers to the bench, found two more cups and filled each with a measure of water and wine.

As Claudia and Murranus settled at the table, the veterans introduced themselves as Stathylus, Crispus and Secundus; their Latin names belied both their appearance and their accents, which clearly showed them to be provincials. They acted full of confidence, old soldiers who'd seen all the horrors of war and could not be surprised by anything new. Claudia had met their kind before: leathery-skinned, sharp-featured, still wiry despite the folds of fat round the belly and face. They were dressed simply in tunics, belts and sandals. She noticed the war belts heaped in the corner as well as the cudgels and walking sticks lying on top of their cloaks. They were friendly enough, explaining how they met here regularly to share bread and wine and toast former comrades, recall long-forgotten battles and pay homage to their guardian Epona, horse goddess of the Iceni, a tribe which lived along the eastern coastline of Britain. They revelled in their former membership of the Fretenses, and were proud to be called the Vigiles Muri.

Claudia let them chatter on as the wine flowed. Stathylus, sitting at the top of the table, had been a junior officer, a decurion. He was hard-faced, with close-set eyes; he remained both watchful and hostile, aware of what Claudia was doing. Now and again he'd urge his two companions to drink slower or mix more water in their wine cups. Claudia, however, gently encouraged them to discuss their earlier careers, and of course, like all old soldiers, they were only too willing to talk. They were all Iceni horsemen from the flat plains of eastern Britain. Horse-lovers, born cavalrymen, they described how they'd been recruited into the Catephracti, the heavily armed cavalry, and been given various postings in that faraway, mist-shrouded province. Eventually they'd been posted to a mile fort along the Great Wall Emperor Hadrian had built in the north, stretching from coast to coast to seal off the province from the wild tribes beyond. They'd fought under a veteran centurion, Postulus, but during the civil wars, mutinies and the emergence of pretenders such as Allectus and Carausius, their numbers had been depleted. They were proud of having fought for Constantine Chlorus, the present Emperor's father, and of supporting the cause of Helena and her son through all their difficulties. They had

as a unit been honourably discharged and given the opportunity to settle outside Rome. Some had brought their wives
and families; others had simply deserted their roots for a
new future at the heart of the Empire.

Secundus and Crispus did most of the talking. Born story-
tellers, they described their service in Britain, conjuring up
images of deep forests, lonely wind-swept moorlands,
freezing winters when all was carpeted in snow, followed
by springs bursting with light and summers which brought
the brilliant green grasslands and cornfields to life. They
talked of warm breezes, a golden sun and rain-washed blue
skies. Above all they described the Great Wall. Many of
the tribes regarded this as the work of the gods with its
soaring crenellated wall, watchtowers, signal posts, mile
castles and great five-mile fortresses. The two men described
the boredom of military life, offset by the terrors which
lay beyond the wall, where savage Picts and Caledonians,
superb fighters, slipped like wraiths through the tangled
heather to probe, attack and ambush. The savagery and
cunning of these tribesmen was something they had never
forgotten, a terrifying nightmare constantly lurking just
beyond the Roman line, ever vigilant, ruthless and merci-
less. Claudia listened fascinated, aware of the day dying,
the darkness deepening, the flames of the oil lamps growing
stronger. She became less aware of the peppery, spicy odour
of the room, with its wisps of black smoke, whilst every
time she looked at the carving of Epona, it seemed more
lifelike. She noticed, however, that all three veterans deliberately skirted the crowning glory of their careers, the
ambush and annihilation of that Pictish war band. At last

Crispus drew their story to a close. Claudia waited for Stathylus to step into her trap, which he obligingly did.

'What has this,' he hissed, leaning against the table, 'got to do with two of our comrades being killed here in Rome?'

'Everything.'

'What do you mean?'

'Look.' Claudia pushed away her wine cup. 'Two of your companions have been brutally murdered in this city. Petilius in his chamber, Lucius in an alleyway. The slums of Rome are full of men and women who take a life as easily as they would snuff out an oil-wick. However, both your companions were killed in the Pictish way, a knife to the belly, throat slit, then their genitals cut off, the penis placed in the dead man's hand. I understand the Picts do the same to dishonour enemy dead.'

All three men, eyes on Claudia, nodded. Crispus muttered a curse under his breath; Claudia ignored it.

'So why,' she continued, 'have two of your companions been killed in such a barbaric fashion? The logical conclusion is that it has something to do with your service in the Fretenses along the Great Wall. Some demon from the past has come prowling through the darkness to hunt you.'

Stathylus made a rude sound with his lips and quickly picked up his cup. Claudia could see he was frightened; the gesture was meant to divert her.

'Something else.' Claudia tapped the tabletop. 'General Aurelian recently invited you all to a reunion at his villa. You attended?'

'Of course we did.' Secundus spoke up. 'General Aurelian always favoured his men; this year it was our turn.'

'Yet afterwards, Petilius went to see the General about something urgent but the General was too busy to grant him an audience. Do you know what Petilius wanted?'

'We asked that ourselves,' Stathylus replied, 'but Petilius kept a close mouth; he was always like that. Perhaps he wanted to keep the information to himself so as to get some reward; we never found out.'

'But it followed that reunion,' Claudia insisted. 'Did any of you see anything untoward, something from the past?'

A chorus of denials greeted her words.

'Anyway,' she sighed, 'let's go back to the past, the Great Wall. The destruction of that Pictish war band.'

'Some eighteen years ago,' Secundus declared, ignoring Stathylus' warning look. 'It happened eighteen years ago.'

'And yet,' Claudia insisted, 'all this time later, two of your companions have been brutally murdered, in a manner very similar to the abuse perpetrated by your Pictish enemies. Now,' she smiled faintly, 'there are no Pictish warriors in Rome. Why such deaths? True, they might be Pictish slaves, but,' she shrugged, 'how would they recognise you eighteen years later? Moreover, doesn't the report say the entire war band you trapped was wiped out?'

Again there was agreement.

'The ambush also took place at night,' Murranus declared. 'I've seen Catephracti, their helmets are like those I wear in the arena, covering the head and protecting the face; even if one of those Picts did escape, how could they recognise a face, only glimpsed in the dark, some eighteen years later?'

'What did happen,' Claudia asked, 'that night of your great victory?'

'Why do you want to know?'

'I can't really answer that,' Claudia replied, 'except I have a feeling that you don't want to talk about it. I can't understand that. After all, it was a great achievement. More importantly, the grisly murder of your comrades, executed in a way so reminiscent of the Picts, may have something to do with the massacre of so many of their people. A matter of logic,' Claudia added, 'unless there is something else you haven't told me.'

All three refused to meet her gaze.

'Ah well.' Stathylus rubbed a hand across his face. 'I'll tell you.' He filled his wine goblet, gulped greedily from it and slammed it back on the table.

'In the winter of our ninth year of service, eighteen years ago last July, the Fretenses, an *ala* of cavalry attached to the Second Legion Augusta, were guarding a mile fort along the Great Wall. There were only twelve or fifteen of us, under our officer, Postulus, a Gaul from Lyon. We were skilled fighters, a crack mounted force, but we were virtually leaderless. Civil war raged in Britain.' Stathylus raised a hand. 'This pretender, that pretender. The wall was stripped of men; cohorts and units greatly reduced. At one mile fort there were only three men left; we were the lucky ones. Now we learned that a Pictish war band was on the move, heading south to probe our weakness. Postulus? Well,' Stathylus shrugged, 'he liked to drink . . .'

'So you were left in charge.'

'Yes.' Stathylus nodded. 'I hate Picts, I always have, cruel bastards, sly and treacherous. By then Postulus was totally inebriated. Anyway, I was in charge, and I thought of a plan. We rode out searching for that band and killed a few.'

'To provoke the blood feud?' Murranus asked. 'To draw them further south? I've heard of that being done.'

'Precisely,' Stathylus agreed. 'Once we had their attention, we retreated back to our mile fort. The Picts followed us south and launched an attack; it failed. Shortly afterwards Postulus died from his drinking.' He grinned sourly. 'In official dispatches, he was classed as killed in action, but that was simply to honour his name. We didn't have time to dress his corpse so we left it there, abandoning the mile fort.'

Stathylus paused to drink; his two companions had turned slightly away from Claudia as if they didn't want her to study their faces. She was sure a lie was being told, just by their posture. Stathylus, more absorbed with his wine, was now back in time at that lonely fort along the Great Wall.

'We left the beacon burning; we even left the pay chest in the cellar. We'd also secured the northern door so it couldn't be opened from the inside. We then pretended to retreat through the southern gate of the fort. The land beyond dropped. At night we sheltered around a fire in the lea of a hill and waited. The Picts found the fort deserted except for the pay chest and jars of posca.' Stathylus shrugged. 'You know what that's like, horse piss and just as strong. They drank and, being hungry for more booty, poured out of the southern gate. I thought they would. We waited until they were out in the open, disorganised and separated, then we charged. The weather had been dry, so we fired the bracken. We could see them clearly and rode them down. There was only one way for the Picts to retreat and that was back through the fort. They did that, hoping to escape through the northern gate, but we'd locked it fast.' He spread his hands. 'We cut many of them down and pinned the rest, together with their leader, within the fort.'

'It was so easy.' Secundus spoke up quickly. 'We were mounted archers, there was no escape.'

'No prisoners?' Claudia asked. She stared at them curiously. Their answers were so quick, they reminded her of actors delivering well-rehearsed lines, words tripping off the tongue, though to be fair, this must have been a story told time and time again. 'No prisoners at all?' she repeated.

'That's what war along the frontier was like.' Stathylus got to his feet. 'Life for life and a fight to the death.' He scratched his stomach. 'I've drunk a lot,' he muttered. 'I've got to go out for a while.' He stumbled to the door.

Secundus whispered something about getting extra food and left, stomping down the stairs. Claudia turned to Murranus and winked. Crispus seemed to be absorbed, busy tying a thong on his sandal; she raised a finger to her lips for Murranus to remain silent. Crispus was definitely uncomfortable. He straightened up, playing with the wine cup on the table, then began to hum a tune beneath his breath. He kept looking longingly at the door. Eventually the silence proved too much, and he flung a hand out.

'You don't believe us, do you?'

'I do believe you,' Claudia conceded. 'I think you are telling the truth, but not all of it. Something happened along that wall, something that has come back to haunt you all, but why now, eighteen years later?'

She studied Crispus carefully. He was younger than the rest, and she noticed the small bead of sweat running down from beneath his close-cropped hair.

'What are you frightened of, Crispus?'

'The past,' he mumbled, and stared up at the smoke-blackened ceiling. 'Always the past! You don't know what it was like out there, desolate, empty, nothing but the grass bending under the wind, the lonely call of birds, the cry of animals at night and, when the civil war raged in the south, the wall being stripped. We had this nightmare, or at least I did, that the Picts would stream across the wall and surround us, cut us off, take us prisoner. If we fell into their hands . . .' He stared at them and blinked. 'If you fell into the hands of the Picts, they'd take weeks over killing you. I've seen their work: men nailed to trees, prisoners slowly tortured . . .' He wetted his lips, turning his head as if straining for a sound, then muttered something.

'What was that?' Murranus asked. He got to his feet, went closer to the veteran and sat down. 'What is it, Crispus? I have not been a soldier but I know what it's like to fight, to be wounded. What is it you're hiding?'

Crispus opened his mouth to reply but shut it when he heard a sound on the stairs.

'You can't answer, can you?' Claudia asked.

Crispus closed his eyes and shook his head.

'I daren't,' he whispered. 'It had nothing to do with me.'

'You were at General Aurelian's party,' Claudia continued. 'What happened?'

Crispus, relieved at the change in questioning, shrugged and swallowed hard.

'You know the General, or perhaps you don't,' he replied. 'Generous, a great man, a good leader, he looked after his troops. Well, over the years he invited all those who'd served with him to a banquet in his garden. They were marvellous occasions, beautiful lanterns hanging from the trees, serving girls, ladies of the night, musicians, actors, tumblers. This year it was our turn. None of us wanted to miss such an exciting evening. We gathered just before dusk and the celebrations went on well into the next day. The General is a hospitable man; those who wanted to could sleep in the gardens, and when they woke up to quench their thirst, there was more food and wine.'

'Did you see anyone,' Claudia persisted, 'or anything which reminded you of the past?'

Crispus closed his eyes, thinking hard.

'Anything at all,' Murranus insisted. 'Anything untoward.'

Crispus opened his eyes. 'I swear,' he pointed to the Lares on the table, 'I swear by that. I saw nothing, I heard nothing.'

'And the rest?' Murranus asked. 'Stathylus, Lucius, Petilius, Secundus?'

'Petilius may have.' Crispus paused to recollect his thoughts. 'I'm not too sure what he wanted to see General Aurelian about. We presumed it was something that happened at the party, because it was only after he saw him that he began his petitioning. It could have been something else. As for the rest of us,' he shook his head, 'nothing untoward was noticed, nothing at all.'

'Nothing what?'

Claudia looked round. Secundus, a platter of bread and

cheese in one hand, his other resting against the doorpost, was staring threateningly across.

'What's going on here?' Secundus strolled across and slammed the platter down on to the table. 'If you've got any questions, wait for our officer to return.'

Murranus got to his feet and squared up to him.

'Do you want to die, Secundus?' he asked quietly. The veteran blinked. 'Do you want to die?' Murranus pushed his face closer. 'Because I'll tell you this, someone in Rome is killing former members of your cavalry troop. Your friends are dying in a barbaric way. How do you know you won't be next? I don't think we've been told the truth.' He gestured at Claudia. 'She is the Empress' representative. If you want, we will invite you back to the palace and we can continue our conversation there.'

'We've done nothing wrong!' Secundus blustered. 'You can't arrest us.'

Murranus seized the man's face between his hands. Secundus had the sense not to resist. 'Listen, you fool,' Murranus whispered hoarsely, 'we are not arresting you, only trying to protect you.'

'Where's Stathylus?' Crispus half rose. 'I thought he'd gone out to relieve himself. He should be back by now.'

Murranus took away his hands. Secundus walked to the table, drew the dagger from his waistband, cut himself a piece of bread and cheese and started chewing noisily. Claudia was about to return to her questioning when she heard a cry from below. She hurried to the door and stared down the wooden stairs. The tavern-keeper stood listening to a grimy-faced maid who was hysterically pointing to the half-open door. Claudia hastened down, followed by Murranus and the rest. The girl, gibbering with fright, led them out of the tavern and down to a small alleyway, a needle-thin passageway running between the houses. The tavern-keeper carried a lantern. At first Claudia thought the girl was pointing to a bundle of rubbish, old clothes – until the tavern-keeper placed the lantern on the ground. The light within strengthened, and the tavern-keeper swung away, one hand to his mouth.

Claudia slowly approached. She lifted the lantern and peered down. Stathylus lay wedged almost in the corner of the wall and the dirty rutted trackway, head tilted, his throat like a bloody gaping mouth, a terrible gash along his belly, his right hand thrown back holding what looked liked a piece of severed bloody meat. Claudia felt her gorge rise and hastily retreated. She leaned against the wall trying to control her stomach, half listening to the others' exclamations, the girl still whimpering, the tavern-keeper retching.

It was Murranus who imposed order. He returned to the tavern and came back carrying a large piece of sacking, shouting at Secundus and Crispus to help. Stathylus was lifted on to the piece of sacking, which was wrapped tightly about him, and taken across the tavern yard to an outhouse, where he was placed on an old trestle table. Lamps were brought. Claudia went out with the rest to study the corpse, but it was too much, the look of terror on Stathylus' face, those awful wounds to the throat and the belly, the great bloody mess between his legs. She could take no more and, hand to her mouth, hastened back to the tavern and its upper room. She sat for a while shivering. The lights before the Lares were now burning low; one was guttering. She stared at that bronze statue, the sinister helmeted figure, cloak billowing around the rearing horse.

'Now,' she muttered to herself, 'now they'll believe me.'

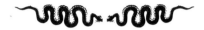

Chapter 4

Hoc volo, sic iubeo: sit pro ratione voluntas.
I will do this deed, so I order it done. Let my will
  stand for my reason.

Juvenal, Satires

Claudia hastily refilled her goblet of wine and drank it a
little faster than she'd intended, half listening to the sounds
from downstairs. She peered at the statue and recalled
Murranus' question at the Temple of Hathor. If the truth
be known, she believed in no religion. She could accept
there might be a God, but all this bloodshed and horrid
death, the sheer cheapness and brutality of life, how could
Presbyter Sylvester explain all that? Noises on the stairs
alerted her. Murranus, Secundus and Crispus came into the
chamber, followed by the tavern-keeper bringing what he
said was his best wine, along with four clean cups. He put
the tray down and hastily retreated. Murranus filled the
cups and raised his in the direction of the Lares.

'May his God look after him,' he toasted. 'May Stathylus be brought to a place of light. He deserved a better death.' He drank and refilled his goblet.

Claudia stared at the two veterans, men who had now had the fight knocked out of them. They seemed to have aged in such a short while; their unshaven faces had paled, cheeks almost sunken, their eyes held the haunted look of beaten slaves.

'So quickly!' Crispus murmured. 'He went out for a piss, that's all he did!'

Claudia, her stomach now settled, told Murranus and the others to wait and went downstairs. The tavern-keeper gave her his lantern and she returned to the alleyway and the place where Stathylus had died. She placed the lantern on the ground and searched carefully, gingerly picking her way around the congealing blood. She stared down the alleyway and glimpsed pinpricks of light beyond. In the end she could find nothing, so, picking up the lantern, she returned to the tavern, washed her hands in a vat of water just beneath the stairs and went up to join the rest. Crispus and Secundus were now drinking as if facing their own deaths.

'How could it happen?' she asked. 'Crispus, you're a soldier, a veteran; whoever killed Stathylus must have got very close and taken him by surprise. Another man, a boy?'

Crispus shook his head.

'Who then?' Claudia asked. 'A woman?'

'Of course,' Secundus slurred. 'Stathylus is like the rest of us. Our wives are dead, or back in Britain; any woman who offers herself would be taken. Stathylus had been drinking, he wouldn't remember, he wouldn't realise the danger until it was too late.'

Claudia leaned against the table, staring down at the food and wine stains. She tried to visualise what had happened. Stathylus had staggered out of the tavern wishing to relieve himself; he'd gone up that alleyway. Someone had known he'd be here tonight. Someone was waiting. It didn't matter who came out; in the eyes of their killer, the fate of these veterans was already sealed. Stathylus was an old soldier, a man who lived by himself, apparently; with a belly full of wine, he wouldn't realise the danger. Some pretty whore comes tripping along, drawing close; she stabs him with a quick thrust to the stomach. The shock alone would paralyse Stathylus, then the rest. Claudia lifted her head.

'Are you going to tell us,' she asked, 'what you have omitted, something very important, from your story? If you want to live, you'll have to tell us, and tell us now.'

Secundus tried to stop him but Crispus, wide-eyed with fear, struck away his companion's warning hand. 'I'll tell you,' he declared. 'Stathylus' story was true, but there was a great deal missed out. We were on the wall under Postulus. No, no, shut up, Secundus, do you want to die like a pig in an alleyway?'

Secundus let his hands fall away and sat, head down.

'As I said,' Crispus' voice grew strong, his tone bitter, 'in the beginning it was a good life. Postulus was a fine officer; he liked his wine but he cared for us. Then we were dispatched to that mile fort. I hated it! A haunted place! The skies seemed to press down on you, and either side of the wall there was really nothing but gorse, bramble and long grass. There was fighting in the south between the different pretenders, units were leaving, but we decided to stay, it was safer. Anyway, there was bad blood between Postulus and Stathylus, they hated each other. Postulus was of the old school, a little bit of a snob; he thought he should be in charge of more men but, of course, cohorts, units, even legions had been drastically reduced. Nevertheless, he was competent enough, and he made sure we were paid, fed and well protected. We heard rumours of Pictish war bands prowling in the area so we decided to go out and reconnoitre. With Postulus there must have been,' he pulled a face, 'about fifteen or sixteen of us. Our horses were good, we were well armed and provisioned. Postulus led us out. We almost stumbled on that war band, they were sheltering in the hollow of a hill. Perhaps they thought that, because of the confusion along the wall, they were safe. We attacked at night, riding into their camp, slaughtering to the left and to the right. There were more of them than we thought, so Postulus decided to call it a day, but we had two captives: a young man – we cut his throat; he was so badly wounded Postulus said we couldn't take care of him.'

'And the other prisoner?' Claudia asked.

'You'll never believe us.' Crispus stared directly at her. 'The Picts are small, dark and wiry. They had allies to the north, the Caledonii, and, across the seas to the west, the Scoti. Some of these are extremely fair-haired. To cut a long story short, the Pictish chieftain had a woman, a young wench, perhaps no more than sixteen or seventeen summers old. She was cloaked and hooded but when we returned to the fort we discovered she was a great beauty. One of our number knew the Pictish tongue, or at least a few words. We tried to make sense of what she said. She was very frightened and claimed she was a princess, the Pictish chieftain's new wife, and that he'd be angry and would come looking for her. We asked for her name but all she told us was that she was the Golden Maid – that's what her name meant – and she'd been given to the Pictish chief as a bridal present, to seal an alliance between the tribes.

'Usually when we took women captives they were shared out and then sold in the marketplace, but this was different. Postulus and Stathylus were both deeply smitten. At first the Golden Maid was frightened, but she soon realised there was very little difference between Pict and Roman, we all have our brains where our balls are, so she played one off against the other. At the same time our scouts reported increased activity amongst the Picts. Furious at their loss, they were hurrying south, a war band of between thirty and forty men. They launched one attack upon the fort but we beat them off. An argument broke out between Postulus and Stathylus about what should be done. Postulus was all for handing the girl back and making a peace treaty, buying the Picts off with some silver from the pay chest and a few jars of posca. They'd be content and leave us alone. Stathylus was different. He accused Postulus of treason, of conspiring with the enemy. Postulus became very drunk. I don't know what truly happened, but he retreated to his chamber. Stathylus took over and did a really stupid thing. He sent out a scout to find out exactly what was happening, and the poor bugger never returned. We later discovered the Picts killed him before they came after us. Stathylus knew the mind of the Picts; the Golden Maid was their woman, so if they found out she'd lain with Romans they'd kill her too. Stathylus, well, he was . . .'

'He was persuasive.' Secundus spoke up. 'He was very eloquent. He pointed out that Postulus had failed to be a good officer. If he was so drunk, we should leave him alone, trap the Picts, kill them and claim the glory. The rest of our story is true.'

'Is it?' Claudia asked. 'You are sure you butchered every single Pict?'

'According to Stathylus,' Secundus spoke up, 'we did.'

'What do you mean, according to Stathylus?'

Secundus gestured at Crispus. 'After the fight, we were sent out on a scouting mission. When we returned, the dead Picts lay heaped in a great pile outside the southern gate. They were drenched in oil and burned. There were no prisoners.'

'And the Golden Maid?' Murranus asked. 'What happened to her?'

'When we attacked the war band,' Crispus replied, 'the Golden Maid had been shackled in a wood. Stathylus made the stupid mistake of bringing her down to see the dead. She was truly beautiful,' he whispered. 'She had hair as gold as ripened corn, pale ivory skin.'

'Have you seen Cassia?' Claudia asked. 'The former courtesan? She's a close friend of Urbana, General Aurelian's wife.'

'Yes, I have.' Secundus half smiled. 'Beautiful.'

'Was she like that?' Claudia asked.

'A little,' Secundus conceded, 'but Cassia is not the Golden Maid. For a start she is too young; secondly she doesn't look like her. More importantly, I know what happened to the Golden Maid.'

'What?' Claudia asked.

'As I have said, Stathylus brought her down. She looked at the dead and cried. We celebrated. We found old Postulus hacked to bits, but of course we all kept quiet; technically we were guilty of mutiny. We burned his corpse as well. The reason we all agreed to it is that Stathylus had promised how, once we'd annihilated the Picts, we'd abandon the mile fort and march south to search out General Aurelian. Postulus had wanted to stay on the wall. Once he was dead, we'd won our great victory and were only too pleased to go.'

'What happened?' Murranus insisted.

'Well, as I've said, we celebrated. We had some wine and food. Stathylus lay with the Golden Maid. We heard her shrieks as he pleasured her. We'd camped outside the mile fort; next morning we found the Golden Maid had hanged herself from a beam inside.'

'Hanged herself?' Claudia asked.

'Shame.' Crispus spoke up. 'Because of her, her husband and his entire war band had been destroyed. She knew what would happen next. Stathylus would either sell her in the market or pass her on, so she'd taken a piece of rope and hanged herself.'

'You are sure she was dead?'

'I am certain. We burned her corpse and rode south, and that was the last time we ever saw that mile fort, the Picts or the Golden Maid. We became heroes, saviours, warriors. No one dared tell the truth. Strange,' Crispus mused. 'I always felt more guilty about Postulus than the Golden Maid.'

'I have asked this before,' Claudia said, 'but is it possible that someone from that Pictish war band survived?'

Secundus shook his head.

'Impossible,' Crispus declared. 'We killed them all. Stathylus was insistent on that. He wanted to make sure that no one survived to describe how Postulus had been killed; that was very important. No Pict escaped, and as your friend said,' he pointed at Murranus, 'the battle took place at night. There was some torchlight, but even then our helmets and cloaks hid our faces. More importantly, it was eighteen years ago.'

'Have you searched?' Murranus asked. 'I mean, to see if there are Pictish slaves in Rome?'

'Of course there are,' Secundus sneered. 'Slaves from every tribe and country under the sun, but no one has ever approached us. Anyway, why now, after eighteen years?'

Claudia realised there were no further questions to be asked. She got to her feet, picked up her cloak and stared at the two veterans. 'We have to go. There is nothing we can really do at the moment, but I warn you of this, never be alone, never allow any woman to approach you. If you do that, you might survive!'

'Will you tell General Aurelian?' asked Crispus. 'I mean about Postulus?'

'I certainly think there's a need,' Claudia replied. 'Not immediately, but when I need him . . .'

'His blood is not on our hands,' Crispus declared stridently. 'We were not party to his death, that's why we kept the secret. Now Stathylus is dead, I don't mind if the truth comes out. We had no hand in Postulus' death.'

Claudia thanked both men, then she and Murranus went down the stairs and into the street. Darkness had now fallen. Shapes flittered across the mouth of an alleyway; strange sounds and cries filled the air. They walked down into the nearby square, where the mercenaries still lounged about; they'd fixed a cresset torch into the wall of a house and were sharing out a jug of wine. Across the square, a warlock dressed in a feathery black cloak was crooning above a bowl of fire; an old woman crouched next to him sprinkled some powder over the flame, making it leap and crackle. Voices shouted curses. Somewhere a child cried, followed by a woman's shrieking laugh. Claudia put her arm through Murranus' and drew him close. A whore came stumbling up clutching a lantern, which she raised. In the faded light her face looked repulsive: no forehead, a short podgy nose, nostrils dilated, mouth curled as she muttered a curse.

'What are you doing here?' she accused Claudia.

Murranus pushed her aside, and immediately another

95

figure lurched out of the darkness: a thickset man with an owlish, cunning face, huge slobbery mouth, fists ready to punch. He stopped, looked Murranus up and down and, grasping the woman by the hair, pulled her away. Claudia and Murranus walked on. The air reeked of the stale odours of cooking, fried fish, coarse bread and rancid meat-dripping. Musicians stood in a pool of light and with rebec and fife encouraged wild dancers, dark, shadowy figures, to whirl and turn. Claudia was relieved to approach the She Asses tavern. Murranus stopped just at the mouth of the alleyway leading down to it.

'I've been thinking,' he murmured.

'Dangerous!' Claudia teased.

'No.' Murranus glanced down at her. 'We questioned those two veterans about that Pictish war band: has one survived, come to Rome, recognised his tormentors and decided to take revenge? However, there is another possibility: Postulus. Did someone close to him, a lover, a member of his family, discover he'd really been murdered by his own men?'

Claudia stood on tiptoe and kissed Murranus on the cheek. 'Yes, that is a possibility and one we must investigate.'

They continued down the alleyway into the square fronting the She Asses. Claudia glimpsed the two Vigiles, swords drawn, standing either side of the doorway.

'Oh no!' she moaned. 'Now what!' They hurried across. One of the Vigiles went to stop her then recognised her and stood back; he smiled at Murranus and waved them through the half-open door. Inside the eating room the captain of the Vigiles sat at a table with Poppaoe, Polybius and Apuleius; all three looked worried, whilst the captain appeared distinctly uncomfortable, as if something had happened that couldn't be bribed away.

'What's wrong?' Claudia walked towards them.

Polybius refused to hold her gaze.

'What's wrong, Uncle?'

'Tell her!' Poppaoe whispered, head down. 'You'd best tell her.'

'I won't just tell.' Polybius, much the worse for drink, staggered to his feet, swaying backward and forwards. 'Come with me.'

They climbed the stairs and went along the gallery to a guest chamber. Claudia's agitation deepened at the splinters of the wood lying outside. Something dreadful must have occurred. The door to the chamber had been forced, its bolts and clasps broken, shards of wood everywhere. Inside the small, narrow chamber, on a cot bed, sprawled the corpse of Theodore. One glance told her what had happened. The former actor looked ugly in death, his face podgy and white, mouth open, tongue sticking out, eyes popping.

'No!' Claudia groaned. 'Uncle, what happened?' She walked slowly across to the bed and felt the corpse's cheek; it was cold, almost wax-like. She knelt down, pushing the corpse more securely on to the bed. Murranus helped her. She sniffed at the mouth and smelled nothing suspicious, but she could tell by the popping eyes, the rictus, the way the lips were forced back that Theodore had been poisoned. Death must have been fairly swift.

She got to her feet and turned round. Uncle Polybius stood in the doorway, one hand on the Vigiles' shoulder to steady himself.

'What you see is what we know,' Polybius pleaded. 'We were having such a marvellous celebration downstairs. The kitchen was doing a busy trade. Theodore left, saying he felt distinctly unwell, and came up here. I decided to invite him back down to keep an eye on him as you asked. So I came up, banged on the door, but he wouldn't answer. I got Oceanus to force it.' He gestured. 'It happened an hour ago, and now we've got trouble! I didn't ask him to come here, Claudia!'

'He's been poisoned.' Apuleius came up behind Uncle Polybius and forced his way through. 'Look around, Claudia.'

Claudia glimpsed the wine cup. It had rolled against the wall, a pool of wine around it. The stool next to the bed had also been knocked over as if Theodore had been lying on the bed and then become agitated, arms flailing, tipping over both the wine cup and the stool, trying to get himself up before collapsing back on to the bed.

'Do you know the cause?' Claudia asked.

Apuleius dug into the purse on his belt and handed the captain of the Vigiles a coin; the officer promptly disappeared. The apothecary and Polybius walked into the chamber, forcing the broken door shut behind them and placing the broken stool against it. For a while they helped Claudia and Murranus arrange Theodore's corpse along the bed, folding his hands over his stomach. Claudia had seen enough death that evening and, taking a coloured cloth from the wall, she covered the dead actor's face. She then sat on the floor, her back to the door, and stared up at her uncle.

'What caused this, what happened? I thought you'd look after him.'

'We did.' Polybius squatted down, sitting cross-legged like a schoolboy. 'We were enjoying ourselves. People were flocking in to see the Great Miracle. Apuleius was here. Theodore complained of a sensitive stomach. Anyway I could see he was beginning to sway, and I said perhaps it was time for a lie-down, take it easy for a while, so he came upstairs, and the rest you know.'

Claudia pointed at the corpse. 'Are you sure he was poisoned?'

'I think so.' Apuleius sat on the edge of the cot bed and stared sorrowfully at her. 'I don't know what noxious potion, some plant, but he has definitely been poisoned.' He gestured at the wine cup. 'I've checked that carefully, it's not to blame.'

'So that means somebody came into this tavern,' Claudia said slowly, 'and poisoned his wine or food.' She rose, picked up the wine cup, sniffed at it, ran her finger around it and tasted the faint dregs. 'Nothing but the best,' she muttered. She handed the cup to Apuleius, who scrutinised it again and pronounced the same conclusion.

'Ah well.' Claudia stared down at the corpse. 'What do we do now?'

'I'll get Narcissus the Neat to have a look at it.' Polybius clambered to his feet. 'Some of the lads owe me money; they can take the corpse to the nearest death house.'

Claudia nodded, and Polybius opened the door for her. She went out on to the landing, down the stairs and into the moon-washed garden. She stood for a while, allowing the cool breeze to fan the heat of her face. Murranus came up behind her and placed his hands gently on her shoulders. She turned, stood on tiptoe and kissed him on the lips.

'Sleep well,' she whispered and tweaked his ear. 'I've talked and listened enough for one evening – tomorrow it's General Aurelian's . . .'

Claudia and Murranus left just as dawn was breaking. They slipped out of the She Asses and along the dusty trackways leading to the Via Tusculana, which cut through the Severan Wall. Even though the sun had yet to rise, the city had come to life. At the top of the alleyway, Torquatus the Tonsor was busy preparing for business behind his stall under the gnarled sycamore tree, sharpening his razors on what he boasted was a special stone imported from Syria. He was full of chatter about magical stones, herbs and animals. He was already pontificating to a small group that had gathered. On any other occasion Claudia would have stayed to listen. Torquatus was fascinating, a born actor with an inexhaustible fund of stories, but General Aurelian, being an old soldier, would surely be an early riser, and it would be best to see him before the business of the day began.

The streets were filling with merchants as well as water-carriers, sweepers and rakers. The sewer men were out with their wheelbarrows emptying the latrines and cesspits, all shouting good-natured abuse at each other. The grimy cook-shops were open, the portable stoves and ovens being set up at judicious places to attract those who'd risen, as one notice brazenly proclaimed, 'with an empty stomach and a dry throat'. A funeral procession was gathering with professional mourners, priests and an Egyptian choir dressed in blue and scarlet head-dresses. A group of dancers from Spain, ejected from some tavern and desperate to earn money to buy from the water-carriers with their fresh supply, were offering to do a dance for anyone who'd pay them a couple of coins. Linen-clad, shaven-headed priests of some Babylonian god went by, guzzling wine, blowing horns, their long curled hair whirling in the breeze. Scholars, eyes swollen with sleep, staggered out for morning school whilst their mothers stood in the doorways of apartments and houses with brooms of green palms or twigs of tamarisk, heather and myrtle. Already the heralds were busy proclaiming what was on sale in the city, particularly the latest wigs, which could be found in a shop near the Temple of Hercules.

The day's heat was beginning to make itself felt, and by the time they reached the city gate, Claudia's lips and throat were bone dry. She and Murranus stopped at an ale booth to refresh themselves and wipe away the dust with cracked cups of fruit juice. They remained silent, not talking until they were out into the countryside, following the via as it cut through fields of ripening corn. After taking directions from a farmer, they left the road, going along a trackway which wound past cypress, plane and pine trees. On either side meadows and harvest land stretched up to the main gate of Aurelian's villa. Here the porter carefully inspected the seal Claudia carried bearing the imprint of the Empress and, on the reverse, an instruction ordering everyone on their allegiance to help its bearer with her enquiries. The gates were promptly swung open, and Claudia and Murranus entered another world, of pebbled paths, lawns, orchards, small copses of trees, fountains, pools of purity, all carefully laid out on either side of the path which swept up to the atrium of the magnificent villa.

At the house, servants greeted them with bowls of perfumed water so they could wash their hands and faces. Afterwards they were taken through the atrium, a splendid affair with a small lake beneath an opening in the roof, then down a porticoed walk to the inner chambers. Claudia was aware of beautiful stone walls decorated with paintings and frescos in yellow amber, bronze, Damascene copper; pillars of Phrygian marble, doors and lintels inset with malachite and tortoiseshell, ceilings sparkling with gold and precious objects. Everything was cool, fresh and sweet-smelling.

For a while they had to sit in a chamber with a wood-laced ceiling of Lebanese cedar; on the walls beautiful paintings celebrated the triumphs of Ceres, Goddess of Spring. Claudia tapped Murranus on the thigh and put her finger to her lips as a warning to remain silent. She knew that many of these villas, built specially for their owners, often had secret eyelets or gaps where people could eavesdrop on any conversation taking place. Claudia leaned back against the cool marbled wall and closed her eyes. The previous night's sleep had not been good, her mind still tortured by images of Stathylus lying in that filthy alleyway and Theodore sprawled out on the bed, his face twisted in agony. She wanted to be by herself just to make sense of the chaos in her mind, but this meeting was important and she had to prepare herself. She half listened to the sounds of the villa coming to life: servants hurrying by along the corridors and passageways, the distant sound of a flute, the cries of serving girls, the neigh of horses from the stables. A chamberlain brought some bread, grapes and watered wine. Claudia and Murranus ate hungrily, and still they waited. Eventually, after what seemed to be an eternity, an arrogant freedman curtly ordered them to follow him.

He led them deep into the house, to what he called the Chamber of Mysteries, a beautiful room with mosaics on the wall celebrating the life of Dionysius and his travels across the world. General Aurelian was waiting for them almost enthroned on a blue and gold stool. His wife Urbana sat on his right with Cassia next to her, and to his left was a young man with close-cropped auburn hair and a smiling face, clad in a light green tunic belted firmly around the waist. Aurelian looked what he was, a former general, a soldier, a tough, wiry man, white hair straggling down a furrowed face like that of a hunting falcon, a sharp-beaked nose above thin, bloodless lips, and eyes that never seemed to blink. He looked much older than Claudia had expected, and she reckoned that Urbana must be twenty or thirty years his junior.

The General welcomed them in clipped tones and asked if they'd eaten. He hardly bothered to wait for their reply but immediately introduced his son Alexander, muttered that they had already met his lady wife Urbana and the Lady Cassia, whom he dismissed with a flick of his eyes, then turned back smiling to his son. Claudia learned a great deal in those few seconds. The relationship between the General and his good wife was, perhaps, not what it should be, whilst Cassia was good-naturedly tolerated. The General's attention was solely on Alexander, a pleasant-mannered, happy-faced, gentle-eyed boy who gazed adoringly at Murranus and had to be restrained by his father from a spate of questions about the arena and the gladiator's great triumphs there. Instead the General, as if barking orders to his tribunes, listed Murranus' duties.

'Do you understand?' he ended, leaning forward. 'Do you fully understand what I ask?'

'Yes, sir,' Murranus replied. 'I am to be your son's shadow.'

The General's severe face broke into a faint smile. He jabbed his finger at Murranus. 'I like you, man, that's the answer I wanted. Where he goes, you follow, and you're always armed. You've brought your war belt?'

Murranus explained how the General's servants had taken his weapon bundle as soon as he'd entered the house.

'They won't do that again,' the General retorted. 'Where you go, your sword, dagger and club are always with you, and where my son goes, you go as well, be it the baths, the latrines, a swim, the Campus Martius, a ride on a horse, even climbing a tree.'

Murranus again reassured the General that he knew exactly what his duties were. The General stretched as if he'd resolved a great problem.

'And Senator Carinus?' He turned to Claudia, looking her up and down. 'No news about Antonia?'

'No, sir.' Claudia barked back the reply so sharply that Urbana and Cassia lowered their heads to hide their laughter; beside her Murranus stiffened quickly, a warning to her not to mock the General. Aurelian narrowed his eyes.

'You're only a child,' he muttered, 'a mere slip of a girl, yet the Empress is using you.' He clicked his tongue. 'But that's Helena! She always does what you least expect; she would have made a good general. In fact,' he pulled a face, 'she was; she advised both her husband and her beloved son.' He added quickly, 'You want to tell me something, girl, don't you?'

'Yes, sir. The Vigiles Muri, the veterans from the Fretenses?'

'Ah, yes.' Aurelian's face grew severe. 'You are to find their killers. A difficult task for a slip of a girl.'

'Another one was murdered last night.'

Aurelian ignored the sharp hiss of surprise from the two women beside him.

'Who?' he exclaimed, hand cupping his ear as if finding it difficult to hear what Claudia was saying.

'Stathylus,' Claudia replied. 'I met him, Secundus and Crispus at a tavern; their funeral club meets in its upper chamber.'

The General nodded, eyes staring hard. 'Then what happened?'

'Stathylus went outside to relieve himself. He was murdered, barbarously, just like the rest.'

For a brief while the General put his face in his hands.

'Murdered!' he exclaimed, lifting his head, 'with an imperial agent close by?'

'We could not save him,' Claudia replied. 'Stathylus brought his own death upon himself. General, it's time you learned the truth.' In sharp, brief sentences she told him what she'd been told the previous evening. Once she'd finished, Aurelian sat, chin cupped in his hand, staring at the floor as if fascinated by the mosaic depicting Mars in triumph. He glanced up.

'And Secundus and Crispus?' he asked. 'Are they guilty of murder, of deliberately slaying their officer?'

'No, sir.' Claudia shook her head. 'At the time it happened, neither was party to it. Postulus died because of Stathylus, because of the bad blood between them, because Postulus was a drinker, but most of all because of the Golden Maid.'

'If I had known this yesterday,' the old General commented, as if issuing a decree, 'I would have had Stathylus scourged. He would have been fortunate not to end up on a cross. I'll summon those other two here. I have questions for them and they'll be safer in this villa!' The old General recollected who was with him and, turning, whispered an apology to his wife, who'd sat throughout studying Claudia closely. Beside her, Cassia was not as amused or as merry as yesterday, but stony-faced and hard-eyed. Claudia realised that both women were consummate actresses, deferential and welcoming as

106

far as they could be in the presence of the Empress, but here in General Aurelian's villa very much the patrician ladies.

'Tell me again,' Aurelian demanded, 'about what truly happened along the Great Wall.'

Claudia did so. Every so often the General would interrupt with a question, then allow her to return to her narration. At the end he tapped his sandalled feet.

'I'll ask Secundus and Crispus to shelter here. I agree with your conclusion, girl: when those men were killed, the only person who would have been able to get close would be a whore, and one armed with a dagger.' He turned to ask Urbana a question, but the door opened and Leartus walked in, black hair carefully combed, his olive-skinned face oiled. He was dressed in a dark red tunic edged with green, reed sandals on his feet. He carried a posy of flowers in one hand, an elegant ivory-tipped wand in the other. Despite his status, the General appeared to like him. Aurelian smiled, gesturing him forward to the stool next to his mistress, and briefly told the eunuch what had happened. Leartus sat sad-eyed and listened attentively, nodding every so often. Aurelian remembered Claudia and abruptly gestured at her.

'Well, girl, are there any questions you wish to ask me?'

'Do you know anything?' Claudia asked. 'Can you add to the report I've given?'

Aurelian spread his hands. 'You are talking of the province eighteen years ago. It was like an overturned beehive, people streaming along the roads, towns and villas deserted. Our greatest enemy was fear. No one knew precisely what was happening, which general was in charge, which units could be trusted. Had pirates landed on the coast? Were the Picts through the wall? Had the Scoti breached the western defences? Which tribes were in revolt?' He glanced at Cassia, smiled and stretched out a hand. 'Poor Cassia here was caught up in it. Days of blood, nights of horror; she still can't really recall what happened.'

The former courtesan smiled tenderly at the old general, who seemed flattered. He sighed loudly.

'Ah yes, it took years to reimpose order. We were only too pleased to see the Fretenses. Of course, when we heard of their great victory, rewards and praise streamed like a river towards them.'

'Did you hear of them taking prisoners?'

'None whatsoever,' the General replied definitely. 'They were moving fast, their possessions lashed to their saddle horns, no carts, only the soldiers and their mounts. They'd even left their own wives and children.' He glanced sharp-eyed at Claudia. 'Next question.'

'Are there Pictish slaves in Rome?'

'That's a hard question.' Aurelian rubbed his chin. 'The Picts,' he said, 'it is years since we've had a campaign against them. I don't know. I suppose I could ask the Aedile or the Prefect.' He glanced at Urbana. 'Can you help here?'

His wife shook her head, her eyes never leaving Claudia's face.

'I'll make enquiries.' The old general sighed. 'But I follow your logic, girl. If that Pictish war band was wiped out, if the woman they called the Golden Maid hanged herself, who would know, who would remember?'

'Do you know anything about Postulus?' Murranus asked. 'The murdered centurion. Did he have a wife and family?'

'Not that I know of,' the General replied. 'Postulus was a loner, that's why he drank. He had a wife once but I think she died; no children, nobody here in Rome. If he had, they'd have been along to see me seeking this favour or that.'

'And Petilius?' Claudia asked. 'You invited him here for a reunion, and shortly afterwards he began to pester you, demanding an audience.'

'Yes, yes, he did,' Aurelian replied.

'Do you know why he wanted to see you?'

The General stared at the ceiling, breathing out noisily, scratching the lobe of his ear. 'I don't really know,' he replied slowly, 'but it must had been something to do with our days of glory.' He smiled. 'Claudia, do you know anything about Petilius?'

Claudia shook her head.

'He was a scout. Now when you're a scout in the cavalry, girl, you not only have to be a fine horseman, you need a very good memory and a sharp eye for land and faces. Petilius was like that. He was also a born lecher; not a whore in Rome was safe from him. I can see how he was killed. Petilius would put himself in danger for the mere smell of a woman. At our reunion he must have noticed something which reminded him of the past so he wanted to discuss it with me. Anyway, that's all I can say.'

The General rose to his feet, rearranging his old-fashioned toga about him, and came across and touched Claudia gently under the chin.

'Claudia, that's your name, isn't it?' He patted her on the shoulder. 'You're so small! You look tired; you're worried, aren't you, whilst your friend here has to settle and make himself at home?' He beamed down at her. 'According to the auguries, it's going to be a beautiful day. Perhaps you should stay for a few hours, before you return to Rome. I will arrange an escort for you later in the day.' He turned. 'My good friend Leartus, you'll look after Claudia, won't you? My wife will be too busy with her hymns.' The General turned back. 'So, let this house be your house. You brought me news, Claudia, something I didn't know. I've got to think about it.' And, wagging a finger at her, he spun on his heel and walked away.

He'd hardly left the chamber when Alexander, who'd sat motionless and silent as a statue throughout, leapt to his feet and rushed towards Murranus with a litany of questions. What was his best fight? Had he ever fought a lion? Was it true that a bull was the most dangerous animal?

Leartus came over and gently took Claudia by the hand. 'Come, Claudia.' He leaned down, face smiling. 'I'll show you the villa.'

Urbana and Cassia were chattering between themselves, but as Claudia rose to her feet, Cassia turned and smiled at her. Urbana appeared more relaxed and waved in a friendly fashion, mouthing that they were busy, but perhaps they could meet later.

Chapter 5

Probitas laudatur et alget.
Honesty is praised and left out in the cold.

Juvenal, *Satires*

Leartus took Claudia on a tour of the villa. They first visited a two-storey tower in the gardens with a viewing platform at the top. From there Claudia could look out over the scenery on either side, and she realised how much it varied. She glimpsed the road she'd travelled on as it narrowed through copses of wood; on either side stretched broad meadows where flocks of sheep and herds of horses and cattle grazed. She could see the different-coloured gardens and flowerbeds of the villa, how the whole complex was in the shape of a 'D'. Leartus pointed out the courtyards, the porticoed walks, the various rooms, the cubicula, the banqueting room, the small apartments, the sun terraces and the heating chambers. He chattered away in a soft, pleasant voice, explaining how the General greatly loved evergreen shrubs and rosemary, whilst he had a special fondness for mulberries and fig trees which grew so luxuriously in his gardens because the soil was especially fertile.

From the tower he took her down into a small garden where the trees were planted in a stylised arrangement reflecting the regular rhythm of the columns and other features of the surrounding buildings, with flowerbeds positioned precisely between different statues or trees. Leartus, laughing softly, explained how Aurelian was a disciplinarian, a military man even when it came to laying out a garden, whilst the Lady Urbana was an expert on herbs. Claudia was fascinated by the different flowerbeds; she was able to recognise many plants: the lily, the violet, the myrtle, the acanthus, the rose, as well as the hybrids and a range of other shrubs. They sheltered under a small cupola overlooking a pool of purity, its water gleaming blue and gold in the sunlight. Leartus explained how the fresco at the bottom of the pool reflected the sun god Mithras, Aurelian's favourite deity, and how the old General refused to become a Christian, claiming he would have nothing to do with the teachings of a criminal who'd been crucified on the far edges of the Empire.

'And you, Leartus?' Claudia leaned forward to sniff a rose. 'How come you're here?'

'I was born in a small village,' Leartus squinted up at the sky, 'near the River Granicus. My father died young and my mother sold me into service. I became a eunuch as a boy and then, of course, there was war. A Roman raiding party came to the village. You know what happens: the women were abused, the men killed. The farmstead I was working on was burned to the ground. I was taken prisoner and brought to Rome. I must have been then no more than fifteen or sixteen.' He rolled back the sleeve of his tunic and showed Claudia the impression of a slave merchant. 'I was put on sale, but because I was a eunuch, very few people had time for me, particularly as I was ill-educated and hardly knew the Latin tongue. But then the Lady Cassia – she's much older than she looks – visited the marketplace. She was looking for someone like me and took me home. One of her patrons, a Pythagorean from Athens, a scholar, a very wealthy man, educated me and taught me the sign language, and ever since, I've been in her service. Where she goes I follow; what she does I watch. A few years ago she met the Lady Urbana; Cassia became a Christian and so did I.'

'And are you happy?

Leartus screwed up his face, and Claudia noticed how young and athletic he looked. He smelled faintly of some delicious perfume; his hair was slightly ringleted and carefully cut, his hands and nails scrubbed clean, his every move elegant and refined.

'Happiness,' he declared, 'is a state of mind, or so Plato would have us believe. Happiness is relative, I suppose. If I had not been made a eunuch, not been captured, not enslaved, perhaps life might have been different, could have been better. And you, Claudia?'

She was about to reply when a servant appeared in the garden calling Leartus' name.

'My mistress summons.' Leartus smiled. 'Claudia,' he gestured at the servant to keep quiet, 'would you like to stay here or go somewhere else? Is there anything more you wish to see?'

'I've seen so many things recently.' Claudia grinned up at him. 'I move from one extreme to another. Yesterday I was inspecting a corpse in a stinking alleyway; this morning I am sitting in a beautiful garden, the air rich with perfume, nothing to listen to except the birds and the dull hum of bees searching for pollen. Have you ever read Pliny's description of his villa?'

The eunuch nodded.

'Just to read it is soothing enough,' Claudia declared, 'but being in a garden like this is paradise. Ah well!' She sighed. 'The day goes on, and work has to be done. I would like to see the library, there are things I must do.'

Leartus quickly agreed. He told the slave to wait and took Claudia back into the villa, along its elegant, beautifully decorated galleries to a chamber called The Hermes. It had a shiny wooden floor and white-plastered walls, most of which were covered by carefully erected shelves of Lebanese cedar holding stacks of parchments, some recent, others yellow with age, all carefully listed and tagged. A long trestle table, polished and gleaming, ran down the middle of the room. At the far end, under an open window, sat a dusty-faced freedman whom Leartus introduced as the librarian. When the eunuch explained that Claudia was the General's personal guest, the librarian could not do enough to please. Leartus departed, and for a while Claudia moved amongst the different manuscripts taking down the works of Terence and Petronius. There were even some Christian writings, including a copy of a letter from their great teacher Paul, transcribed elegantly in both Latin and Greek.

'Is there anything else you need?' The librarian kept following her like a shadow.

'Yes, there is.' Claudia smiled. 'I'd like a fresh piece of papyrus, a pumice stone, a quill and some ink and I'll be very happy.'

A short while later, in a writing carrel placed beneath a window, Claudia sat, face in her hands, and stared at the dust motes dancing in the light. What had she actually discovered so far? She took a sharpened quill, dipped it into the ink and carefully wrote her ciphered conclusions.

Primo. The hostages were wealthy young men and women snatched from their doting parents, gagged, bound and held for ransom. The amount demanded, 25,000 in gold coins, was heavy but not too onerous. None of the hostages could determine where they'd been kept, except their cell was fetid and rather cool. They were held there whilst the abductors sent their parents threatening messages to deliver the gold to that rambling cemetery along the Via Appia. The money was always delivered, the young man or woman always released. Claudia paused, then continued writing. The more she reflected on this, the more certain she became that the cemetery along the Via Appia was not only the place where the hostages were released, but that they were actually detained in some catacomb cavern beneath. The abductors were certainly a gang. Theodore had talked of a group of masked men invading that garden. Was their leader someone who knew all the movements of those they kidnapped? Such information could become common knowledge in great households such as those of Senator Carinus or General Aurelian; slaves, servants, freedmen, people hired for a special occasion, they could all be bought. And why were the youngsters abducted? Was it purely for profit, or was the leader of this gang trying to bring the rule of Constantine and his mother into disrepute? Claudia dipped her pen in the ink again.

Secundo. Theodore. She felt a pang of sadness; she'd worked with men like Theodore. A good man at heart, absorbed in his own art, the love of drama, the play, the lines, the world of make-believe into which she had once retreated. Theodore had been with Antonia the night she'd been abducted. Claudia could understand a young woman being seduced by Theodore's learning, his affected ways, his flattery. Had the actor been part of the gang? Or were the abductors led to the Fountain of Artemis by someone else, a traitor inserted into Carinus' household? Theodore claimed he had tried to resist, that he'd plucked a mask from one of the gang and would recognise his face again. Yet he was not that brave. Surely, if the gang of abductors had realised that one of them had been unmasked, they would have dispatched Theodore, a mere actor, there and then? So why had Theodore developed that story? To pose as the hero, to win the favour of Senator Carinus, or something else? He had been taken to the palace, interviewed by the Empress and later became an enforced guest at the She Asses tavern. Why had he been killed? What did he see? What did he know? Claudia put her quill down and nipped her thigh.

'That's for not being sharp enough,' she muttered. 'You should have questioned him.'

'Pardon?' the old librarian called from his stool at the far end of the room.

'Nothing.' Claudia smiled. 'I'm talking to myself.'

'I know the feeling,' the librarian quipped.

Claudia went back to her reflections. Theodore had definitely been poisoned. He had not eaten or drunk anything since he'd left the palace. She had watched him visit the Temple of Hathor, his quick words with that sharp-featured priest Sesothenes. He had been murdered at her uncle's tavern, but how? Someone had certainly followed him to the She Asses and managed to sprinkle a deadly poison either in his food or his wine, yet the cup he'd been drinking from was untainted, she was sure of that.

Claudia reread what she'd written. One word caught her attention: 'masks'. She underlined it. What if, she argued with herself, Theodore had not dragged the mask from one of the attacker's faces but recognised the actual masks? She felt a faint thrill of excitement. 'Of course,' she whispered, and glanced up at the window. Actors' masks were fairly expensive, especially those which covered the entire face and head. Had Theodore recognised those masks as belonging to a specific troupe or being sold in a certain shop? Claudia sprang to her feet, walked to the library door and went out to stand under the shade. She recalled her own days as an actress: one thing they were most careful about was the masks; they were the tools to convey the drama. Had the masks been bought, or had the person who organised these abductions hired a troupe of actors to perpetrate the crimes? Again Claudia reflected on her own troupe. Many of them had a great deal to hide and could be hired

117

not just to stage a drama but to do anything else a wealthy patron might desire. In fact, that was why Claudia herself had returned to Rome: her manager had become bankrupt and the other actors were being hired for activities she could not stomach.

Claudia glanced across the well-groomed lawn at a strutting peacock, its feathers all arrayed to catch the sun like some gorgeously bejewelled coat. 'Theodore was like that,' she murmured, 'all shadow and little substance, but in this case, what was the little substance?' Returning to the library, she smiled: the manuscript on the desk had been moved. Doubtless the old librarian had come across to see what she'd been writing. However, Claudia often wrote in her own script, intelligible to no one; sometimes she lost her temper with herself when even she couldn't decipher it, but not this time. She would remember the mask! She sat down, grasped the pen and continued to write.

Tertio. The death of the veterans. Three had been killed: one in his chamber, two in alleyways; the killer was undoubtedly a woman, a prostitute, a whore. Old soldiers were vulnerable; they would be wary, but a pretty woman was a different matter. Claudia could imagine the assassin snuggling close, the man putting his arms around her, leaving himself exposed to that swift dagger thrust to the belly. The shock and the pain probably forced him to his knees, then the killer would slip behind him, pulling back his head, cutting his throat before carrying out those heinous abominations upon his corpse. Claudia was certain that the murders were linked to what had happened in the north of Britain some eighteen years ago; that Pictish war band being massacred in the mile fort, the Golden Maid, the rivalry between Stathylus and Postulus. But what had happened now to summon ghosts from the past? What had Petilius seen? Why did he wish to meet his old general again? To tell him something confidential? Something secret? But why didn't he share this with his friends? Of course! Claudia glanced up. All those veterans were frightened. General Aurelian had put his finger on the heart of the problem. Postulus had been a Roman officer, maliciously murdered by his own men; for such an abominable crime they deserved crucifixion or some other horrific death. Did Petilius see something, or someone, at that reunion and realise their secret might not be as carefully guarded and protected as he thought? Was that why he didn't share his information with his colleagues but wanted to see Aurelian? Claudia sat for a while studying what she'd written, reflecting on what she'd seen and heard. Her mind returned to the She Asses tavern, and she picked up the pen again.

Quatro. Sancta Fulgentia – where had that corpse come from? Claudia knew enough about the Christians and the great emphasis they laid on miracles. She'd heard stories of bodies found in the catacombs, especially young women who'd been killed and buried before the Edict of Milan, when Constantine had issued his Decree of Toleration for the Christians. Some of these tombs had now been opened, and according to popular rumour a few of the bodies within had not decomposed, a true sign of God's favour. Was this corpse one of these? Claudia concentrated on what she'd learned. The body had definitely been buried with Diocletian's coins on its eyelids; these dated the woman's death to about nine or ten years ago. It had been buried in a part of the garden, certainly not by Polybius, who hadn't owned the tavern then. Apuleius, a man of integrity, had guaranteed that the body was singular in aspect and appearance. Yet if Fulgentia had been a girl taken from a family outside the city, brought into Rome for questioning and murdered, why not bury her in the cemetery along the Via Appia where her corpse would never be found? Or, as had happened to so many, throw her into the Tiber or bury her beneath one of the many wastelands and commons in and around Rome?

She tried to recall the events as they had happened. The corpse had been found by Venutus the Vine-dresser, who'd chosen the wrong part of the garden to work. He'd started in the poor light and Polybius, busy in the tavern making sure the ovens and stoves were fired, didn't notice. The corpse had been found in that chest, the coins pressed on the eyes and those faint marks on her throat and along her shoulders. It hadn't decomposed. Claudia closed her eyes. Polybius had naturally taken control and sent for someone skilled in medicine. Apuleius was the natural choice. He and his wife arrived. They declared Fulgentia was possibly a martyr and should be revered. No clinical explanation could be given for the preservation. The corpse was swathed in fresh linen, placed back in its coffin and taken down to the cool cellar. Polybius, never a man to miss a profit, then proclaimed the Great Miracle throughout the quarter. Men like Mercury the Messenger spread the news and the curious flocked in; they bought wine and food as well as paying to gape at the Great Miracle.

Claudia gritted her teeth. There was something wrong. Polybius was a rogue, but Claudia knew her uncle and Poppaoe would never stoop to any real wickedness. Mischief perhaps, evil no. And then there were the witnesses: Narcissus the Neat, Oceanus, and, above all, Apuleius. She paused as she heard the sound of women singing, straining her ears she caught the words.

'To the Lord of Light on the eastern horizon, Risen Lord, clothed in might, come Lord Jesus, come.'

'What is that?'

The librarian, dozing on his stool, lifted his head. 'Ah, that will be the Lady Urbana and the other Magdalena. They often meet here, in that part of the garden set aside for them.'

'Can I see?'

'Come with me.' The old librarian, huffing and puffing, got off his stool, came around his table and led Claudia out into the bright sunlight. After the smell of vellum, parchment, ink and sand, the garden smelled even more fragrant. The librarian, grumbling under his breath, led Claudia along a portico where beautiful medallions, attached by cords between the pillars, swung lazily in the breeze, each displaying the head of a god or goddess. On the lawns peacocks screeched, and from gilded cages a brilliantly coloured flock of songbirds thrilled the heart and pleased the ear. A veritable paradise of dappled greens, shrubs from every part of the Empire embedded in the richest soil. They passed grottoes and statues, went through a cherry orchard and out on to another green lawn stretching up to a corner of the curtain wall. A group of women dressed

121

in white gowns, stoles pulled up over their heads, knelt on marble slabs all facing what Claudia first thought was a rockery, a pile of earth in which polished stones had been set. On the top stood a wooden cross and next to that a small artificial cave. She immediately recognised the symbols: the crucifix of the Lord Jesus and the cave in which He lay buried for three days before He rose from the dead. The women, Urbana leading from the front, were still singing their hymn, a soft, melodious chant, rising and falling, exhorting Christ, the Lord of Time and Space, begging him to come again.

The librarian quickly retreated; Claudia heard a cough and turned to her right. Leartus stood beneath a tree, smiling at her. He raised his hand and then turned back, joining in the hymn as it reached its final doxology giving Glory to the Father, the Son and the Holy Spirit. The singing tapered off. The women knelt, heads bowed to the ground. Urbana rose to her feet. She was about to address her companions when she glimpsed Claudia, smiled and softly clapped her hands.

'Sisters,' she said, 'we have a visitor.'

The rest of the ladies rose and turned to greet Claudia, faces smiling, pushing back the stoles from their heads. Claudia recognised some of the faces from the court; they all looked severe, no cosmetics or jewellery, no ornamentation, simple and pure in their dress. Urbana moved amongst them talking softly, and the group broke up, drifting away across the garden, whilst Urbana and Cassia took Claudia and Leartus over to a portico crowned with flowers and creeping ivy. Inside it was cool and refreshing.

Urbana sat down on a seat, leaning back against the wall, breathing out noisily.

'I'm glad you're here, Claudia. It gives us a respite from the heat and our duties.'

Leartus was watching Cassia's fingers make their symbols and signs.

'What is it?' Claudia asked.

'My lady,' Leartus replied, 'wonders what you're doing here. Would you like to become a Magdalena?'

'Who are the Magdalena?' Claudia teased back.

Urbana went to intervene, but Cassia held her hand up rather imperiously and continued her silent conversation with Leartus.

'You're not a Christian?' Leartus asked.

'I think you know that,' Claudia replied. 'I've learned something of your faith, what they call the Way, your Scriptures.'

'Well,' Leartus gestured at Urbana and Cassia, 'these are the Magdalena. Mary Magdalene was a woman in the Gospels possessed by seven demons which Jesus cast out. She later became one of his closest followers and followed his ministry throughout Galilee and Judaea. When the Lord Christ was crucified, she stayed in vigil beside his tomb. According to our Scriptures, she was one of the first to whom the Lord Jesus appeared after His resurrection. She was the Lord's ideal disciple. The ladies Urbana and Cassia have renounced their former lives, their wealth, their position, their status. They, like Mary Magdalene, have left the past behind them, and are dedicated solely to the Lord Jesus and spreading his name.'

'And what does that actually mean?' Claudia spoke directly to Cassia.

'It means,' Leartus intervened, speaking as he watched Cassia make her signs, 'that we must make the name of the Lord Jesus known in every corner of society, be it the hovels and filthy alleyways of the slums, or the palaces and villas of the great and mighty. The Magdalena participate in a range of good works, hospitals, and medical facilities, but above all they encourage those who walk the streets and sell their bodies to renounce such sin and turn to the Lord Jesus.'

'There is something else,' Urbana declared, smiling at Claudia. 'The Augusta searches the Empire for relics of the Divine Saviour, Our Lord Jesus. Well, we're no different. We have accepted the spirit of Mary Magdalene, we wish to minister to Christ in all His people. But,' she smiled thinly, 'we also wish to discover more about her. We know that she came from Bethany outside Jerusalem. After the Lord Jesus ascended into heaven, Mary Magdalene stayed in Judaea for a while, but due to the conflict with the Romans and the persecution of the Christian faith, she fled to Gaul. She landed at Marseilles, moving deep into the countryside there. We have this great dream, this ambition, this vision, to find her remains and bring them back here to Rome. We've heard rumours,' Urbana shrugged, 'that when she fled from Judaea, Mary Magdalene was joined by others of Jesus' disciples, Nicodemus and Joseph of Arimathea. Even more importantly, after she went to Gaul she married: a prophecy proclaims that her children will be the seed of a future

124

line of glorious kings, but perhaps such tales are mere fairy stories. Anyway, this is what we are, Claudia. What business do you have with us?'

Claudia pointed at Cassia, who was staring intently at her.

'We are faced with many, many crimes, Domina,' Claudia used the formal title, 'and I am perplexed. Young men and women are abducted, veterans are murdered. I ask you, with no insult intended,' she spoke slowly and clearly, 'you must know people from your former life, you must listen to the rumours from the city: do you have any information which could help me?'

Urbana scowled at her. Cassia lowered her head, but those beautiful eyes came up and held Claudia's, and just for a while she stared coolly at her. Then she began to talk with her fingers, Leartus watching intently.

'My mistress,' the eunuch began, 'does not resent your insinuations but she knows nothing about what you say. The hostage-taking, the destruction of veterans, what is that to her?'

'Then let her tell me about her former life in Britain. She came from the same province where these men served.'

'That's ridiculous!' Urbana cut in. 'Cassia cannot remember much. Moreover, we come from the Iceni in the eastern part of that province. We had no dealings with Picts.'

'Where were you last night?' Claudia cut in quickly. 'After dark, when the curfew had been proclaimed and the horn sounded.'

Cassia turned to Urbana, smiled and shrugged.

Urbana glowered at Claudia. 'Are you insinuating,' she

said, 'that we have anything to do with the death of that veteran in some stinking alleyway?'

'I didn't say that, Domina,' Claudia replied tactfully. 'I simply asked where you were.'

Urbana sprang to her feet and, with an irate glance at Claudia, walked away. She returned with a grey-haired, solemn-faced man whom Claudia immediately recognised as one of the chamberlains.

'Tell the lady your name,' Urbana urged. 'What is your name?'

'Why, Domina,' the fellow stuttered a reply, 'my name is Dimisces. I am a chamberlain at your husband's villa.'

'Tell this lady,' Urbana flung her hand out at Claudia, 'where we were last night.'

'Why, Domina,' Dimisces replied, 'everybody knows you were here, you and the Lady Cassia, from before sunset until the early hours. The Magdalena were also with you. You prayed, then you retired.'

'Thank you.' Urbana dismissed the chamberlain with a flick of her fingers and turned on Claudia. 'So, what further questions do you have to ask?'

Claudia, discomfited, excused herself and went to say goodbye to Murranus. He was in the palaestra with young Alexander, teaching him the rudiments of fighting with the short sword and square shield. Murranus, dripping with sweat, followed Claudia out into the cool colonnade, held her close and kissed her on the brow before turning away. He paused in the doorway, looked over his shoulder and grinned.

'Well, at least I'm not entering the arena!'

Claudia held up her hand in salute and went to the stables, where two of General Aurelian's slaves were waiting with a gentle cob. They left the villa, going along the winding path through the gates and on to the trackway which would lead them down to the main thoroughfare. The day's heat was dying, and soothing evening breezes had sprung up. Above the grass on either side butterflies floated. A thrush started to sing its clear liquid song, the sky was scored red, the lowing of cattle echoed rather sombrely from behind the fringe of trees; above it the sound of a child laughing and screaming carried on the breeze. The cob plodded sturdily along, the two escorts walking ahead, chattering amongst themselves. Claudia half dozed. On the way to the villa, she'd found the countryside familiar. She remembered that, as a young girl, her father had taken her, Felix and their mother along here, out into the countryside, simply to get away from the stench and heat of the city. She recalled those days and how her life had changed. Her father and her mother had become Christians but they had never made her convert. Claudia started awake and blinked. That was one thing she would remember them for: loving, ever-present, but never forcing their beliefs upon her.

She wondered if one day she and Murranus would come here with their children and sit under the shade of the outstretched branches of an oak tree to picnic, to immerse themselves in the ordinary, everyday things of life. Sometimes, on an evening like this, with the sun sinking in the west, the birds singing, the breeze fanning the sweat from her skin, she resented what she had to do, how she lived, the dangers that threatened her. Yet on the other hand, she could not suppress that feeling of excitement, that tingling, that sharpening of the brain as she waited to encounter some threat, some danger, in order to resolve a problem. She found it fascinating to observe, record and study human conduct, to pick at the loose threads and pull them free so that a whole tapestry of lies would collapse and reveal the truth behind. She often wondered if the attack and rape on her, coupled with the murder of her brother Felix, had unbalanced her wits, forced her soul to go in another direction. Nevertheless, she was now on that path, and she would journey along it as far as she could.

Claudia glanced up at the sky and wondered what would be awaiting her at the She Asses. Abruptly she heard a cry and reined in. The escorts had also stopped, shading their eyes and peering into the distance at the three figures, staffs in their hands, walking briskly towards them. One of the slaves carried a sword; he drew this from its scabbard but then his companion muttered something to him. The sword was put back and hands were raised in greeting as the retainers of General Aurelian recognised each other. Claudia, peering through the dust haze, realised that General Aurelian had been true to his word. The two veterans Crispus and Secundus had been summoned to the villa. They met where the trackway curved. At first the two veterans looked rather shamefaced, slightly apprehensive. Claudia greeted them and made to go on, but Crispus came up, grabbed the cob's halter and peered up at her.

'You told General Aurelian?'

Claudia stroked the neck of her cob and shrugged. 'I had no choice, he had to know.'

'We are innocent,' Crispus declared defiantly. 'We were not party to Postulus' killing.'

'I know,' Claudia replied, 'and so does General Aurelian.'

Secundus had a word with his escort and came over. 'We would like to talk to you,' he said. 'I mean, before we part.' He held up the leather bag he carried. 'We have some wine, it's ripe Campanian. General Aurelian sent it. We also bought some fresh bread from a bakery just near the city gate.'

Leaving General Aurelian's retainers to talk amongst themselves, Claudia and the two veterans settled in the shade of a tree overlooking a small pond covered in green slime. Dragonflies hovered above it and the dull buzz of bees hummed from the gorse which ringed the pool. They shared out the bread and passed round the wineskin. Claudia took two or three mouthfuls and handed it back.

'You wanted to talk to me?'

'It wasn't as we said,' Crispus mumbled between mouthfuls.

'What wasn't?'

'After the attack.' Secundus spoke up, wiping his mouth on the back of his hand. 'Once the massacre was over, Stathylus wanted to enjoy himself. We hunted the war band down in the heather, killed those in the fort and slung their bodies out, burned every single one, a stack of corpses piled like bloody wheat sheaves, but the chieftain was different. We spent the next day, or rather Stathylus did, torturing him. We crucified him against the wall and cut his flesh.

At first the man was brave, he kept his mouth shut, but, of course, everyone has their limits, and by the late afternoon he was screaming with pain, begging to die. Every one of us was a hardened soldier; we've done things, Claudia, you wouldn't dream of, but even we grew tired of it. Stathylus eventually cut the Pict's throat and that was the end of the matter.'

'What was worse,' Crispus took a generous sip of the wine, 'was that Stathylus brought the Golden Maid to watch what he called the "fun". She fainted at least twice and was roused to watch again.'

'Why are you telling me this?' Claudia asked.

'We agreed,' Crispus replied, 'that whatever happened at the wall, on that night and the following day . . . well, I've heard the stories about the Furies of Hades pursuing their quarry.'

'And what are the Furies here?' Claudia had to pinch herself. Here she was sitting in the shade of a lovely evening, the shadows lengthening, the birdsong clear, butterflies floating, the noise of the crickets in the grass, with two men describing a nightmare which occurred years ago on some lonely heathland beneath that great brooding wall in the north of Britain. Something happened that day which, as Crispus said, had released a hatred that prowled like some vengeful ghost seeking its quarry.

'Are you sure that everyone was killed? I mean in that Pictish war band?'

'The chieftain had a son,' Crispus narrowed his eyes, 'a young boy probably no more than thirteen or fourteen summers. We learned that while we were torturing the father. Stathylus sent us out to search the heather; we found the boy's corpse, we recognised it by the torque round the neck and the arm bracelets. We dragged it back. The sight of it only increased the chieftain's humiliation and despair, as it did that of the Golden Maid.'

'Are you certain,' Claudia persisted, 'that everyone was killed? That no member of that war band survived to study and remember your appearance?'

'Mistress, most of the Picts were fully fledged warriors, mature men, and that was some eighteen years ago. They were killed, no slaves were taken.'

'Are you sure of that?' Claudia demanded harshly.

'Of course we are,' Secundus declared. 'Stathylus was no fool. We abandoned the mile fort, burned our surplus supplies and rode south. Now remember, Crispus and I weren't party to the decision to abandon Postulus. After it was all over, both of us were left behind for a while when Stathylus and the rest rode south.'

'For how long?'

'About two days in all,' Crispus replied. 'We were each given a fresh mount and told to ensure there were no survivors, that no one came creeping back. I tell you, mistress, those were the loneliest two days of our lives, out there in that deserted fort, next to it a stack of corpses burned to nothing but charcoaled flesh. The smoke and stench from it still fouled the air. We saw nothing, we felt nothing, and yet . . .'

'And yet what?' Claudia asked.

'We didn't tell you this either. Eventually we rode south-east until we reached Colchester, where other troops were mustering. We reported for duty. By then of course Stathylus had told of his great victory and was being applauded by all. The camp was overflowing, so we took lodgings in the town near the ruins of the old Temple of Claudius. Oh, it must have been about two weeks after our arrival. One of our number, I forget his name now . . .' he looked at Secundus, who just shrugged, 'went missing . . .'

'Missing?' Claudia asked. 'What do you mean?'

'He was never seen alive again. His corpse was later found in a ditch outside the town—'

'Let me guess,' Claudia intervened. 'His throat had been cut, his belly slit, his testicles severed and placed in his right hand.'

Both men swallowed hard and nodded. Crispus refused to meet her eye.

'You see, mistress,' Secundus declared, 'all of Britain was on the move, refugees here and there, every tribe in the province trying to flee. It's possible . . .'

Claudia held up her hand, staring at a tangle of gorse. 'It is more than possible,' she conceded, 'that somebody did survive that massacre and followed Stathylus' troop south, seized his opportunity, killed a veteran, and disfigured corpse, but then what? Why not strike at the rest? Is there anything else?' she asked. 'Are you frightened of meeting General Aurelian?'

'We'll declare our innocence,' Crispus declared. 'Postulus' blood is not on our hands. Why, mistress, what do you think will happen?'

'The General will question you,' Claudia got to her feet, brushing the crumbs from her tunic, 'but I think he wants to keep you safe.'

132

'It was Stathylus' fault . . .'

'Don't worry.' Claudia stared into the darkening trees. She was lying! In her heart, she conceded that these two veterans were like beasts chosen for sacrifice. Some furious ghost from the past had marked them down for death. Only fortune, or mere chance, could save them from the vengeance haunting their every step.

Chapter 6

Canta bit vacuus cum latrone viator.
The foolish traveller will sing with a thief.

Juvenal, *Satires*

Claudia bade the two veterans farewell. She and her escort continued their journey into the city. Darkness was falling when they reached the She Asses and Claudia's stomach lurched as she entered the square and stared across. In the doorway clustered a group of German mercenaries. The Empress had decided to visit the Great Miracle! The German guards crowded around Claudia like snuffling bears, almost carrying her into the tavern, which had been emptied because of the imperial visit. Poppaoe was busy with a cloth wiping tables. Sorry, armed with a tamarisk twig broom, was sweeping the floor whilst Caligula the cat sprawled like an emperor on one of the benches. Burrus was in the kitchen, one hand on the hilt of his broadsword, the other holding a chicken leg which he was tearing to pieces, smearing his moustache and beard with grease. He still insisted on hugging and kissing Claudia, then gestured with his head indicating that the Empress was in the garden beyond.

'Your man,' he grunted, 'the warrior, where is he?'

'Murranus is at General Aurelian's villa. He has taken up his new duties.'

'Good.' Burrus bit at the chicken leg, glaring at her fiercely, eyes almost watering. 'He should stay there. To guard someone important is a great honour. The Empress has come to visit you, little one. She waits for you.'

Claudia stared into the captain's light blue eyes. Burrus blinked and glanced away, holding the chicken up as if inspecting it carefully.

'You know what I'm thinking, Burrus,' she warned. 'This is my uncle's tavern. Tell your lovely lads out there, nothing must disappear, promise?'

Burrus nodded and returned to the chicken leg. Claudia slipped by him, out through the kitchen and into the garden. At the far end, in Polybius' favourite spot, Helena sat enthroned in the tavern-keeper's great pride and joy, his large chair, its arms covered with gilded leather. Before her, Polybius, Apuleius and Narcissus knelt on the grass; on a stool behind the Empress, half hidden in the shadows, sat Presbyter Sylvester, his saturnine face only faintly distinct in the flickering light from a lamp on the table beside the Empress. Helena sat like some priestess over her oracle, her head and face almost concealed by the hood of her silver-edged mantled robe. She glanced up as Claudia approached and indicated that the girl should kneel next to her uncle. Claudia, suppressing a sigh, obeyed and stared up at the Empress' face. Helena was not pleased; her eyes were hard, her lips thin, pressed tightly together. She stared at Claudia for a while, registering her displeasure at the deaths of Stathylus and Theodore.

'Augusta?' Claudia bowed.

'We have been talking about the Great Miracle,' Helena snapped. 'How God preserved the body of the virgin martyr Fulgentia.' She indicated the heavy leather pouches on the table beside her. 'I have decided, and your uncle has agreed, this is no place for such sacred remains.'

Claudia glanced quickly at her uncle. He seemed very pleased with the bargain, beaming from ear to ear. He turned quickly and winked mischievously at her.

'As you know,' Helena continued, staring up at the clear sky, the stars bright as jewels against their velvet background, 'my son has decided that certain palaces will be handed over to the Christian Way; they will become basilicas. Such basilicas will house the relics that I am searching for, sacred objects belonging to the Great Faith.' She paused, eyes half closed, as if listing for herself those miraculous finds for which she had ransacked the Empire.

'Fulgentia's corpse will be one of these. Your uncle and his friends,' Helena indicated with her head, 'will be well paid for their labours. My guards will remove it tonight. Do you not agree, Presbyter?' She half turned, and the priest nodded slowly, eyes intent on Claudia, a half-smile on his face. 'Good,' Helena clapped her hands softly, as she always did when business was finished. 'Now take your money, Polybius, and go back into your tavern. Keep an eye on my lovely boys and give them a flagon of wine, but make sure they don't keep the cups.'

Polybius scrambled to his feet, seized the clinking pouches from the table and, followed by his two companions, raced across the grass back into the tavern.

'And Presbyter?'

Sylvester stepped forward.

'Go,' Helena murmured. 'Go into the tavern, arrange for the remains of the blessed Fulgentia to be taken in a litter back to the palace. We'll decide then what is to happen.'

Sylvester did not demur at being so courteously dismissed, but came towards Claudia, hands out, and raised her to her feet. 'Claudia, it's good to see you.' He clasped her hands and Claudia felt the piece of papyrus being pushed into her palm.

Helena watched Sylvester walk away, then pointed to one of the small stools.

'Claudia, bring it closer. Sit down. Let me hear about what's been happening.'

Claudia made herself comfortable and told the Empress what had occurred the previous night: her discussions with Stathylus, Crispus and Secundus, the macabre death of the decurion and her visit to General Aurelian. Helena heard her out, head down, listening intently, and when she'd finished she glanced up and winked at her.

'Stathylus' death was not your fault,' she murmured, 'but you are correct, his murder, as well as those of the others, is linked to something which happened a lifetime away. General Aurelian will be kind to Crispus and Secundus. They'll probably argue that Postulus wasn't loyal to him, my husband or my son. He is a good man, Aurelian, he'll look after them. Perhaps he'll learn more from them with a cup of wine. And Theodore, his death here, you think he was poisoned?'

'Undoubtedly so, Augusta.' Claudia tried to stifle a yawn. She paused, listening to the sounds of the tavern, the noise of laughter, of furniture being moved; Sylvester must be already ordering the removal of the corpse. Claudia was pleased about that; whatever Helena had said, Claudia still entertained the gravest suspicions about Fulgentia, her origin, her death and her uncle's participation in such a miraculous find. Yet she must keep her suspicions to herself. If Polybius had been involved in any mischief, if he had deceived the likes of the Augusta and Presbyter Sylvester, his punishment would be horrific.

'What are you thinking about, little mouse?'

Claudia smiled apologetically.

'Theodore, Augusta! He came here and joined in the celebrations. Uncle is a generous host; Theodore must have eaten and drunk, then retired to his chamber where he died.'

'So somebody here must have murdered him?'

'Not one of Polybius' people,' Claudia declared. 'The assassin must have slipped in and poisoned him. This is the area of the Flavian Gate and the She Asses tavern, where everybody knows everyone else, yet my uncle Polybius noticed nothing suspicious. We know that Theodore was murdered, but who was responsible, how and why remains a mystery.'

'Not the why,' Helena retorted. 'Claudia, wake up, use your wits! Why should anyone kill a wandering actor except for what he saw at the Villa Carina? He must have seen something, Claudia.'

'But what?' Claudia protested. 'Theodore was an actor. He depicted himself as a hero but he wasn't. Undoubtedly he tried to protect Antonia and was knocked to the ground, but if he had seen anything, such criminals would have cut his throat without hesitation. He certainly learned something, but exactly what, Augusta, I truly don't know.'

'Have you discovered anything about Theodore's background?'

Claudia closed her eyes. She would love to go to sleep, but knew that Helena would think nothing of summoning her to the palace in the middle of the night if she did not tell her everything now. She tried to marshal her thoughts, remembering her walk back with Murranus and Theodore, the visit to the Temple of Hathor, how the actor had kept chattering about his past, where he'd been, whom he had met.

'He was from Egypt originally.' Claudia opened her eyes. 'From Memphis on the Nile. He was devoted to the Goddess Hathor, Lady of Drunkenness, the Lady of the White Walls. On our return here, we visited Hathor's temple. He spoke briefly to the High Priest Sesothenes . . .'

'Ah yes, I've heard of him.'

'Theodore wanted to give thanks for his deliverance; he asked Sesothenes to burn some incense, then left. I watched him all the time.'

'The Temple of Hathor,' Helena scoffed, 'a derelict place, full of dirty abominations, the usual rubbish of secret rites and rituals. Anything else?'

Claudia shook her head.

'Then get a good night's sleep, Claudia. Tomorrow, at the ninth hour, Antonia is to be released in the cemetery along the Appian Way. I want you to be there. Do not put yourself in danger, but watch, see what you can discover. Come close, little mouse.'

Claudia moved the stool, and Helena leaned forward.

'All those who have been kidnapped,' Helena whispered, 'have been released there. I've reflected on what you said, Claudia. The cemetery itself is a forest of stones, bushes and trees; beneath it lie the catacombs now deserted by the Christians.'

Claudia moved her hand slowly and pushed the piece of papyrus Sylvester had handed her into the small pocket of her tunic. Helena was so engrossed she never noticed.

'Now, as you know, Claudia, you are one amongst many of my retainers; another is Cassius Chaerea. Chaerea is a very useful man, a Christian who was seized during the persecution, interrogated and condemned to the mines in Sicily, where he worked for at least ten years. He is a great survivor, a farmer by birth; he learned how to survive in the galleries and tunnels of the mines outside Syracuse. I have shown him a map of the catacombs beneath the Via Appia, the best I could get. Presbyter Sylvester gave it to me. Chaerea and I studied that map most closely. He agrees with me,' Helena continued, 'that the catacombs would be the natural hiding place of these kidnappers; they could conceal their victims anywhere in its chambers, galleries, passageways and tunnels. There are so many entrances, not even dogs could search them out.' Helena gathered her stole about her shoulders. 'Chaerea has certain gifts, a legacy from his long service in the mines. He can see his way in the dark. He has no fear of confined or constricted places. He can thread his way through the most elaborate maze. He also has a sharp sense of smell, an animal instinct for danger. He should be busy now,' she murmured. 'The kidnappers may believe that a search would be made during the day, but Chaerea will slip in under darkness, and perhaps he can find something.' The Empress rose to her feet, pushing her hand towards Claudia so she could kiss the ring on her finger. 'Whatever happens,' she leaned down, one hand pressing hard on Claudia's shoulder, 'be in that cemetery tomorrow, long before the named hour . . .'

Chaerea the former slave would have disagreed with his imperial mistress in one respect: his senses were truly sharp, but the memories of the mines of Syracuse always came flooding back when he went hunting. Chaerea was very proud of his past. He had survived the mines, their murky, ill-lit galleries reeking of salt, where death could seize you in many ways: suffocation, hunger, thirst, a fall of rock, the sheer fatigue of hacking away, the cruelty of overseers or the savagery of your companions, who'd kill for a mouthful of stale bread or a cup of bitter water. A hideous time! The memories came surging back now as Chaerea slipped down the narrow, pebble-strewn gully beneath the tomb of the tribune Larentius, who had seen service in Dacia a hundred years earlier. The sharp shale cut at Chaerea's legs but he reached the bottom softly. Oh yes, this did remind him of the mines! The blackness wrapped round him like a shroud; hot, foul air, the constant sense of menace, of lurking danger.

Chaerea squatted for a while, preparing himself. A small, wiry man, sharp eyes above sunken cheeks, his fingers were like claws, the muscles on his legs hard as whipcord. He had prepared himself well for this. He had studied and memorised the trackways beneath the ground. He had made an offering to the white Christ. The small sack he carried contained a lamp, some rope and a dagger. Chaerea was used to such adventures. Helena had often used him in the catacombs to search for precious objects and relics, but this was different. The Empress had warned him about that, and Chaerea was no fool. He knew about the kidnappings in Rome and realised that the cemetery was the kingdom of the Inferni, those men and women, driven from society, who lurked there to prey upon the vulnerable, anyone weak or stupid enough to enter. Chaerea had been promised a lavish reward, enough money to arrange a feast for himself and his friends and hire those plump young courtesans who could delight him so much. He had his heart set on that. His years beneath the ground in Sicily had made him wonder about the power of Christ, and when he had been released, he'd determined to enjoy himself as much as possible. He closed his eyes, calming his breathing, recalling the Empress' instructions. He was not here to free anybody, but simply to discover, search out and report back.

Chaerea had accompanied the Empress on her journeys through Italy and around the Empire in her search for Christian relics. He was secretly amused by her quest; what did it matter about holy bones or sacred objects? The dead were dead, it was the living that mattered. Now he opened his eyes. The blackness was similar to that of the mines, no lamps, no lights; his eyes grew accustomed to the darkness. Two trackways stretched before him, one to the left, one curved sharply to the right. Chaerea knew the one on the left led deeper into the catacombs; that was where the Christians had hidden. He doubted the abductors would conceal themselves there, so he took the path to the right, eyes and ears straining, searching for any sign of danger. He could have stood upright and walked, but he knew that was dangerous, so he crawled like a dog, edging his way forward carefully. Now and again he would pass crumbling skeletons, desiccated corpses which had slipped out of their recesses in the wall to break, snap and crunch under his careful tread. He pushed aside skulls, hardened bones; these did not concern him. It was no different from the mines, where the dead were buried where they fell.

He must have crawled for about an hour, cutting and grazing his hands, arms and knees, when he sensed a change. The air had been hot and murky, reeking of dust, but he now became conscious that it was fresher, and that other odours, out of place, mingled here: the smell of a burning oil lamp, of hot fat, grease, even perfume. Chaerea crawled on. On one occasion he paused, one hand on a skull, the other on a crumbling rib cage. He had reached another place of the dead, some long-forgotten cemetery, but he was sure he'd heard something. Was it from above ground, the bell-like howl of a dog? He felt sweat pricking the nape of his neck and let it run. He always shaved his head, blackening the skin of his face, arms and legs so no light would catch the glint of sweat. He drew himself up against the wall, one hand on the ledge of an opened tomb, and closed his eyes, breathing in deeply. Yes, those fresh smells were back: sweat, tallow candle, oil lamp, fat. People had been here recently, congregating close by. He followed the tunnel, reminding himself to ignore those needle-thin runnels which branched off leading to dead ends.

Chaerea turned a corner and froze. Further on, deep in the tunnel, he caught the glow of a lamp for just a few seconds before it disappeared. He squatted down, moving slowly, feeling his way forward. When he reached the place where he'd seen the lamp, he turned a corner and crouched. Ahead was a deserted gallery where sconce torches had been lit and fixed into niches. Chaerea should have welcomed the light, but he hated it. He hadn't anticipated this. He edged forward, keeping close to the shadows. On either side of the tunnel rising above him were the recesses of ancient tombs, some still sealed by their plaster coverings, while others had crumbled, revealing piles of dusty bones, shards of pottery. Similar rubbish strewed the ground before him. Again he heard the sound of a dog, not the yip of a mongrel but the deep howl of some mastiff. He paused, biting his lip, wondering what to do. He knew he should retreat, he'd seen enough, but the prospect of even more silver and gold, of being lavishly rewarded, patronised by the Empress, made him thrust aside his usual caution.

Chaerea crawled on. He was now moving from one patch of shadow to another. He passed a small hallway and looked in: nothing, but a torch burning. Then he smelled it, the smoke from a brazier, and he heard the sound of voices echoing eerily along the gallery. He paused, opened the sack he carried and took out the long stabbing dagger. He coated the shining blade with dust and grasped its wire-coiled handle. His body was now soaked in sweat. He had reached a crossroads when he heard a moan to his left. He crossed quickly, edging his way along the wall, and reached the corner of one of those chambers where priests or mourners used to celebrate the funeral feast. He edged round and looked quickly inside. A torch burned in the corner, and a figure huddled beneath it, head covered with sacking. He peered closer and heard the clink of chains and a faint moan. As he stood wondering what to do, a sound behind made him whirl round. A figure stood at the crossroads, in one hand a sword glinting in the poor light, in the other a heavy club. The sound of the dogs drew closer.

Chaerea had no choice; he leapt forward, driving hard with his dagger. The man ducked. Chaerea did not stay to continue the struggle but turned and fled back the way he'd come. He dropped his sack and, grasping only the dagger, ran wildly, tripping over shards of bone, pieces of pottery. Now there was no subterfuge, no skill, he simply had to reach the place where he had come in and escape. Sounds and shouts rang out behind, but what froze his blood was the long-drawn-out howl of the dog. He was being hunted! He stumbled blindly on, slipping and slithering, only to realise he had taken a wrong turning. Where was he? He paused and felt the wall – nothing! He moved his hand and felt a carving, and his fingers made out the shape of Anubis, the jackal-faced God of the Dead. He racked his memory. He must be in the passageway described as the Gallery of the Night, heading towards an entrance deep in the cemetery known as the Gates of Hell. He cursed. He'd made a dreadful mistake in dropping that sack; the dogs would use it for scent.

Chaerea raced on, memories flowing back about the mines, about that old witch cackling how he would die as she would, deep in the dark beneath the earth. He had always hoped that he would end his days with dignity, his friends grouped around him, his corpse embalmed, his feet towards the door, ready to be escorted with honour through the streets to be cremated, but that would not happen now. The air felt very hot, as if the Manes, the souls of the dead, had crossed back over that infernal river and were crowding around him. Chaerea paused, fighting for breath. The dogs were drawing closer. Eyes burning, mouth gasping, throat dry, he ran into a wall; he had made another wrong turn! He was lost! He turned. A pool of light was fast approaching, and Chaerea screamed at the sinister sight of the mastiffs loping towards him . . .

Claudia stood on the broken steps leading up to the crumbling Temple of Minerva, which stood off a square near the Coelian Gate. The wooden door of the temple was flaking, the columns on either side chipped, their plaster cracked. In the colonnade to the right, a spell-caster squatted on a stool, a horrid-looking mask over her face. On the cloth before her lay a range of curse tablets, some prepared, others blank. The woman waited, metal pen in hand, a pot of ink open before her. Claudia walked up the steps.

'Happy the man who remains far from the world of business.' The harsh voice behind the mask quoted a line from the poet Horace.

'But who shall guard the guards?' Claudia replied with a famous verse from Juvenal.

'He'll be here soon,' the guttural voice retorted.

Claudia nodded, pushed open the door and walked into the long hall of the temple. It was a desperately shabby place. The pillars down each side were battered and chipped; the floor, once tiled, had been badly damaged by looters from the nearby tenement blocks. Nothing which could be removed remained, and the rest had been vandalised, the doors of the vestibule on either side of the sanctuary were badly scorched, whilst rats and vermin scurried in the shadows. Flies danced in the light pouring through the windows high in the wall. Claudia stood and looked round. Such places fascinated her; she was intrigued by the history of Rome. This place had once been a sanctuary of power thronged with worshippers, particularly the nearby fullers, who regarded it as a holy of holies, the shrine of Minerva, the patron goddess of their art. The shabby portico still displayed a battered chip carving of fullers trampling woollen cloth in a vat; above them floated an owl, the symbol of Minerva.

Claudia studied this for a while, then walked up the left-hand portico. She was safe here: the spell-caster outside was one of Sylvester's spies, and there would be other men around the temple, Sylvester's guards. The Presbyter might not move through Rome with all the power of a consul, but he still had those he could whistle up to protect himself. Claudia stood by a pillar and smiled to herself. She was fascinated by that. Sylvester preached the word of the gentle Christ, and yet, not two years out of the catacombs, the Christians were beginning to surround themselves with all the trappings of power: spies, guards, wealth and places of worship.

Claudia recalled the events of the previous night. Once Helena had left, Polybius and his cronies had begun to celebrate. Claudia was too tired and had retired immediately to bed, waking before dawn to wash and dress herself, break her fast in the kitchen and slip out here to the Temple of Minerva to meet Sylvester as he'd demanded in that cryptic note he'd pushed into her hand. She wondered what he wanted.

'A place of death.'

Claudia glanced up sharply. The figure at the far end of the portico, leaning against a pillar, walked slowly towards her. Sylvester's pace quickened as he approached, his face wreathed in a smile, hands out in friendship. Claudia met him and clasped his hands. Sylvester put an arm around her shoulder and gently guided her further up the temple.

'A place of death, Claudia, but fascinating, isn't it?' He paused and gestured around. 'The old Rome is dying, and that's good.' He grinned. 'The ancients could never make up their minds which god to worship. Look.'

He pointed to a fresco on the wall depicting the Egyptian God of the Sun, Horus, with a hawk's head, a sceptre in his right hand and an ankh, the symbol of life, in the other;

to the left of this was a painting of the god Api with a crescent moon between his horns. They moved further down the temple to another faded scene celebrating Dionysus leading a procession of satyrs, cupids and panthers. In another fresco the wine god sprawled in a chariot pulled by a centaur whilst above this dancers were engaged in a frenzied ritual, robes open, cups in one hand, laurel wreaths in the other. The colours were faded but they vigorously celebrated the rites of one of Rome's favourite gods.

'All dying.' Claudia caught the note of triumph in Sylvester's voice. 'The gods of Rome are dying. Soon there will only be the one true God.'

'Is that why you brought me here?' Claudia asked. 'To gloat in triumph over old gods dying and new gods rising?'

Sylvester laughed and squatted down at the base of a pillar, gesturing at Claudia to join him. He opened the small leather pannier looped around his neck and brought out a linen cloth, which he delicately unfolded. He broke the bread and cheese, then, dipping into the satchel again, brought out a wineskin. Claudia, hungry, ate quickly, taking drinks from the watered wine, still staring round this deserted place of worship.

'You haven't answered my question,' she said.

'You know why I have asked you here.' Sylvester paused between mouthfuls. 'The virgin martyr Fulgentia; is she one of Uncle Polybius' tricks?'

'I don't know,' Claudia replied.

'If she is,' Sylvester wagged a warning finger, 'he'll feel the Empress' fury.'

'We shall all feel the Empress' fury,' Claudia replied

wearily. 'Presbyter, I cannot answer that. What Polybius has told the Empress seems to be the truth: the corpse was discovered in his garden.'

'Very good, very good,' Sylvester soothed. 'But do tell me,' he glanced at her sharply, 'if the full truth emerges.'

'What will happen to her corpse?' Claudia asked curiously. 'The Empress talked of a church.'

'That's what I am telling you, Claudia. All over Rome, places like this are being given to us. Imperial palaces, old temples, including the Pantheon, will be blessed with the presence of the Christ Lord, and all this will be forgotten. Just as these frescos commemorate Dionysus, so our churches will be full of Christian art, of the Fish, the Keys, the memories of those who died for their faith, like Fulgentia or our great Apostles Peter and Paul.'

'And you support that?' Claudia asked curiously. 'The Empress' hunger for relics? The manger Christ was born in, the clothing of the Apostles, the bodies of dead virgin martyrs?'

'It all helps, Claudia,' Sylvester replied. 'Anything to fortify, strengthen, encourage the faith of the people; miracles like that of Fulgentia are useful to us.'

'But it is not just that,' Claudia said. 'You have brought me here for something else.'

'Of course!'

Sylvester folded the piece of linen and put it back in the leather satchel, then picked up the wineskin, and offered it to Claudia, who shook her head. He took another deep gulp and put the stopper back.

'These abductions,' he began.

Claudia was tempted to tell him to mind his own business, but she needed Sylvester as much as he needed her, to discover certain matters in the mind of the Empress.

'Well?' he asked. 'I know the Empress has placed great trust in you, and these abductions worry her deeply.'

'And why should they worry you, Presbyter?'

'Because,' Sylvester took a deep breath, 'because whatever upsets the Empress and her son upsets the Church of Rome. Look at these paintings.' He waved around. 'They are made up of little scenes: a figure, a garden, a wine press, all brought to life and connected by the brush of the artist. So it is with Rome, Claudia. What concerns the Empress in one area might affect another.'

'Do they have so much power,' Claudia asked, 'the powerful ones, the senators and their like?'

'Not really,' Sylvester scratched the back of his neck, 'but they can be a distraction. Constantine, as you know, is building up his army, settling affairs at home so he can march east. There must be no delay. Licinius in Nicomedea must be brought to battle and destroyed. Constantine needs the support of these bankers, generals, merchants, men and women with great influence.'

'And the Lady Urbana and her good friend Cassia?'

'Ah.' Sylvester's face broke into a smile. 'If Helena is a committed Christian, so are Urbana and Cassia. True, both, how can I put it, enjoyed vivid lives, dramatic careers, before they converted, but those two are very powerful, particularly the Lady Urbana. She is more zealous in the Christian Way than even the Empress. You know about the Magdalena?'

152

Claudia nodded.

'Lady Urbana believes that Mary Magdalene may have married, and from her will spring a great dynasty of kings, but more importantly the Lady Urbana is searching the southern cities of Gaul for the corpse of Mary Magdalene to bring it back to Rome. If she did, it would be a veritable triumph, the body of a woman so close to Christ.'

'Do you believe all this?' Claudia tried to keep the cynicism out of her voice.

'If the Lady Urbana believes it,' Sylvester retorted coldly, 'then she has my support. What you must do, Claudia, is make sure the Empress' business is brought to a successful conclusion.'

Claudia got to her feet and tightened the cord around her waist, adjusting the needle-thin dagger sheath on her belt. She'd left her cloak at home and forgotten her walking stick. She felt strangely vulnerable staring down at this powerful priest who was studying her so closely; she also felt angry. Who was he to give her orders? She was not of his faith. She squatted down close to Sylvester and held his gaze.

'Are you threatening me, priest? Why should I help you? Why should I keep you informed? Think on that.' She rose, spun on her heel and walked hot-faced towards the door.

'Claudia,' Sylvester's voice was friendly, 'Claudia, let us not part in anger. Come back.' He paused. 'Murranus, Polybius . . .'

'Murranus, Polybius,' she turned, 'what about them? Don't threaten me, Sylvester, I warn you, and don't threaten those I love. I will have you as my friend, my ally, but if you threaten me, you will be my enemy.'

The priest chewed his lip. 'I wouldn't want that, Claudia.' He rose and came towards her, stretching out his hand and touching her lightly on the cheek. 'I have a great deal of respect and admiration for you and for what you've been through. I knew your father—'

'Don't mention him!'

'I will mention him, Claudia, because I have a responsibility for you. I tried to help you before and I will now. So listen carefully.' He grasped her hand and held it between his. 'I mean you well, Claudia. Your uncle Polybius is a great rogue; he likes to dabble in this and dabble in that. He is also borrowing money.'

'What?'

'You know Torquatus the Tonsor, the barber who sets up his stall near the She Asses tavern?'

'Of course.'

'You also know that he has the ear of some quite powerful bankers, courtiers and senators. To be blunt, Torquatus speculates . . .'

'Oh no!' Claudia groaned.

'Oh yes,' Sylvester retorted. 'Torquatus is a money-lender. He is not an evil man, but he has invited Polybius into certain business ventures which have failed. Polybius owes Torquatus a lot of money.'

'Is he in any danger?' Claudia asked.

'Not really.' Sylvester narrowed his eyes. 'Torquatus is one of us, a Christian; well, at least he shows the outward signs of being a Christian. He is really more interested in the She Asses tavern.'

'Of course,' Claudia whispered. 'It's near his stall and—'

154

'Precisely,' Sylvester agreed. 'Torquatus would love to own it. If Polybius gets deeper into debt, if he can't repay his loan, Torquatus might foreclose; that's why I asked you about Fulgentia. Polybius is not a villain, but he's a rogue. If he can worm his way out of mischief he will, although this time he is treading a very dangerous path. The beautifully preserved corpse of a young woman was found on his property. Now there may be another reason for that, but Polybius has sold it to the Empress as the mortal remains of a blessed virgin martyr, a miracle, proof of God's intervention in the affairs of men. If that was proved to be a deliberate lie, Polybius would suffer, despite whatever influence you have. So you must, I beg you, Claudia, make sure that Polybius is protected, that what has happened is the truth, built on rock and not on crumbling sand.'

Claudia moved her head, easing the tension at the back of her neck. She felt like screaming, running out of the temple, going back to the She Asses tavern and confronting her uncle, but that would be futile. Unless she had proof, evidence of his roguery, Polybius would simply bluster.

'And Murranus?' Claudia asked. 'What about him?'

'Oh, Murranus,' Sylvester replied, 'champion gladiator, the glory of the amphitheatre.'

'What about him?' Claudia snapped.

'I know you have a great fear of Murranus returning to the arena, and you are right. Murranus is a champion, but every day he grows older; eventually he will enter the amphitheatre and meet someone younger, faster, swifter, more deadly. The mood of the mob is fickle. Today they will clap Murranus on the back, buy him a goblet of wine, women will offer themselves to him.' He shrugged. 'I apologise. I am not saying Murranus would accept, but that is the way of the world. One day Murranus will make a mistake. He'll lie sprawled on the sand, mortally wounded, begging for his life from the mob who, simply because they don't like the way he fought, would consign him to death.'

'The Empress would intervene.'

'The Empress is a politician, Claudia; she will do what the mob wants, you know that as well as I do.'

'So what are you saying?'

'The Church of Rome needs, how can I put it, protectors, bodyguards. My master, the other powerful bishops of this region, must have their own military escort. Murranus would be an ideal choice as a captain.' He smiled as Claudia relaxed. 'See, I'm not all threats and menaces. I am trying to help you.'

'But Murranus is not a Christian.'

'He is better than that. He's a man who can't be bought. He can be trusted. So, Claudia, if we remain allies, even better, friends, whatever authority I wield, whatever power the Church exercises, will be used on your behalf and that of Murranus.'

'And Polybius?'

'As I've said, Polybius is a different matter, he is following a very dangerous path. The Empress is devoted to her relics, the antiquities of the Christian past. If it came out that a tavern-keeper near the Flavian Gate had fooled her . . .' His words hung like a noose.

Claudia stretched out her hand; Sylvester clasped it. 'You have my word,' she promised. 'I will do what I can, and if

I discover the truth about Fulgentia,' she chewed her lip, 'you'll be the first to know. Oh, Presbyter, there is something else.'

'What?'

Claudia quickly described the murders of the veterans, their service in northern Britain, the savage desecration carried out on their corpses.

'I've heard something of this,' Sylvester murmured, 'but how can I help you? Such deaths have no connection with the Christian Church.'

Claudia laughed abruptly. 'Very little, Presbyter, but I need your assistance. Many followers of your way are slaves or servants; I want you to make diligent enquiry for me amongst them. Are there any Picts in Rome? I need to talk to someone who knows their tongue, customs and culture.'

'Perhaps a survivor from that attack?'

'No, Presbyter, there were no survivors. Or at least I don't think so. I just need someone to describe for me the Pictish way of life, explain what could be happening here.'

Sylvester held up his hand. 'I will do all I can, Claudia.' He smiled. 'You know Sallust the Searcher and his family?'

Claudia grinned; she certainly knew Sallust!

'I'll employ him,' Sylvester declared, getting to his feet. 'He can find anything in Rome . . .'

A short while later, just as the water clock of the tavern she'd left indicated the seventh hour, a different Claudia entered the cemetery which stretched along the Appian Way. She had gone to a seller of perfumes and powders, cosmetics and paints for ladies, and bought herself a dye and some powder. Afterwards, she'd stopped at a second-hand clothes-seller and purchased a few rags, a pair of battered sandals for her feet and a polished walking cane. She'd sheltered in a tavern near the city gates and changed, dusting her hair and face, rubbing ash on to her hands and arms before putting on the smelly, tattered rags. She had perfected the walk, the slight stoop of an old crone, from her days as an actress.

Now she followed the winding path into the jungle of undergrowth, tombs, monuments and sarcophagi which stretched to the great heathland in the far distance where she could glimpse the arches of the Claudian Aqueduct. To her right rose the dust from the Appian Way, as farmers, merchants, traders and tinkers either left or made their way into the city. She could still hear the hum of conversation, the creak of wheels as she fought her way through the tangle. Eventually all sounds faded except for bees buzzing above the wild flowers and the occasional scuttle of some animal fleeing from her approach. Claudia was used to visiting the cemetery. In the past, she'd often met Sylvester in the catacombs to the north, though there was now little need for such subterfuge; their recent meeting at the deserted Temple of Minerva proved Sylvester's growing confidence in being able to carry out his affairs when and where he liked. Claudia paused, resting on her staff, and closed her eyes. She must remember that. When she'd first begun her relationship with Sylvester, the Christian Church had only recently come out of the catacombs and Constantine's Edict of Milan had been fresh in everyone's minds. Since then, the Church had worked vigorously and swiftly to reinforce its authority as well as to gain patronage and favour at court.

Claudia started from her reverie at the harsh cawing above her; glancing up, she glimpsed the buzzard circling above her. She continued on her way. She was now approaching the main part of the cemetery, walking slowly, using the stick to drive away the tangle of bramble, gorse, wild grass, and nettles which scored her ankles and made her gasp in pain. Yet she kept up the pretence, stopping every so often to look at the various funeral tombs, as the old do, as if still relishing their hold on life: a fresco of a man set in a wreath, a small cremation chest to mark his wife, the pitiful sarcophagus of a child, carved figures lamenting around the deathbed of a young girl, a dead woman portrayed as Venus triumphant, a married couple exchanging vows. Some of the stone was pure marble from the Sea of Marmara, other monuments were of rough stone hewn from a local quarry. Most of the tombs, sarcophagi and memorials were at least a hundred years old and slowly crumbling under the lashing rain, winter frosts and summer heat. The tomb of the tribune where Antonia was to be released lay on the far side of the cemetery, deep enough in this tangle of stone and bramble for the gang to free their hostage and escape unscathed. Now and again Claudia paused and looked up. Across the cemetery grew different trees, many in weird, grotesque shapes; any of these could house a lookout posted to spot approaching soldiers.

Claudia, aware of the oppressive, brooding silence, paused at a tomb of a young man, his likeness carved on the front in the form of the sleeping Endymion. She leaned against this and turned slowly in the manner of an old woman. She was certain she was being followed; just a coldness on the back of her neck, a slight agitation in her stomach. She listened intently, scrutinising the brambles and tangled gorse behind her for any sign of movement. Only silence, nothing but that buzzard still cawing noisily above her. Had it been disturbed, forced to flee whatever morsel it had been plucking at? Claudia sighed, her face and body now coated in sweat, then pushed on along the trackway. She entered a clearing and was about to cross it when four figures emerged from behind a chest tomb. She immediately recognised what they were: Inferni, dirty, dishevelled men dressed in rags but armed with wicked-looking knives and clubs. They blocked her path.

'Hello, old one.' The pig-faced leader stepped forward. 'What are you doing here? Haven't seen you before.'

Claudia leaned on the stick and peered at them, assessing their strength. She felt fear, but at the same time she could throw off her disguise and run faster than any of these. The one on the far left had a slight limp; the others looked fat, with the unhealthy colour and sagging cheeks of men who drank copiously of cheap posca and other foul wines.

'Well?' The leader edged forward.

Claudia stepped back.

'Come on, old lady, let's see who you really are. Let's have a look at your hands.' He made an obscene gesture with his groin. 'You can still work your wonder here.'

Claudia was about to turn and flee when Burrus and five of his companions slipped out of the undergrowth as if they'd come up from the very earth itself. Despite their size and bulk, they moved swiftly and deadly. The four Inferni didn't even have a chance to resist. For a short while the silence of the clearing was shattered by grunts and moans as Burrus and his companions dispatched them. Claudia watched, horror-struck. Within a few heartbeats, all four men lay dead, their throats cut. Burrus and his companions squatted down, cleaning their swords and daggers on the long grass. The captain glanced up and winked at Claudia.

'We've been watching you, little one, ever since you left that tavern. We knew it was you.' He and his companions laughed softly and came crowding round this little woman whose bravery they admired.

Claudia put down the cane and wiped the sweat from her face.

'You've been following me?'

'Of course, little one. This is no different from our forests in Germany. An entire war band could move around here and not even disturb the birds on the branches.' Burrus crouched down and stared into her eyes. 'You're unharmed, little one. They were tracking you. You're not as old as you look.' He grinned and tweaked her cheek. 'Go on, we will be behind you.'

Claudia crouched down, gesturing at Burrus and the others to join her.

'Why are you here, to protect me or to hunt the kidnappers?'

'Both,' Burrus replied, squinting up at the sky. 'The Augusta thought that if any soldiers could get close, we were the ones. None of the fancy boys from the guards; they'd go blundering about like a child in water. We are different. There are more of us, at least two dozen out there heading towards that tomb.'

Claudia suppressed a chill of fear and pointed to the trees. 'You could be seen from there.'

'I doubt it,' Burrus declared. 'We'll be crawling on our bellies.'

Claudia was about to reply when one of the guards lifted his hand.

'Look, look!' he urged.

Claudia glanced to her right. Black smoke plumed against the blue sky, followed by flames darting greedily up. Such fires were common in summer along the dry heathland round the city, but this fire had started too quickly. Claudia followed Burrus as they hurried back through the tangled undergrowth, no longer bothering to conceal their progress, tripping over cracked pots, pieces of masonry, making their way round the tombs towards the fire. One of the German guards paused, sniffing the air like a lurcher, then Claudia smelled it, that horrid stench of burning flesh. They hurried on. The flames were dying but the foul smoke made them cough and splutter. They reached a small glade in front of a large tomb, and found a tangle of wood heaped around a burned corpse, its flesh bubbling. The smell was awful. Covering her nose with her tattered cloak, Claudia followed Burrus over and stared down.

'He has no head!' she proclaimed, and turned away as her stomach heaved.

The corpse, whoever it belonged to, was nothing more

than blackened remains. Burrus grasped her by the shoulder and led her away from the smoke. He made her crouch down while he and one of his lieutenants went to inspect the gory remains more carefully; they turned the corpse over, muttered to each other and came back.

'It's definitely a man,' Burrus declared, cupping Claudia's chin in his hand. 'Not Antonia, perhaps a quarry of the Inferni, but why they took his head then burned the rest, I don't know . . .'

'Do you think—'

Claudia's question was cut off by a chilling scream. Burrus leapt to his feet and, with Claudia following, hastened down a narrow winding path into another clearing. A young woman sat with hands and feet bound, though she'd managed to remove the blindfold over her eyes and was staring in horror, shaking, trying to knock away the severed head nestling in her lap.

The Germans cut her bonds, pulling her to her feet. Burrus lifted the severed head, inspected it carefully and, taking one of his companion's cloaks, wrapped it up.

'Who is it?' Claudia asked.

'The Augusta's man, Chaerea,' Burrus replied, his voice thick and guttural. 'She sent him here. By the marks on the head and face, he was mauled by dogs before being decapitated.'

Chapter 7

Omnia Romae cum pretio.
Everything in Rome comes with a price.

Juvenal, *Satires*

Claudia groaned and turned back to the girl. She was plump and very pretty, but now her face was tear-streaked and dirty, her hair a tangled mess, the tunic she wore stained and frayed, her legs and arms cut and bruised. Claudia forced the young woman to kneel well away from the blood-stains and, cupping her face in her hands, stared at her. Antonia was about to start screaming again. Claudia smacked her gently on the cheek.

'You are safe,' she whispered. 'I am Claudia; these are German guards sent by the Augusta. How long have you been here?'

Claudia could make no sense of what the young woman told her. Antonia was shocked, horrified, talking as if in her sleep about dark passageways, men who touched her, that severed head in her lap. In the end they took her back into the city, Burrus using his authority at the city gates to hire a litter. The young woman was carried up to the Palatine Palace, where Senator Carinus, together with the Augusta and other leading courtiers, were waiting to receive her. In an adjoining chamber Claudia quickly described what had happened. Helena cursed like a trooper at the fate of Chaerea and vowed vengeance on his killers, but snapped how that would just have to wait. Claudia told her about the attack by the Inferni, how Burrus had intervened, the fire, then finding Antonia.

'They must have seen you,' Helena declared, walking up and down.

Claudia sat still on the bench.

'They must have seen you and decided to take Chaerea's head and burn his corpse to distract you. What hour was it?'

'Shortly before the eighth,' Claudia replied wearily. 'I don't really know.'

'They must have guessed you were coming,' Helena repeated. 'Now we'll have to wait.'

Claudia was refused permission to leave the palace but had to kick her heels in either the imperial gardens or one of the small refectories adjoining the kitchens. Slaves brought food and wine but she had little appetite. She learned from a chamberlain that the Lady Antonia had been stripped, bathed, anointed and perfumed, given a sip of drugged wine and put to sleep.

Later that day, Senator Carinus, one arm round his daughter, who now looked much refreshed, joined Claudia and the Augusta in a small enclosed garden. They sat in a flowered arbour. Carinus was eager to leave, but Helena was insistent that Antonia answer Claudia's questions. At first the young woman found it difficult to speak. She shook her head and blinked. Now and again she would lapse into silence or stare at her father as if recognising him for the first time. Claudia recognised the symptoms of shock, of sleep deprivation. She spoke softly, gently, pointing out that she needed Antonia's help, and at last the young woman, fortified by a cup of white Falernian, answered her questions, though she could give very little information. She had been taken from her father's garden, blindfolded, gagged, bound hand and foot and carried somewhere. It was always dark and cold. She was given food, something to drink and a slop bucket to serve as a latrine. She talked about one man fondling her and of him being killed; about her own terrors and fears. Helena intervened. Did Antonia know anything about the death of Chaerea, whose severed head had been placed in her lap? Antonia shook her head.

'There was some commotion last night,' she said, 'but they gave me some drugged wine. I woke once. Men were shouting and dogs howling, that is all I remember. This morning they came and told me that if I behaved I was to be freed. My father had paid the ransom. I was pulled to my feet and taken along tunnels. Some were narrow, others broad; now and again the stones scored my arms and feet, then I was out into the fresh air. It smelled so good, the sun was on my face. I was pushed ever so gently and taken to where you found me.' She gestured at Claudia. 'I was told to count to ten eight times, and only then was I to lift the blindfold. I was terrified, I don't know if I counted or not. I smelled the smoke, that hideous stench. Something was put in my lap. I could feel the wetness through my tunic.' She stopped, fingers to her mouth. 'I thought it was a wineskin, something to drink or eat. I lifted my wrists and forced the blindfold off, and saw those dead eyes staring up at me, the gaping mouth.' Antonia staggered to her feet and ran off to retch and vomit behind a bush.

'I think she has said enough.' Senator Carinus leaned forward. 'Augusta, Claudia, I must take my child home.'

'In a short while,' Claudia murmured. 'There are other questions I must ask.' She got up, went over to Antonia and patted her gently on the shoulder. 'You've been very brave,' she whispered. 'It's all over now, but there are a few more questions I must ask. You know Theodore is dead?'

Antonia nodded, wiping her mouth.

'Come.' Claudia slipped her arm through Antonia's, but instead of returning to Senator Carinus, they walked across the lawns. 'Look around, Antonia: the plants, the roses, the flowers; see that peacock over there with its tail extended in such beautiful colours. Stare up at the sky. Don't you feel the evening breeze? It's all yours again.'

'Theodore,' Antonia asked. 'Was he killed defending me?'

'No, no.' Claudia swiftly described what had happened. Antonia began to cry again and Claudia hugged her close. 'I want to avenge his death as well. Tell me, Antonia, did Theodore remove the mask of one of your attackers?'

'No, no, he didn't!' Antonia replied. 'He leapt forward but was knocked down. By then I was seized and they were thrusting a gag into my mouth while the blindfold came

down across my eyes, but no mask was taken off. Why do
you ask?'

'Theodore claimed differently.' Claudia half smiled. 'He
said that he removed one of the kidnapper's masks. That may
be why he was murdered, because he recognised somebody.'

'Well he didn't!' Antonia snapped. 'That was Theodore!
He was forever telling stories, always telling lies.'

'What other lies did he tell you?' Claudia asked.

'Oh, where he'd been, where he came from.'

'Let me ask you another question.' They paused under
the outstretched branches of a sycamore tree; above them
songbirds in gilded cages sang hauntingly as if grieving over
their imprisonment. 'Is there anything Theodore did not
lie about, anything constant in his life, family or friends?'
Claudia made the young woman sit down on a bench fitted
against the trunk of a tree, and squatted before her. 'Please,
Antonia, was there anything constant?'

'Theodore believed everybody loved him, including me.
He was a ladies' man. He boasted about what plays he
knew, which stage manager would help him, how one day
all Rome would know his name, but yes, there was one
constant. He had great devotion to the Lady of Gleefulness,
of Joy, I forget her name.'

'Hathor of the White Walls.'

'Yes, that's it, Hathor of the White Walls. He was always
talking about his devotion to her. How she'd favoured him
in his career, how pleased he was that he had found a
temple dedicated to her in Rome. He repeated that time
and again.' She smiled ruefully. 'On reflection, perhaps that
was the only truthful thing he said.'

169

'Thank you.' Claudia got to her feet, brushing twigs and grass from her tunic. 'One more question, Antonia.'

'Mistress, I am very tired.'

'You are sure that you were imprisoned in the catacombs?'

'It must have been.' Antonia shook her head. 'When I was freed, I only walked a short distance. Perhaps no more than from here,' she pointed across at the palace buildings, 'to there, then I was out in the sun.'

'Anything else?' Claudia enquired. 'Smell, taste, touch, voices?'

'Just one voice,' Antonia replied. 'I'll never forget it, threatening, telling me what to do.'

Claudia left the palace and made her way back into the city. Daylight was fading, traders were closing up shop, the taverns and eating houses were busy. Just as she entered the Flavian quarter, Claudia noticed a man dressed in goatskins, with unkempt beard, hair and moustache, standing on a stone plinth, in one hand a staff, in the other a crude wooden cross. She paused and stared at him. The man was addressing passers-by, few of whom paid him attention, but Claudia caught his words.

'Man is conceived with tainted blood,' this fanatic claimed, 'through the ardour of lechery.' On and on he ranted. Such preachers were becoming common in Rome, religious fanatics inveighing against anything and everything.

Claudia moved on, pushing dispiritedly through the noisy throng. At the corner of the street leading down to the She Asses tavern, Torquatus the Tonsor was busy putting his implements into a leather sack: razors, knives, hair-pluckers, whetstone, leather straps, oils, unguents, powders and creams. He stored these all carefully away. Claudia watched him neatly tie the string around the neck of the sack before clearing away the folding stool and table.

'Torquatus?'

He glanced up and peered at her.

'Why, it's Claudia, what do you want?'

'I'd like to buy you a drink.' Claudia indicated with her head towards the tavern standing on the corner of an alleyway, the House of a Thousand Dreams.

Torquatus grinned and, putting his fingers to his mouth, gave a sharp whistle. Two boys came hurrying over. He handed them his sack, table and stool and instructed them to remain under the sycamore tree until he returned, then he and Claudia entered the tavern, a dingy hole with narrow windows above the counter at the far end. It smelled like a stable. In the centre stretched a deep pit where two blood-spattered cocks, cheered on by their respective owners, fought like gladiators with beak and spurred claw; their screeching cut the ear as they turned in a whirl of feathers and puffs of dust. Torquatus led Claudia out through the rear door into a quiet garden with a range of drinking arbours tastefully fashioned out of pine logs and festooned with crawling ivy and wild flowers. A lawn stretched the full length of the garden. In the centre, a gracefully carved fountain displayed three marble dolphins, mouths open to the sky, through which water spurted.

'The best of both worlds.' Torquatus grinned at Claudia's surprise. He ordered jugs of wine and water and cups of crushed apple juice. The raucous sounds from the tavern echoed faintly. Claudia relaxed in the last golden burst of sunlight, relishing the evening breeze as it brushed the flowerbeds, and wafted fragrance towards her.

'What do you want, Claudia?'

'I know what *you* want.' Claudia sipped at the apple juice. Torquatus, moon-faced under his matted, straw-coloured hair, gazed back all innocent, lower lip jutting out, one finger scratching at the dimple on his clean-shaven cheek. 'You want the She Asses Tavern. You've lent Uncle Polybius money, he can't pay you, and now you wish to foreclose—'

'I did lend Polybius money,' Torquatus interrupted. 'He heard of my recent business venture.'

'What was it?'

'To import spices from Punt—'

'Ye gods!'

'The venture was not successful; our ship sank. Polybius owed me his share, I advanced that for him.'

'And now you think you have my uncle cornered?' Claudia demanded. She stared at this most skilful teller of tales. She'd always liked Torquatus, a character of the quarter, ever friendly and cheerful with his never-ending list of tales and a catalogue of medical cures which even an imperial physician would envy. She immediately regretted her words when she saw the look of hurt in Torquatus' eyes.

'Claudia, Claudia.' Torquatus took a deep drink of his wine before adding some water. 'You're tired. I know you have other business.'

He gazed at her meaningfully, and Claudia wondered if he was also employed by the Empress.

'Your uncle doesn't owe me any money. He's paid it back, thanks to the Great Miracle at the She Asses.'

Claudia sighed with relief. 'I am sorry!' She put her hand across the table. 'Torquatus, you know Polybius; he's attracted to mischief as a cat to cream.'

Torquatus clasped her hand gently. 'Of course, I would love to own the She Asses. It's in a prime location, it has a good eating room with a well-furnished kitchen and a garden that's even better than this. However, Polybius has repaid every single denarius. He owes me nothing, thanks to the Great Miracle.'

Claudia sat back in her seat and stared at the shadows lengthening across the grass.

'But of course Polybius,' Torquatus continued, 'literally jumps from pot to fire and back into the pot again. You've heard about Ophelion?'

Claudia suppressed a shiver of fear and sat up straight. Of course she knew Ophelion! He was one of Helena's most trusted spies, a snooper, a collector of trifles, a born eavesdropper, sharp of eye and keen of wit.

'What about him?' she asked tersely.

'Well, he's been snooping around.' Torquatus leaned closer. 'He has been making very careful enquiries about the corpse found at your uncle's tavern.'

'But you know the result,' Claudia declared. 'The Empress herself has paid Polybius; she recognised the body as that belonging to a virgin martyr, a manifest miracle by God.'

Torquatus grinned at the sarcasm in Claudia's voice.

173

'I hope so,' he declared, and leaned across the table. 'I'm a friend, Claudia, I mean you well. I like Polybius, he's a rogue born and bred. As you say, he has a natural penchant for mischief. May the Lord of Light help him,' Torquatus' voice turned hard, 'if he has fooled the Empress. Can you imagine, Claudia,' he paused and grimaced, 'whatever your relationship with the Empress, if your uncle has fooled her, or lied to her, the punishment would be great.'

'What has Ophelion been asking?' Claudia asked.

'The usual questions,' Torquatus replied. 'He is digging in the past, any young girl around here who disappeared, you know how it is . . .'

Claudia bit her lip and watched the butterflies hovering near the fountain. 'But that is ridiculous,' she murmured. 'Young women disappear from the slums every month and no one cares.'

'I am not concerned about those,' Torquatus replied quickly. 'All Ophelion needs is to find one. You must remember, Claudia, the authorities now have their corpse, and they will examine it carefully.'

Claudia finished the fresh apple juice; she was going to take a sip of wine but changed her mind. 'Can you help me, Torquatus?'

'Any way I can.'

'You seem to know a great deal about medicine.' Claudia edged closer. 'Is there any logical explanation for what Venutus discovered?'

'I've thought of that myself.' Torquatus ran his finger round the rim of his cup. 'I cannot think of any, but the

174

imperial libraries hold many manuscripts. Perhaps you should look there?'

Claudia finished her drink, thanked Torquatus and left the tavern. She found the She Asses rather quiet; it was still daytime, and many of the usual customers were either busy about their usual mischief, sleeping off what they'd drunk during the day or waiting until dark so they could slip through the street without being spotted by some sharp-eyed Vigiles who might remember a misdemeanour they'd committed. The eating room was swept and clean-smelling, the ovens in the kitchens cold. Januaria the servant girl sat on the steps leading into the garden; she declared that Poppaoe and Polybius had retired against the heat of the day. Claudia was about to go up to her own chamber when Januaria called her name and pointed down the garden.

'I am sorry, mistress, you have two visitors.'

Claudia found Sallust the Searcher sitting under the shade of a tree sharing a jug of spiced wine with a squat, thick-set man seated across the table opposite him. Sallust looked the same as ever, dressed in shabby, dusty clothes; he had a lined face under a shock of white hair, his tired, rheumy eyes forced a smile, while his podgy nose sniffed the air as if he was still searching for something. Sallust, however, was not what he looked; he was in fact a very prosperous searcher-out-of-things, a man who could find anything in Rome if he was paid enough. He had backed the wrong side in the recent civil war between Constantine and Maxentius, but due to Polybius and Claudia had regained imperial favour. With his extended family, Sallust had amassed a fortune which was belied by his personal appearance, his austere eating habits and his shabby attire.

The Searcher clasped Claudia's hand as if he were her physician, nodding understandingly as Claudia apologised for keeping him waiting, and then introduced his guest. Celades was of medium height, thickset, with a dark face, though most of this was hidden by a tangle of white hair and a luxurious beard and moustache. He greeted Claudia in a guttural voice. Sallust explained that Celades was a Pict, a former slave, now a freedman.

'Indeed, so free,' Sallust concluded, 'that he is able to do anything. His patron has died so Celades is now looking for fresh employment.'

Claudia asked both men to relax and refilled their cups, adding that she'd drunk enough herself but was pleased to see Sallust. She enquired after his family, his cousins, brothers, uncles, sisters, sons and daughters, all of whom helped him in his searches throughout Rome. At last the conversation turned to the business in hand. Claudia asked Sallust if he'd heard about the kidnappings. Sallust nodded.

'Of course,' he murmured, 'everyone has.'

'And have you ever been hired to look for the hostages?'

Sallust shook his head. 'Not the pond I'd fish in,' he declared. 'Too dangerous.'

'What do you mean?' Claudia asked.

'Well . . .' Sallust paused, searching for his words.

Claudia glanced quickly at Celades, a gentle man with tired eyes and full lips, his nose slightly twisted. She realised the moustache and beard hid a deep scar along his right cheek which ran under his chin and down to his neck.

'Yes, that's it.' Sallust spoke up. 'Whoever is organising these kidnappings is a gang-leader – I stay well away from that. Anyway,' he sighed, 'here is Celades, former Pictish warrior, captured south of the Great Wall fourteen years ago and brought to Rome. He was sold as a slave to the house of Valerius Gratus, where he excelled himself as a cook. Freed by a grateful master, Celades was about to set himself up as a chef when his would-be patron abruptly died. Valerius' son and heir has no interest in him and refuses to support him. So Celades has bought his own stove and grill to become an itinerant chef. He is well known in the Coelian Hill quarter.' Sallust gestured with his hand. 'When Presbyster Sylvester asked me to find someone from the Pictish nation, it wasn't hard. My family have often been nourished by the best of his dishes; an excellent cook.' He added wistfully, 'Very good indeed.'

Claudia stared curiously; the Pict gazed sadly back. He had tried to present himself as cleanly and tidily as possible, but his tunic was frayed and stained. She noticed a burn mark on his left arm smeared with grease, probably goose fat.

'You weren't always called Celades?' She smiled.

The Pict grinned back in a fine display of hard white teeth, some sharpened like those of a dog. 'My tribal name is Ogadimla,' he declared harshly. 'I come from a clan which lived far to the north of the Great Wall.' He paused and shrugged. 'I wasn't much of a warrior.' He smiled again, 'Oh, I can tell you fearsome stories, but the truth is, our chieftain, a fool born and bred, relished my cooking.' Celades paused as if collecting his thoughts. His command of the lingua franca was excellent, although he had diffi-culty with certain letters and words. 'My chief liked his food, so I was always included in the war band. Oh, I looked a sight.' He tugged at his beard. 'This was black as night. I painted my face and body. I could grunt like a boar, snarl like a wolf.' He abruptly lunged forward, face towards Claudia, and roared. 'Be as fearsome as a bear.'

Claudia laughed and clapped her hands.

'Anyway, by your reckoning, fourteen, fifteen years ago, our tribe heard how the Romans south of the wall were still fighting amongst themselves, so cattle, women and treasures were all to be had. War bands were already returning laden with loot, and our chieftain thought he would try his hand. So south we trotted, brave warriors all. As we approached the Great Wall, the fort was deserted, the gates open. We slipped through, down into the open countryside but there really was little to be had. We jour-neyed on, travelling in the morning or late at night, keeping away from the highways and the roads. Now and again we came across the occasional deserted villa, which we looted. We all wanted to go back, there was something very wrong, but our chieftain was insistent: he'd declared he'd return home laden with riches, and that was what he intended.

'Our end came soon enough, and it wasn't the Romans. We struck east to the coast, hoping to attack the fishing villages or the occasional villa, and were ambushed by a group of pirates. We fled, and that was the beginning of our troubles. We'd had enough of playing the warrior; we wanted to go back to our village, so we retreated north, but of course we were weakened and became lost. Eventually

we encountered a troop of Roman cavalry scouring the countryside, and you can guess what happened. We were caught
out in the open; there was nothing we could do. I'd had
enough of fighting. I simply threw down my club and
crouched on the ground. The Romans came back, tied ropes
round me and I became a slave, sold to this person or that.
At first they thought I was a fearsome warrior, but I soon
proved my skill at cooking. Anyway, the troops were leaving,
the civil war was coming to an end. I was slave to a tribune
working in the military kitchens, and he took me back to
Rome, but he didn't want me, so he sold me on. Valerius
bought me, the only truly good man I've ever met.' The
Pict added sorrowfully, 'A kindly man. He actually taught
me the Roman method of cooking. I excelled, but now he's
dead, and once again I am wandering under heaven.'

'Has Sallust told you why I wanted to meet you?'

Celades, lower lip jutting out, shook his head. 'Perhaps
you want to hire a cook?'

Claudia glanced back over her shoulder at the tavern; a
thought occurred to her.

'Perhaps I do,' she smiled back, 'but first let me tell you
the reason for this meeting.' She quickly described the
murder of the three veterans and the abuse inflicted on
their corpses. Celades heard her out, now and again grunting
to himself.

'What do you want me to do, mistress?' he asked when
she'd finished. 'I am no assassin. I've told you I am not a
warrior.'

'Is that the Pictish way of abusing the enemy dead?'
Claudia asked.

'Yes and no. Let me tell you. First, mistress, I've heard of this story.'

Claudia leaned forward. 'You mean about the Golden Maid?'

'Oh yes.' Celades nodded. 'Don't forget, although we lived out in the heathland, the tribes were constantly trading with each other. To the west, across the sea, were the Scoti; often they were red-haired, while we Picts are as dark as our own souls. We traded with the Scoti, made treaties and marriage alliances. Some of their women,' he added wistfully, 'were truly beautiful, totally different from ours, fair-skinned, blue-eyed, hair like the sun. We heard about a chieftain who'd married one of these princesses, but it was one story amongst many. At the time, all the tribes were looking hungrily south, hoping for rich pickings.'

'And the murders?' Claudia asked. 'The castration?'

'Killing is all the same under God's sky,' Celades replied. 'It doesn't really matter, does it?' He raised his eyebrows. 'A cut to the throat, a slit belly, a hand hacked off, it always ends the same, cold as a piece of pork on a butcher's slab. I've done with my warrior ways, mistress, I don't want to fight. I don't even want to see another corpse.'

'But these murders, the abuse?' Claudia insisted.

'Well, to answer your question bluntly . . .' Celades picked up his goblet, sipped from it and smacked his lips. 'If you really want to know, mistress, such abominations were carried out by our womenfolk on prisoners. You see, the Romans often came pillaging and burning. If they captured one of our women, they'd rape her, so if we captured one of them, a rare enough event, or indeed anyone we considered

180

guilty of rape or sexual abuse, we'd hand them over to the women of the tribe, who'd kill them and then castrate them. So, the person you are looking for has invoked the blood feud. He, or she, believes those men are responsible for heinous crimes, especially rape, against themselves or someone they love, someone tied to them by blood.'

'But here, in Rome? Do you know of any Picts?' Claudia asked. 'I mean amongst the slave population or freedmen?'

Celades shook his head. 'I'll be honest, mistress. I have no desire to talk to anyone from my people. If I thought there was a Pict sitting in your tavern, I'd do everything I could to avoid him or her.'

Claudia nodded, distracted by the song of a thrush. She heard sounds from the tavern. Was that Polybius' voice? She stared up at the sky, wondering what Murranus would be doing.

'Mistress,' Celades sat forward, 'do you know of anyone who would hire or need a Pictish cook? I am skilled in everything.'

'What is your speciality, Celades?'

'Fried liver from livestock, especially fattened on figs; that's how the athletes like to eat it. It's best to avoid the liver of a pig, it's coarser than calves' or lambs', and I prefer frying rather than grilling; the meat tends to stay succulent and fresh. Mix it with mint, coriander, salt and you have a fine dish. What my people would call *narifa*.'

'*Narifa?*' Claudia queried.

'Victory!' Celades grinned. 'Victory served up, victory for the senses, for the stomach, for the tongue, for the palate. So, mistress, do you know of anybody who needs a cook?'

'Yes, I think I do.' Claudia smiled. 'Celades, come with me!'

The veteran Secundus stared at the tympanum above the porticoed entrance to the luxurious baths at General Aurelian's villa. Dawn was imminent, the eastern sky lit up a red-gold; a breeze, soft and cool, whispered among the trees, spreading the perfume from the flower banks. Secundus could just make out the carving of the extravagant roundel containing a fearsome head with flowing hair and beard, all surrounded by winged Victories and helmeted Tritons. He climbed up the steps and into the shadow-filled portico. He pulled at the bolts on the top and bottom of the door and walked into the darkness. A mixture of smells greeted him: soap, oil, perfume and salted water. He took a taper and lit the row of oil lamps in their copper containers before the carving of the Four Seasons, dominated by the goddess Luna. He lit more oil lamps, noticing how they were carved in the shape of proud stags, the antlers spreading out, the space in between for the wick and oil. He would rest a while; after all, Crispus had not yet arrived and it was still very early.

Secundus had slept badly. He wanted to reflect, recollect himself and think about last night's meeting with General Aurelian. Both he and Crispus had been summoned into the villa's library, where his old commander sat behind a desk, as he used to behind that table in the imperial pavilion. Aurelian had greeted them coldly and barked one question after another. Secundus and Crispus had prepared their story very carefully. They described the macabre events so many years ago at that mile fort along the windswept wall in the north of Britain. They conjured up the loneliness, the desolation, the brooding weather, the sudden storms and the fear of attack. They described how Postulus and Stathylus had clashed over the woman, the so-called Golden Maid. How Postulus' drinking had become worse, and he had begun cursing and swearing, leaving all commands to Stathylus.

The General had heard them out, muttering under his breath as he nodded, that eagle-like face brooding as if summoning up the ghosts from the past. Crispus and Secundus would not tell the full truth. How they had not really been sent out scouting, but decided to escape the tension and the growing sense of menace in that fort; nor did they want to talk about the woman. She had been truly beautiful, really no more than a girl, but she'd captivated Postulus and Stathylus. Most of the garrison realised it would end in bloodshed, and they'd all been very worried. They were cut off, not another soldier in sight, just that desolate heathland. They'd even heard reports that villas and farms many miles to the south were deserted. In the end they had been secretly relieved that Stathylus had taken the law into his own hands, leaving their drink-sodden officer on his own in the abandoned mile castle. Postulus had been killed whilst they'd wreaked vengeance on the Picts, then galloped south as fast as they could. It was a pity the girl had died. Aurelian had questioned them about that. They didn't talk about the torture of the chieftain, how the maid was brought to watch his final agonies, or that she'd lost her wits and killed herself.

The old general had seemed satisfied with their answers, but he had clearly been talking to that interfering little nobody, Claudia. He kept coming back to the same question: had any Picts survived that massacre? Crispus and Secundus spoke the truth; they'd scoured the moorlands, nobody had escaped. They'd piled the dead high, soaked them in cheap oil and burned them. They thought the interrogation was over, then Aurelian had turned to the question of Petilius. Why had he been so insistent on trying to see him? Crispus and Secundus, relieved to tell the truth, replied they did not know. Petilius was never one to confide in others. The old general had concluded that they were good soldiers. He was concerned that their companions had been killed, so he had decided to look after them; after all, he needed good servants, and what better than former companions, men who'd stood with him in the battle line? He would care for them; they'd share a room, eat in the kitchens, be responsible for cleaning the baths and receive fresh livery and an allowance.

Afterwards Crispus and Secundus had congratulated themselves on their good fortune; there was little for them in Rome, whilst the General had assured them that they could stay at the villa as long as they wished. They'd gone down to the kitchens, where Crispus had drunk so deeply that Secundus found it difficult to rouse him this morning. After fitful, nightmare-filled dreams, Secundus had grown tired of lying on the cot bed. He'd got up, splashed some water over his face and was now here. They were to sweep and scour, check the water, go downstairs into the cellar and clear the hypocaust. General Aurelian had assured them that the baths would not be needed until the day after next.

He had ordered them to be closed down so that the water could be purified, the filters emptied and cleaned, every tile, as he put it, scrubbed to gleaming. Secundus put his face in his hands and wondered how long this would last. Surely Aurelian and that little busybody Claudia would find out who was behind these murders? Ah well, he wouldn't start work yet, not until Crispus arrived.

He jumped as the door was flung open. A woman, dressed in a long tunic, sandals on her feet, a veil about her head, came rushing in carrying a jar, muttering to herself. She didn't notice Secundus, but continued on across the vestibule, up the steps, pulling open the door leading into the first pool. Secundus heard the crash as the pot was dropped, followed by an exclamation. Cursing beneath his breath and forgetful of all warnings, he sprang to his feet and hurried up the steps. As he opened the door, he blundered straight on to the knife, which pierced his belly. He tried to step back, but his attacker followed, the veil a mask across her face. Only her eyes were visible. The hideous pain spread from his chest and down his legs. Blood was bubbling at the back of his throat. He stretched out his hand. He was growing so weak; he felt hot, yet cold. He slumped to his knees, staring fixedly at those familiar eyes. He now knew what it was that Petilius had seen. He felt the knife drawn out; he heard the suck as the blood spurted out of his belly wound. Secundus realised he was a dead man. The figure before him disappeared, then his head was yanked savagely back and a dagger sliced his throat.

A short while later Crispus hurried up the bath steps. He felt hot and sweaty, slightly sick. He'd drunk too much wine the night before, yet he wanted to keep in the General's good books. As he entered the vestibule, he noticed the lamps glowing before the fresco of the Four Seasons in those strange candle stands carved like stags. In the flickering light they looked rather sinister.

'Secundus,' he shouted, looking around. The door leading into the pool was half open. He hurried up the steps, into the wet darkness. The sun had not yet risen, so the windows on either side only allowed in a grey light. Crispus paused and stared in horror at the pool, where a body floated face down. It was Secundus, his blood billowing out like a red cloud around him. Something was lashed to his right hand. The body turned slightly. Crispus glimpsed staring eyes and a gaping mouth; more blood was flowing out of the wound in Secundus' throat and from between his legs.

As Crispus panicked and opened the door to flee, a figure seemed to spring from the darkness, a lithe form, face hidden, a smell of perfume. The dagger went straight into his belly, again and again. His attacker danced away, light and swift, silent as a shadow. Crispus, groaning at the pain in his stomach, staggered down the steps and collapsed to his knees. He looked around, but could see no one. As he stared down in horror at the blood spurting out, he felt a blow to the back of his head. He crashed forward, face hitting the hard marble floor, and someone was beside him, lifting his head, holding a dagger to the side of his throat . . .

Murranus and Alexander left the villa long before dawn. They'd taken their horses from the stables, saddled them, and, with two grooms walking before and two behind, gone down the snaking trackway through the villa gates, opened by a sleepy-eyed porter, and out on to the country road. Murranus still felt tired, and his head ached slightly, not that he'd drunk much the night before, but he had slept badly in his new quarters, whilst Alexander, although a very pleasant young man, was full of questions about this and that. Murranus had hardly finished dressing, splashing water over his face and snatching at the bread, cheese and olives the servant had brought, when Alexander, his freshly shaved face oiled, sandals on his feet, sword belt strapped proudly round him, arrived to ask a new spate of questions. Murranus realised that to keep this young man quiet he would have to keep him moving. The evening before, he'd asked General Aurelian's permission to take Alexander down to one of the gladiatorial schools in Rome, where they could practise with wooden swords and shields. Murranus hoped the journey would distract his protégé, but Alexander, fired with curiosity, had a further litany of questions. At first Murranus found it difficult to reply; at last he decided to take the initiative. He grasped the reins of his horse, trying to close out the sounds of the countryside coming to life, the birds singing in the hedgerows, the wood pigeons cooing so insistently. The morning mist was thinning, the sky turning red-gold, and a cool breeze brought the smell of the farm, manured fields and wet grass. Murranus had decided to leave early so they could avoid the heat and bustle of the city and practise long before noon. Now, to divert his zealous pupil, he launched into his famous lecture about the Thracian gladiator confronting the *retairius*, the net-man.

'You see,' Murranus gathered the reins in one hand, holding up the other to demand silence from Alexander, 'the net-man is dangerous not because of the trident but because of the net; people often forget that! The trident is sharp, three-pronged, and the novice watches that, but it's the net which will trap him, it is the net that will kill.'

Alexander, however, was not so easily quietened and immediately interrupted with a description of his last visit to the games. Murranus grunted absent-mindedly, half listening as he looked out across the fields on either side. The soil was bare of any crops, baked hard under the sun. He wondered what it was like to be a farmer. Perhaps that was what he and Claudia should do: leave the bustle of the city and buy a small farm out in the countryside, grow crops, raise livestock, well away from the intrigues of the court and the constant mischief of the She Asses tavern.

Murranus looked around; he felt safe and secure. The two servants in front of them were walking briskly, the two behind, holding staffs, were playing some sort of game, trying to rap each other's ankles. Murranus glanced ahead, where the road narrowed between two dense clumps of trees. In the field to his right, a farmer was at his plough, the two oxen straining under the yoke. The farmer probably wanted to use the coolness of the day, finish the back-breaking work before the heat really made itself felt. Murranus smiled wryly. Perhaps he wouldn't be a farmer!

A flock of birds broke out of the trees and went crying and whirling above him. A prickle of fear cooled the sweat on his neck. The birds wheeled and turned but there seemed nothing wrong. The farmer was leaning over his plough, the oxen still straining. Murranus shouted at the servants walking ahead to be vigilant and, turning in the saddle, scowled at the two young grooms still clicking their sticks together. They entered the dark shade of the clump of trees. Murranus stared through the greenery. Now the farmer was resting on the plough, but he wasn't dressed like a farmer, no homespun tunic; wasn't that a leather kilt and a sword belt he wore?

Murranus reined in, shouting a warning to the servants ahead, but it was too late. They spun round. One of them immediately took an arrow in the back, the other in the neck; both collapsed, coughing on their own blood. The two young grooms behind, instead of retreating, almost hurried into a hail of arrows as demon-like figures, armed with swords, clubs and axes, swirled out of the trees. Murranus grasped the reins of Alexander's horse. The attackers in their grotesque masks milled about them. Murranus and Alexander drew their swords, lashing out, but it was futile. They were pressed together, the men closing in, clubs and daggers falling. Murranus, threatened by one attacker, heard a gasp and glanced round in alarm. Alexander, staring at him white-faced, eyes black pools of despair, was clutching at terrible wounds in his thigh and stomach. The young man opened his mouth to speak, then lurched to one side and fell off his horse. The red mist of battle fury descended. Murranus lashed out. His attackers pressed in, a thick pole swung at him, and in avoiding that, Murranus ignored the other from behind. A sickening blow to the side of his head sent him swaying in the saddle. The shouted clamour echoed distantly, almost drowned by the roaring in his ears as he slipped with a crash to the pebbled trackway . . .

Claudia was breaking her fast in the garden when the sweaty-faced messenger arrived at the She Asses with the hideous news that Alexander, General Aurelian's only son, had been stabbed and murdered in an ambush on a country road outside the villa. Four servants had also been killed, and Murranus had been injured, whilst General Aurelian and his wife Urbana were beside themselves with grief. Claudia pushed away her platter and cup, and listened in freezing horror as the servant described the attack, the death of the young heir, the murder of the four escorts and Murranus' head injuries; how the gladiator had survived, stumbling back to the villa with Alexander's corpse before he collapsed. The messenger also described the deaths of the two veterans, gruesomely murdered at the baths in the gardens of the villa. Claudia felt her own fears about to burst out, but she could neither scream nor cry. She wanted to crawl off to her own chamber and hide, but she had to sit, breathing quickly, as the messenger declared that Lady Urbana needed her. The Empress herself was also journeying to the villa. Polybius, who overheard the conversation, offered to accompany her. Claudia did not refuse, simply adding that Oceanus had better come too, heavily armed.

They hired horses from a nearby stable and made their way through the morning streets. Claudia was aware of nothing. She did not hear the passers-by shouting salutations or the noise and clatter as stalls and booths were opened. The creak and screech of winches on building sites, the myriad different colours as the crowds surged out to greet the day meant nothing to her. She wanted only to reach Aurelian's villa, ensure that Murranus was well, and try and make sense of the horrors that had occurred. She uttered not a single word on the journey, and looked neither to the left or the right, unaware that she'd even passed the city gates or of the countryside spreading around her. Polybius tried to draw her into conversation, but Claudia remained steadfastly silent.

When they reached Aurelian's villa, the signs of mourning were already displayed. Cypress branches had been placed on top of the pillars, black drapes hung over the gates; the porter was heavy-eyed, clothes rent, his tear-streaked face stained with ash. The same was true of every servant they met as they made their way along the trackway on to the great open space before the magnificently colonnaded villa, now turned into a haunt of nightmares.

Chapter 8

Rara avis in terris.
A rare bird in all the earth.

Juvenal, Satires

Stewards and servants hurried down to greet them. Claudia handed the reins to a groom and, followed by Polybius and Oceanus, walked up the steps into the vestibule. All the signs of mourning were displayed: black drapes, cypress branches, ashes strewn, fires banked, all candles and lamps extinguished, the shutters of every window opened so that the departed spirits could move freely. No water to wash or greetings were offered. Somewhere cymbals clashed, a fife played mournfully, the sounds of keening and lamentation echoed along the passageways. It was truly a house of mourning, a place of foreboding and gloom which darkened the spirit.

The steward led Claudia to view the dead. First Alexander, laid out in a chamber off the vestibule. The young man's corpse had been washed, oiled and perfumed, and dressed in a snow-white tunic; he lay, head on a cushion, bare feet pointing towards the door. His servants and retainers knelt around, hair, faces and shoulders strewn with ash. A priest softly chanted prayers. Claudia couldn't discern whether he was praying to some pagan god or the Lord Christ. She gazed down at the waxen face and grieved for the youth, the sheer waste and horror of his death. If it had not been for the whiteness of his skin, Claudia would have thought he was sleeping, lips still red, eyelids closed, the lashes still fresh. She bowed towards the corpse and left.

The steward led her out of the house and across the grounds to the baths. Armed servants stood on guard; these stepped aside as the steward led Claudia up into the vestibule and the chamber beyond. While Alexander's corpse had been treated with every honour, Crispus' and Secundus' looked as if they'd been dragged from a battle-field, the mauled remains soaked in blood and gore. Flies hovered around. The stench was offensive. Claudia felt her stomach pitch. There was no need for any questions. The steward, standing behind her, whispered how both men had been brutally castrated, their throats cut and bellies slit; they had been found in the baths, floating in the water, which had now been drained off.

'Like a butcher's yard,' he murmured. 'Blood everywhere. Such hideous deaths, mistress!'

Claudia didn't reply, and the steward led her out. Once outside, she paused, closed her eyes and sighed deeply, drawing in the freshness and fragrance of the gardens.

'I need to see Murranus,' she murmured. 'I need to see him now.'

They returned to the villa. Murranus' chamber stood at the side of the house, overlooking one of the lawns; its shutters were open. Murranus lay stretched out on the cot bed, a linen sheet pulled up to his chin, his head resting on folded drapes. A physician with two attendants was dressing the wound on the side of the gladiator's head. Claudia pressed her hand against Murranus' cheek.

'How is he?' she whispered.

The physician's red-rimmed eyes held hers.

'In no physical danger,' he replied. 'There are some bruises.' He pulled back the sheet.

Claudia gasped. Murranus lay naked except for a loincloth. All along both his arms were angry welts and bruises, and the same on his belly and thighs. The physician pulled the sheet back up.

'They're nothing,' he whispered, 'they'll soon fade. We must concentrate on this.' He turned Murranus' head slightly and Claudia glimpsed the wound and contusions; the gladiator's wiry red hair was stiffened with blood. 'This again is nothing.' The physician picked up a swab and gently pressed it against the wound. 'What I am concerned about is any injury within. If his skull is thick, then he is safe. He is still unconscious; we'll know possibly in the next hour or so. There is nothing you can do here.'

Claudia leaned over the bed, kissed Murranus on the brow, lips and cheek, then left. She stood for a while in the passageway, as if fascinated by the mosaic on the wall celebrating the legend of Sleep, the Brother of Death, the Son of Night, who lived in a mysterious cave on the isle of Lemnos near the land of the fabulous Cimmerians. The artist had conjured all this up, conveying a dark, misty picture of the waters of Lethe, the river of forgetfulness, flowing through the cavern where Sleep stretched on a feather-soft couch surrounded by an infinite number of his sons, the Dreams. The entire painting had been executed in sombre colours with the occasional flash of brilliance, vivid spots like bursts of sunlight on a dark day. The painting reflected Claudia's own mood. In truth, she was confused. The news, the sights she had seen, had dulled her wits. She had difficulty concentrating on anything. Murranus was injured. Aurelian's son Alexander was murdered; would Murranus be blamed? Four servants had died, not to mention those two veterans. How could all this happen in or near this beautiful villa surrounded by open countryside? How could the abductors have known that Alexander was being escorted into Rome? That must have been where Murranus was taking him, perhaps to one of the gladiatorial schools, the exercise gyms or even the baths. Only Murranus would be able to tell her for certain.

Claudia was about to return to the garden to sit and reflect when the villa was rent by more hideous screams and cries which drowned out the lamentations of mourning. She remained rooted to the spot as the heart-rending sounds echoed from the back of the house. Servants, slaves and freedmen, shocked from their own grief, hurried towards the fresh crisis. A short while later the steward returned, accompanied by Leartus; the expression on both their faces announced further tragedy.

'It's General Aurelian,' Leartus gasped. 'He's been found dead of a stroke or heart attack. He'd retreated to the library to mourn. Come . . .'

Claudia followed them along the exquisitely furnished galleries to the library. In the pool of light pouring through a window at the far end sprawled General Aurelian. Urbana and Cassia knelt close by, rocking themselves backwards and forwards, so distracted by their grief that neither woman protested as Claudia pushed through the servants standing helplessly by and crouched beside the General. His face was whiteish-blue, his eyes open, mouth gaping in all the horror of sudden death. Claudia glanced quickly around. She could see no wine cup, no food, nothing except a manuscript open on the table. Urbana was sobbing uncontrollably. Cassia knelt close by her, one arm across her shoulder, staring fixedly down at the corpse. Claudia felt the dead man's face; it was cold. She leaned closer and smelled his mouth: nothing but wine. She moved aside as the physician who'd been tending Murranus hurried in with a satchel across his shoulder. He felt Aurelian's throat and wrist; he pressed on the stomach and chest, staring into the glassy dead eyes. Claudia was impressed by the man's quiet skill and reserved manner. He drew away.

'A sudden seizure of the heart,' he declared. 'General Aurelian came in here to grieve; the pain and shock must have been too much for him.'

'Did he have a weak heart?' Claudia spoke over the sobs of the two women.

The physician gestured with his head towards the door before ordering the servants not to move the corpse until he returned.

'Did General Aurelian have a weak heart?' Claudia repeated the question once they'd left the library.

The physician stared up at the ceiling as if fascinated by the carvings. Claudia could see the man was deeply agitated, uncomfortable.

'You know who I am,' she said. 'I am Claudia, servant of the—'

'I know who you are, Claudia.' The physician stared at her, his light green eyes watchful. He was a handsome man, high-cheekboned and thin-lipped. He struck Claudia as sharp, a man who observed closely, said little and kept his own counsel. 'I know who you are,' he repeated. 'General Aurelian told me about you. I am British by birth; my name is Casca. I have studied at the schools of Rhodes, Salerno and here in Rome. I've served the General ever since he retired. I was not only his physician but a close friend, his adviser; someone would even say a personal steward.' The physician chose his words carefully. 'Now, mistress,' he stepped forward, 'to answer your question. General Aurelian was a very good man; beneath his crusty ways he had a kind heart, but it was also a weak one. He'd served long and hard in the army both in Britain and elsewhere. Alexander, his son by his first wife, was his pride and joy, and his death meant the death of Aurelian's world, the end of his own life. I suspect, mistress, he did not wish to live any longer, but wanted to join his son in whatever life exists after death.'

The physician walked away, then came back, standing so close Claudia could smell the sweet crushed herbs in which his robes had been washed. He tapped the side of his head. 'I'm a physician, Claudia, I can observe and perhaps tell you what is wrong, but what goes on in the mind, in what they call the soul, I do not know. General Aurelian was devastated by the murder of Alexander; such a hideous death, to be ambushed on a country road and cut down—'

Claudia held her hand up to stop him.

'What's the matter, mistress?'

She tugged at the man's tunic and they walked away from the doorway to stand by an open window overlooking a small courtyard.

'I may be wrong,' she declared. 'I had a suspicion that those who attacked Murranus and Alexander intended to kidnap the young man, but if that was the case, why did they kill him? Is this attack by the same gang who carried out those other crimes in Rome? Or was it just outlaws? No, no!' She paused. 'That's not logical. If it was a gang of robbers, they would choose much easier prey, not a young man armed and protected by the likes of Murranus, not to mention four servants walking with them. I can't understand that! Why was he killed? Murranus might be able to answer that question. Tell me, Casca.' Claudia held the physician's gaze. 'From the little I know,' she continued, 'Murranus, Alexander and their escort left this villa before dawn. They took the road leading to Rome, so they were bound for the city.'

'True,' Casca conceded. 'Everyone knew that.' He half

smiled at Claudia's questioning look. 'Last night,' he continued, 'the General was full of praise for his son. He told anyone and everyone what was going to happen today. How Alexander wished to test his skill against Murranus at the gladiatorial school. How he was interested in arms, that one day he'd make as good an officer in the imperial army as Aurelian had been. The old general announced this to anyone who'd listen, to his guests at dinner, to servants coming and going. Look around you, mistress, this villa is full of people who are recipients of Aurelian's kindness; those two veterans, barbarously murdered in the baths, were only two amongst many. Aurelian always invited people he'd known from his long career. They could stay as long as they wished. People were coming and going, servants travelling here and there; news soon spreads.'

Claudia nodded in agreement. She could imagine the old general boasting the previous night. Anyone could have heard what was intended and slipped away into the city. Once darkness had fallen, despite the villa's gates and curtain wall, they could leave and return and no one would notice.

'What happened last night?' she asked.

The physician blew his cheeks out. 'Well, as I've said, Aurelian was pleased that Murranus had joined us; he felt more secure. He was also satisfied with the story those two veterans had told him, he informed me of that. Anyway, we dined late, General Aurelian, myself, the Lady Urbana and Lady Cassia. Aurelian reminisced about his army days and how Alexander would follow in his footsteps.'

'Did you see or hear anything suspicious?' Claudia persisted. Casca shook his head. 'Would you make further enquiries?' Claudia begged. 'Anything a servant may have seen or heard? Somebody in this villa must know something.'

The physician nodded in agreement.

'Was Leartus there? I mean, at the banquet last night,' Claudia asked.

'Of course,' the physician replied coldly. 'Where the Lady Cassia goes, Leartus always follows. Talking of which, the ladies need me now. I'll remember what you said.' He was about to walk away when Claudia caught his arm.

'The other deaths,' she said, 'the escort?'

'All four were killed instantly,' the physician replied, 'shot by arrows. Their corpses lie in the death house.'

'The two veterans?'

He shrugged. 'According to a slave, Secundus was seen just before dawn walking down to the baths; the General had given him some task. He went in, and the other must have joined him later, but how they were killed so easily, so quietly, I don't know. Now, mistress, I really must go.'

The physician hurried back towards the library, and Claudia went searching for Polybius and Oceanus. She found them sitting on some steps in the kitchen courtyard, surrounded by servants from the sculleries and nearby stables. Polybius was trying to distract them. In the centre of the courtyard was a fountain, the water spout in the shape of a sheaf of corn tied to the tail of a fleeing fox carved out of marble. Polybius was describing the rites of the great festival in Rome when a fox, with burning brushwood attached to its tail, was released at the foot of the Aventine Hill.

'I think the origins,' Polybius declared, who fancied himself as something of a teacher, 'dated from the time when a fox was caught raiding a hen coop. Apparently it was covered in straw and set alight, but escaped with only its tail burning. The sacrifice brought great luck, so ever since then . . .'

He paused as he noticed Claudia, excused himself, rose and hurried towards her, Oceanus stumbling behind. The servants protested that his story wasn't finished, and Polybius shouted over his shoulder that he would tell them the rest one day. Claudia took them both over to a shadowed corner of the courtyard.

'Before you ask,' Polybius smiled, 'I snouted like any good little pig for whatever bit of news I could find.' He gestured back towards the kitchen, where the servants, disappointed that his story hadn't been finished, were filing back to their duties. 'It was a happy household. Aurelian ran it with a rod of iron, but he was very kind and generous. The servants loved him. There were many visitors here. Apparently the old general doted on his son and his memoirs, whilst Lady Urbana and Cassia were devoted to their own good causes and the cult of a woman called . . .' He closed his eyes, screwing up his face.

'The Magdalene.'

'Ah yes,' Polybius opened his eyes, 'the Magdalene.'

'How is Murranus?' Oceanus asked.

'There's a bad bruise to the side of his head and he is still unconscious. I've got to wait until he wakes.' She turned back to Polybius. 'Have you learned anything about the attack?'

'Well, everyone knew they were leaving for Rome. Oh, by the way, someone else was killed, a peasant farmer who worked on the outlying estate. They found his corpse with a feather shaft in his back; he must have been killed by the same people who ambushed Murranus.'

Claudia stared up at the sky. White wisps of cloud were disappearing, the sun growing stronger. 'Let's go there,' she declared. 'I want to visit the place where the attack took place.'

They left the villa, going out on to the sun-baked trackway. Claudia wished she'd brought a hat. The heat was cloying; the cool breeze had disappeared, and sweat trickled along the back of her neck. The trackway was rock hard; the undergrowth, sprouting wirily along the sparse hedgerow, was already alive with insects and the constant clicking of crickets. They reached the place of ambush, dark, cool and shaded by the trees on either side of the road. A place of ghosts, Claudia reflected, where the *manes* of the murdered hovered restlessly. She quickly muttered an incantation her mother had taught her, not knowing if it was Christian or pagan. Oceanus and Polybius stood, hands on hips, staring up at the interlaced branches above them.

'A good place,' Oceanus declared almost in a shout. 'This is where I would attack someone.' He crouched down and drummed his fingers against the hard pebbled soil.

They searched the ground carefully. Claudia detected bloodstains, fragments of arrows; here and there horses had skittered and turned, their hoofs chipping up the soil. Only faint signs remained of the violent attack which had cost five men their lives. She followed Oceanus into the copse on her left; here the undergrowth was tangled and thick but at last they found a trackway the attackers must have used. Oceanus had spent many years in the auxiliaries, and his military training now came to the fore. At first he was bumbling and hesitant, but eventually he began to point out how the attackers had used the trees on either side of the trackway to position archers. Claudia, standing under the shade of a sycamore, realised how clear a target Murranus and his companions must have been. They crossed the trackway and searched the other copse. Little by little they collected scraps of information. Oceanus reckoned there must have been about twelve men, who had sheltered in the copse for some time; they found a heap of horse dung, a stone where a sword had been sharpened, scraps of food, a broken cup and a piece of leather.

'I believe,' Oceanus concluded, 'that the attackers, about a dozen in all, came here long before dawn. They camped, ate and drank and prepared themselves. The trees are closely packed together; the undergrowth is tangled and dense. Even the birds would get used to their presence. They were professional killers, they knew what they were doing. Strange,' he mused, 'they only had one or two horses.'

'And after the attack,' Claudia declared, 'surely they'd be noticed when they went back to Rome?'

'Not necessarily,' Polybius declared. 'If you follow this

trackway it leads down to the crossroads. The attackers could escape down there, break up, mingle with other travellers going to and from the city; as long as they didn't act suspiciously, no one would really notice. Who knows, they may even have been disguised as soldiers, auxiliaries travelling to some garrison. Who would have reason to stop them?'

'I wonder,' Claudia asked, 'what happened to their own wounded, even their dead. Murranus would give a good account of himself.'

Polybius and Oceanus, mystified, just shook their heads.

Claudia walked back to the trackway and stared towards the villa. There was something wrong, but she felt too tired, too confused to put her finger on the knot of the problem. She called Polybius and Oceanus, and they followed her through the trees and out across the field to where the farmer's corpse had been found. The ground here was hard underfoot, dipping and twisting, so they had to be careful they didn't stumble or wrench an ankle. The land rose sharply to the summit of a hill. They found the plough and the wheelbarrow still full of dung; the oxen had been unhitched and taken away. Oceanus discovered a bloodstain. Claudia, standing on the brow of that lonely hill, stared down at the farm that stood at the bottom, a red-brick building surrounded by trees, and wondered what tragedy, what grief the death of that poor man had caused. She stood immersed in her own thoughts as she reasoned what might have happened. The farmer must have come out before dawn, leading his oxen to hitch to the plough. He would work for as long as he could under the boiling sun, breaking up the hard ground. Afterwards he'd push the wheelbarrow along, scattering the manure to fertilise the ground when the rain came. The ambushers must have realised the danger the farmer posed; he might see them, so they killed him, a callous addition to their further cruelties.

All of a sudden Claudia heard the distant sound of a trumpet; she whirled round and caught the glint of sunlight on armour on the trackway between the trees.

'What is it?' Oceanus called.

'The Empress,' Claudia replied. 'Helena in all her glory is coming to the villa.'

'In which case,' Polybius declared, 'it's time we disappeared.'

Claudia whirled round. 'What do you mean?'

'Nothing.' Polybius stared innocently back. 'But that Pict you advised me to hire as a cook, he is proving to be an artist, Claudia. I must return to keep everything in order . . .'

All the power of Rome arrived at General Aurelian's villa. Imperial palanquins, their carved wood gleaming a dark warm brown with gold edging and screened by heavy white drapes fringed with precious stones, brought Helena and Constantine to pay their respects to the dead general's widow. The Augusta and her son were accompanied by leading courtiers and administrators including Anastasius, Chrysis and even Presbyter Sylvester. The imperial guard, both foot and cavalry, also came, resplendent in their magnificent dress armour with sculptured breastplates, greaves, leather-studded kilts, scarlet cloaks and gloriously ornate, purple-crested helmets. They filled the courtyard and grounds of the villa, commandeering outhouses and stables, setting up tents and pavilions on lawns and in the fields beyond the wall, circling the villa with a ring of steel.

Polybius, true to his word, collected his meagre possessions and, with Oceanus hurrying behind, fled the villa. Claudia slipped through the throng to visit Murranus. The servant watching over him declared he had regained full consciousness, but Casca had given him a potion to kill the pain and make him sleep. Claudia, satisfied that he was safe, retreated into the gardens. Burrus and his company had encamped in one of the orchards, where they were already sharing out provisions filched from the kitchens, sitting round a makeshift fire like a group of grunting boars. They rose to greet Claudia ecstatically, making a place for her, pushing a wooden platter heaped with spiced pork into her hands and coaxing her to drink from a wineskin. The Germans loved their food, using their fingers to push the piping-hot meat into their mouths. Burrus ate as fast as the rest, but kept a watchful eye on Claudia.

'The Empress,' he muttered between mouthfuls, 'is like our war goddess Freya, full of fury, seething with anger, so be careful, little one.'

Claudia heeded the warning. She kept to herself and managed to secure a small chamber above one of the outhouses. She glimpsed Helena from afar. The Empress' face was taut with smouldering anger as she proceeded from the atrium along the colonnaded peristyle, one hand holding a gold-edged black fan, the other resting on the arm of her square-faced, bulbous-eyed son, whose flaming red cheeks, slobbering lips and awkward gait proclaimed he had drunk deep. One glance was enough: the Empress was truly angry!

Claudia kept to the shadows as imperial officials took over the preparations for the funerals of those killed. The intense heat of the late summer meant the obsequies had to take place that evening. Funeral pyres were built in the far corner of the villa grounds, six small ones around a soaring central altar for Aurelian and his son. The funeral procession formed in the central courtyard just after dark. Officers of the imperial court, in dress armour, carried torches, their flames dancing in the breeze. Singers and actors, hastily brought from Rome, began their dirge, a mournful, heart-chilling chant which echoed eerily through the dark. Incense, crushed sandalwood and flower petals soaked in perfume turned the air fragrant. A lone trumpet sounded, standards and pennants were raised and lowered and the procession left for the funeral pyres.

The corpses of General Aurelian and Alexander lay on one broad, extravagantly furnished couch; the bodies of the other six on wooden pallets. To the strident clash of cymbals and the mournful sound of a fife, the procession wound its torchlit way around the funeral ground. Lady Urbana, supported by Cassia and Leartus, with Helena and Constantine as principal mourners, stood by the podium. Claudia stayed far at the back, sheltering under the outspread branches of a holm oak. Constantine himself delivered the panegyric from the makeshift rostrum, then, to the sound of lamentation, the pyres were sprinkled with wine and flowers and the dried brushwood at the bottom was fired with torches. At first the flames flickered, but once they caught the dry, oil-soaked wood, the fires were fanned, roaring to the night sky in blood-red shafts of flames.

Claudia had seen enough. She slipped through the dark, back to Murranus' chambers, only to find him still sleeping, as was the servant on a mat of straw in the far corner. Claudia kissed Murranus on the brow. Outside the chamber she paused, listening to the sounds of the funeral lamentations, the crackle of wood. Even from where she stood, she could smell the distinctly oily odour of the pyre. She retired early, keeping well away from the galleries and passageways. Helena and Constantine would attend the funeral feast, and once the rites were finished, the Empress would strike.

Claudia wasn't disappointed. Early the next morning, just after sunrise, Burrus searched her out as she prepared to visit Murranus again. He insisted that she follow him and led her down to the garden beyond the atrium, its colonnaded walk closely guarded by his Germans and hand-picked imperial officers. Helena had set up court; only she and Constantine would preside. The Emperor, still bleary-eyed, sprawled on a specially enthroned chair, scratching his unshaven face and looking longingly at the flagon of wine and tray of cups placed on the central table. He stretched out a hand to fill one of these, only to have it slapped away by his mother, who directed

Urbana, Cassia, Leartus and, finally, Claudia, to some stools facing them. It was a cool, delicious place, close to the pool of purity, which shimmered in the light, the air freshened by the white lotus blossom floating on the surface, petals opening to the rising sun. A silver-edged purple canopy was being erected to shield them all from the heat. Helena sat still as a statue, face and eyes hard as marble, lips slightly twisted by the fury seething within her. She only looked once at her 'little mouse', a darting, angry glance. Constantine, dressed like his mother in purple-hemmed white robes, hid a grin behind his hand and winked at Claudia. Burrus slouched across and, standing behind the Empress, bowed down and whispered in the Augusta's ear.

'Good!' the Empress breathed. 'Bring another stool for our champion.'

Burrus withdrew. Claudia tensed. A short while later a pallid-faced Murranus followed Burrus under the canopy and took his seat. He was dressed in a dark green tunic slightly too big for him. The bruises on his arms and legs were smeared with oil, a poultice bandage tied to the side of his head. He suddenly recollected himself and genuflected before the Emperor and his mother, then turned to greet Claudia who'd half risen.

'Sit!' Helena's voice cut like a whiplash as she pointed to the stool.

As Claudia sat back, Urbana gave a loud sigh. Claudia turned. The widow sat head down, hands in her lap. Claudia couldn't decide whether the sigh was one of grief or anger at the appearance of Murranus.

'Lady Urbana,' Helena smiled sympathetically, 'once again please accept our most sincere condolences on the hideous tragedy which has occurred here—'

'Vengeance,' Lady Urbana broke in harshly. 'I want vengeance and justice, and I want them now!'

'All in God's good time.' Constantine stretched across to the table and filled a goblet of wine so swiftly Helena could not intervene. 'And in Rome's good time,' the Emperor added, taking a deep drink.

Claudia willed herself to relax. Constantine had put his finger on the root of the problem. Any personal tragedy here, at this villa, paled in significance against the harsh politics of the Empire.

'The abductors?' Helena spoke up. 'Those kidnappers—'

'Murderers! Assassins!' Murranus broke in. He extended a hand. 'With all due respect, Augusta, I was there. They made no attempt to kidnap Alexander.' He glanced swiftly at the Empress as Urbana choked back a sob. Murranus apologised for the distress he was about to cause, then went on to describe the murderous assault, arrows whipping out of the darkness, the violent hand-to-hand fighting, the masked men gathering round his horse and that of Alexander. 'It is as I said,' he concluded. 'An attempt not to abduct or kidnap but to kill that young man and possibly myself.'

Claudia sat listening intently. Helena turned to her, cold and hostile.

'Do you agree with that?' she snapped.

'Yes, Excellency, I do.' Claudia then described what she had learned. How General Aurelian had announced that Murranus and his son were leaving for Rome the following day to attend the gladiatorial school. How the attackers could have been alerted by anyone leaving the villa. How they had assembled in that copse long before dawn, killing the farmer and then preparing their attack. Once she'd finished, Helena turned to the deaths of the two veterans. Claudia replied that both men might have been followed from Rome, that the villa was scarcely a fort, that anyone could have lurked in the trees or some desolate part of the grounds and waited to execute their plan.

Helena heard her out, tapping her foot impatiently and nudging her son, who was staring lustfully at Lady Cassia as she communicated with Leartus.

'Your Excellencies,' Leartus leaned forward, looking down at his companion, then across at the Emperor and his mother, 'Lady Cassia asks this. Murranus is a famous gladiator. If that attack was intended simply to murder young Alexander and, possibly, Murranus, why did they leave the cover of the trees? Four of the servants were killed by arrows; the same fate could have befallen both Alexander and Murranus. Why the hand-to-hand fighting with a man famous for being a warrior?'

'There is one possible answer to that,' Claudia said softly. 'Excellency, your servant Chaerea was sent into the catacombs to search for these malefactors.'

'And this is their revenge?' Constantine asked quickly. 'It is as I said, Mother,' he turned to Helena, 'a direct challenge to our authority, an attempt to make us look fools in the eyes of Rome.'

'I don't think so.' Claudia spoke up. Constantine turned to her in surprise.

'What is that, little mouse?' he teased.

'Excellency, I don't think so. Murranus has described the attack, but he has omitted one thing. That is why I wanted to question him first.' She smiled at the Empress, who glared back.

'Ask it now!' Helena retorted.

Claudia got to her feet and moved to kneel beside Murranus. Placing one hand on his knee, she looked tenderly up at him. He was still very pale, dark rings shrouding his eyes, the pallid colour of his skin contrasting vividly with his reddish hair.

'Murranus, can you remember the attack?' she began softly. 'You and Alexander were riding side by side.'

The gladiator nodded.

'The arrows came out of the trees, the four servants fell, then what?'

'A swirl of figures,' Murranus declared, 'masked, dressed like mercenaries, leather kilts, sandals on their feet, well armed, swords, daggers, clubs and axes in their hands. They grouped around us, lashing out. I fought back, so did Alexander, a true soldier.'

Urbana began to sob quietly again.

'Did you kill any of them?' Claudia asked. She heard Constantine's gasp of excitement.

'Of course,' the Emperor breathed, 'some must have died.'

Murranus closed his eyes, head down as he tried to recollect.

'Yes,' he declared, 'I am sure Alexander killed two, I saw the sword thrusts. I must have done the same to two or

213

three; others were severely wounded. It was a bloody mêlée, blade against blade.'

'I saw the bloodstains on the trackway,' Claudia confirmed, then turned to face the Empress. 'Augusta, I have reflected on this. There is every possibility that this attack will be the last; that's why Alexander was killed. Why they attacked so publicly!'

'What do you mean?' Constantine asked.

Helena narrowed her eyes, studying Claudia's face intently.

'Excellency,' Claudia turned to the Emperor, 'when soldiers are part of a punishment cohort, what happens to them?'

'They are always sent into battle first, ordered to prove themselves.'

'What I think happened,' Claudia declared, 'is that whoever led this gang actually wanted to kill Murranus and Alexander, as well as his own followers; that is why they were sent in. The leader had decided that enough was enough. True, he may have wanted revenge for Chaerea's meddling. More importantly, he no longer needed the ruffians he'd employed. What better way than using a man like Murranus to kill those he wanted to get rid of.'

'My mistress agrees,' Leartus spoke up, 'but there is one further problem. You say,' the eunuch paused to gather his thoughts, 'you say the attackers came from Rome, that they waited for their victims in that copse. The attack was launched, Alexander was killed, but what happened then?'

Murranus tapped the side of his head. 'I received a blow

here, I was weak, I fell from my horse but managed to fight my way to my feet, otherwise they'd have killed me. To them I was still dangerous. I remember the sound of a horn, and those attackers who'd survived fled, but I recall them taking their fallen. I picked up Alexander, but realised he was dead. I put his body over a horse and brought him back to the villa, then I collapsed, and the rest you know.'

'The corpses!' Claudia exclaimed. 'Your Excellency, if this gang intended to kill Alexander and Murranus from the start, as well as their own members, where are the corpses of the attackers? Murranus glimpsed them being taken away. True, those who survived could ride towards the great highway leading into Rome, mingle with the crowds and become lost, but corpses are very difficult to hide.'

'What do you suggest?'

'Those clumps of trees,' Claudia replied. 'Excellency, please allow me to send Burrus down there. We need to search thoroughly once again. Perhaps the corpses are still there, hidden away. If we discover them, we might be able to identify who they were, where they came from, some clue to this mystery.'

Constantine, excited, quickly refilled his cup. He slurped noisily, nodding in agreement.

'In which case,' Helena declared, 'we shall adjourn.' She called to Burrus to take his men down to the copse of trees where the attack had taken place and search the ground thoroughly for any trace of the earth being dug. 'You are looking for corpses,' Helena emphasised.

'In this heat,' Burrus bowed, 'the stink, never mind the flies, will lead us to them.'

Once Burrus had left, Helena turned back. 'This is not good,' she whispered shaking her head. 'This is not at all good! Lady Urbana, please, once again accept our condolences. Murranus, you shall stay here. Claudia, you too, while I consider what is to happen. In the mean time,' she rose to her feet while everyone hastened to follow suit, then grasped Claudia roughly by the shoulder, her nails digging into her skin, 'let us hope you are correct, little mouse, that this is the last of the abductions. I want the truth. Whoever is behind this shall die a death all of Rome will marvel at.' The Empress swept out, followed by her son, still gulping from his goblet.

Claudia turned to Lady Urbana and clasped her hands, expressing her own deep regrets and condolences. Urbana was pale-faced, her eyes red-rimmed. She nodded but couldn't resist rounding on Murranus.

'You promised to protect my son,' she hissed, 'but he was killed! Because of his death, I lost my husband. What can I say to you?' She shrugged and walked away.

Cassia and Leartus came up. Although she too had been grieving, Cassia still looked exquisitely beautiful. She caught Claudia's face in her hands, kissed her gently on each cheek then trailed her fingers down Murranus' arm in a gesture of friendship before signalling at Leartus to follow her. Claudia watched them go. Murranus, overcome by weakness, sat down quickly, putting his face in his hands.

'It's not true,' Claudia whispered. 'Murranus, it isn't your fault. Look . . .'

Murranus took his hands away.

'It's not true what Urbana said,' Claudia insisted. 'No one could have expected that. We've been dealing with abductions, young men and women being kidnapped, not brutal assault and savage murder!' She shook her head. 'I cannot understand what is happening,' she continued. 'Everything is shrouded in mystery and lies. But come, Murranus,' she forced a smile, 'keep up your strength.'

She helped him up and insisted that he return to his chamber. She made him comfortable on the bed, sitting on a stool, stroking his face with the tips of her fingers. Murranus tried to talk, but his eyes grew heavy and soon he was asleep. Claudia left him. She felt coldly angry, not just at Helena's public disdain or Urbana's grief and provocative remarks; she and Murranus had been trapped. She was now certain that the abductors had intended all along to kill young Alexander. They'd journeyed from Rome to achieve that, but why? To show their contempt for the Empress? Revenge at Helena's interference in their affairs through Chaerea? Or, as she suspected, to get rid of their own followers?

Claudia sat on the steps to one of the side entrances of the villa and thought about Secundus and Crispus, two more deaths demanding vengeance and justice. She rose to her feet and made her way across to the villa baths. The bloody mess caused by the two killings had been cleared away, the water in the square bath drained off. Claudia studied the tiled floor around the pool and noticed the fragments of pottery pushed between tiles or heaped in niches where the wall met the floor. She went outside and, using her authority, dispatched a servant to fetch Casca the

Physician. She waited in the coolness of the portico until the physician, ill pleased that he'd been taken away from his morning meal, came hurrying up. Claudia apologised for the inconvenience caused.

'Look,' she continued, 'when the corpses of those two veterans were discovered, you were summoned?'

'Yes.' Casca sat down wearily on the ledge beside her. 'A servant girl, curious about a half-opened door, went in and saw the horror.'

'And then?'

'I and the steward were summoned. We found both corpses floating in the pool.'

'Anything else?'

'Blood everywhere.'

'And?'

Casca pulled a face. 'Ah yes, there was a pot smashed. Why?'

Claudia stared out across the lawn. Slaves were now out watering the grass, peacocks shrieked, birds flew over the flowerbeds, across which butterflies lazily floated. A pleasant rustic scene, one much loved by the poet Horace and the naturalist Pliny; such a contrast to the grisly mayhem committed here.

'Mistress?' Casca asked.

'Two veterans were killed,' she replied slowly, 'seasoned soldiers, wily warriors. They must have been ambushed by someone they least expected. Despite the warnings they'd been given, they let their guard slip. I suspect the killer was a woman. Secundus, I understand, came here first. He sat down and waited for Crispus. Old soldiers don't like work. Secundus certainly wouldn't begin without his companion. He'd also been shocked by the change in his circumstances, summoned from Rome, interviewed by the old general. Anyway, he is in the atrium half dozing, a woman enters the baths. It is around dawn, the light in the atrium is poor. She is carrying a jar. Secundus doesn't give her a second glance. She goes into the pool chamber and drops the pot. Secundus, startled, hurries up and walks straight on to the waiting dagger. A short while later Crispus enters, half asleep. He stumbles up the steps, is startled by the horror floating in the pool. He attempts to flee, and when he turns, the assassin is waiting. Again a swift thrust to the belly.'

'You are sure it was a woman?'

'I am certain.' Claudia smiled at him. 'Just like the other murders. Do you think it is possible, Casca?'

The physician spread his hands. 'Under the sun, Claudia, anything is possible. Yes,' he gestured with his hand, 'look around at this villa, people coming and going.'

'The old general,' Claudia asked, 'you truly liked him?'

'You know my thoughts.'

'And the Lady Urbana?'

'You met Lady Urbana, very much the Pontifex Maximus, very much in charge. She was as devoted to Aurelian as he was to her, though they went their separate ways. The General was writing his memoirs. You know how old soldiers are. Lady Urbana was immersed in all things Christian, particularly the cult of the Magdalena. She sent messengers to Gaul. She was going to write her own history of the cult. They didn't really work for their living, not like us. The General had his routine: every morning he rose, he bathed, ate and entertained, then he'd go into the library to write his memoirs. The only time he'd leave would be to talk to Alexander.' Casca got to his feet. 'I must go.' He smiled down at her. 'I have to keep an eye on Lady Urbana, she is not well, and the Lady Cassia too.'

'Did General Aurelian like her? I mean the Lady Cassia?'

'Oh yes, very much.' Casca paused, choosing his words carefully. 'I've not met a man who was not attracted to her. She and Leartus? Well, they are more one person than two. Cassia is kind and gracious whilst Leartus is very courteous, a fountain of knowledge when it comes to medicine, perfumes and the different herbs that are grown. Anyway, Claudia, if you want to know more about General Aurelian, go to the library, his memoirs are there. Ask the librarian, he'll help.'

'Oh, Casca?'

The physician paused on the steps.

'You dressed the corpses of those two veterans for burial?'

'Yes, yes, I did.' Casca grimaced.

'As a physician,' Claudia rose to her feet and came down the steps, 'who or what would cause such abominations?'

Casca tapped his forehead lightly. 'I've told you, Claudia, what happens here is a true mystery.' He came closer. 'But I tell you this, whoever killed those veterans truly, truly hated them!'

Claudia watched him go, then made her way back into the villa. The old librarian was only too willing to help. He sat her down at the table under the window at the far end, asking if she had enough light. Claudia smiled up at him.

'I have enough to read by,' she said. 'Is it possible for me to see the General's memoirs?'

The librarian brought them across as if they were sacred objects from a temple. He laid the collection of scrolls, each carefully numbered, on the table.

'The General wrote them clearly in his own hand,' he explained, 'to be copied out later by me.'

Uninvited, he sat down on a stool at the side of the table and watched curiously as Claudia untied the scrolls. She'd seen the like before. General Aurelian was no different from any veteran officer describing his campaigns in Britain and elsewhere: his opinions about fortifications, troop movements, the defences of the Empire. Claudia moved to the last scroll, undid it and went through it carefully. The General had a neat, precise hand, marking each turn of events with a new paragraph and writing in the margin what each section was about. Again, he was full of all the woes of empire: the weakness caused by civil war, the need to strengthen the army, rebuild the navy, protect the Corn Fleet from Egypt, items that were discussed daily in the forum and elsewhere. There were sections about his family, notably Alexander; another about Christianity, which Aurelian tolerated with good-natured humour. Claudia could find nothing remarkable or significant. She rolled up the scroll and handed it back to the librarian.

'What were you looking for?' the man asked.

'Nothing,' Claudia replied absent-mindedly, 'nothing at all really.'

The librarian moved away. Claudia sat, elbows on the table, staring down the library. She wondered when Burrus would return. She was about to leave when the door at the far end opened and a figure entered. She narrowed her eyes as she recognised the careful walk of Presbyter Sylvester.

'Ah, Claudia,' he called out, 'I've been looking for you. Come, I've something to show you.'

He led her out of the library, down a gallery and into a small garden, where he took her over to a flower-ringed arbour and made himself comfortable beside her.

'You are well, Claudia?'

'You know what's happening,' she replied. 'The Empress is angry. I've made no progress.'

'But I have.' Sylvester picked up the leather satchel he'd been carrying, opened it and took out a dog-eared, yellowing manuscript which he placed in her lap. 'You may keep that.' He smiled. 'It's a rather battered old copy of Celsus' *De Medicina*. Now,' Sylvester crossed his arms and continued conversationally, 'Celsus wasn't a physician but a keen observer of human beings. He was a contemporary of Plutarch; he lived about two hundred years ago. He has a marvellous appendix in his work about the death of Alexander the Great in Babylon. He quotes all the sources, Diodorus Siculus, Justin, Arrian and the rest . . .'

'Presbyter Sylvester, what has this got to do—'

'Listen,' he replied, 'Alexander died at the height of summer in Babylon. Immediately fighting broke out amongst his leading commanders about who would succeed him. A real crisis developed. Alexander's corpse was left unattended for at least a week. When the Babylonian and Egyptian embalmers finally managed to reach it, they found it marvellously preserved.'

Claudia felt a chill. This was not about the hideous crimes committed in this villa, but Uncle Polybius' Great Miracle.

'Now the same sources,' Presbyter Sylvester continued, 'emphasise Alexander's deity by pointing to the fact that, despite the intense heat, corruption hadn't begun. The same authors also provide a detailed summary of Alexander's death at a private banquet some nine or ten days before. They list the symptoms: nausea, violent pain, stomach cramps and high fever. Celsus believes Alexander was poisoned. The great commander had just returned from fighting on the borders of India, where there is a potion, arsenic, which in small doses can also be used to treat stomach pains and even serve as an aphrodisiac. This intrigued me, Claudia, so I read Celsus, Plutarch and other commentators avidly. Arsenic is also a powerful poison, which comes in many forms and colours. Its effect is deadly, but it also slows down, and even stops, the process of decomposition and corruption. Certain symptoms become apparent. If the corpse isn't burned on a pyre, a yellowing of the skin ensues which could appear slightly golden; the corpse also exudes a powder, a thin coating of dust. So, Claudia,' he paused, 'the blessed Fulgentia, I believe, has a great deal in common with Alexander the Great. The Empress and her son have most generously bestowed certain buildings to serve as our churches in Rome. I was,' Sylvester smiled, 'or rather I am, preparing a sarcophagus for the Blessed Fulgentia. Helena regards her as a holy virgin martyr.'

'But she isn't,' Claudia broke in, 'she is not a saint. It's trickery, isn't it?'

'Yes, I am afraid it is. I've had that corpse stripped and washed. I removed the thin wax-like coating from her skin and—'

'Apuleius,' Claudia muttered.

'And,' Sylvester continued, 'as soon as I did, I began to detect a reddish powder between the fingers and toes and in the small of her back. In my view, Claudia, the Blessed Fulgentia is really a murder victim, poisoned by arsenic and buried in your uncle's garden.'

'That doesn't mean Polybius is guilty.'

'The Empress,' Sylvester whispered, 'will not care, and, in a strange way, neither will I.'

'What do you mean?'

'Well,' Sylvester got to his feet, 'it doesn't really matter, Claudia. Sanctity is a matter best left to the good Lord. I don't really care, nor do I want you to think I am threatening you. I am not. Have no worries, your uncle will not be troubled. I will personally see to the burial of the Blessed Fulgentia.' He leaned down, his face close to hers. 'I have assured the Augusta that all is well. The snooper Ophelion? He has been reined in and given a fresh task to do.' Sylvester straightened up. 'There'll be no more awkward questions. What I want you to do, Claudia, is bring this business to a swift end. The Empress calls you her "little mouse". Some mouse,' he added wistfully, 'sharp-eyed and sharpteethed! Go scurrying about, Claudia. Helena wants to know who is responsible for these abductions and publicly punish them, to bolster the confidence of the senators and merchants, the powerful ones of Rome. She also wants the murder of those veterans resolved. Once all this is finished, she will return to more pressing matters.' He pointed at the manuscript. 'Read it.'

Chapter 9

Nobilitas sola est atque unica virtus.
The one and only true nobility is virtue.

Juvenal, *Satires*

Claudia watched the Presbyter walk across the grass and glanced down at the manuscript. She trusted Sylvester. All he wanted was the Empress' attention. If she brought this bloody mayhem to an end, discovered the abductors, the murderers, and handed them over to imperial justice, Helena would be more susceptible to Sylvester's diplomacy. Meanwhile, Claudia chewed her lip, once she returned to the She Asses Uncle Polybius would have a great deal to explain! Claudia leaned back in the flower arbour and thumbed through the manuscript. At first she attempted to read it quickly with a swift study of the appendix, but Celsus fascinated her with his clever, shrewd observations about medicine and potions, the different effects of certain powders. She returned to the beginning, read the prologue and carefully studied everything Celsus had written. The more she read, the more certain she became that Sylvester was correct. The Blessed Fulgentia had been murdered by a powerful poison called arsenic, but how, why, and to what extent her uncle and Apuleius were involved were matters she still had to resolve. Sylvester would protect her. She also thought about Theodore. Something pricked her memory, something she'd remembered.

Once she'd finished, Claudia left the arbour and returned to the villa, finding her way back to the library. The librarian was about to lock up, claiming he was looking forward to his lunch of mushroom bread, lentils and barley soup. Nevertheless, he patiently heard Claudia out, then shook his head.

'We have nothing in our library,' he said, 'about medicines, potions or plants, I assure you, mistress.'

Claudia made to object.

'You can search if you want,' the librarian declared. He handed her the key. 'I leave it to you.'

'Claudia, Claudia?'

She turned. Burrus and four of his companions came hurrying across the lawn, their faces dirty and sweat-stained, hair and beards more unkempt than usual. Burrus unhitched his great shaggy cloak, let it fall to the ground and crouched down, peering up at her.

'I have news,' he gasped.

The librarian slipped away. The Germans had found another wineskin and passed it to each other. Burrus took a mouthful, rinsed his tongue then spat it out.

'I have two messages for you, Claudia.' He stared, blue eyes unsmiling. 'We have been down to the copse. We found no pit, no hole, nothing covered up, but we did find the marks of a cart; that is how they came here, and that's probably how the attackers removed their dead.'

Claudia closed her eyes and beat her fist across her thigh. Of course, the attackers would use a covered cart, pretending to be farmers or merchants, leave the road and, under the cover of the trees, arm themselves and prepare. The same would happen afterwards: the dead would be loaded on to the cart, followed by the masks, armour and swords; in a short while they would be just another covered cart rattling along the busy thoroughfare into Rome.

'And the second message?'

'The Empress is not pleased.'

'I know that!' Claudia snapped.

'She has ordered you to return to Rome immediately to continue your investigation. You are to leave within the hour. You may take your farewell of Murranus, who will stay here. The Empress does not want any distraction for you in Rome.' Burrus delivered the message in clipped, short sentences, then he smiled. 'I am to accompany you. The Empress believes that I will protect you.'

Claudia moved over and patted the huge barbarian on his head. 'I think you are being sent to spy on me, Burrus. To make sure I do what the Empress wants.'

'If the Empress wants it,' Burrus whispered, 'that's how it must be, little one.'

'How soon?'

'We must be gone within the hour.'

Later that day, Claudia sat in Polybius' orchard and watched her uncle, Narcissus, Apuleius and Oceanus finish what had proved to be a delicious meal served by the She Asses' new chef, Celades. Polybius had reluctantly employed the Pict, only to discover he was a real treasure, a skilled practitioner of the culinary arts. Claudia had returned to find the tavern doing a bustling trade, serving a range of cheap dishes cooked by Celades and advertised on a board by Polybius. The local stonemasons, carpenters, tinkers and traders had flocked into the tavern. Now darkness was falling. Claudia had insisted that Celades prepare a sumptuous meal so she could share some news with her uncle and friends. Celades had surpassed himself, serving up hare, hot and spicy, in a sauce stewed from cumin seed, brown ginger, bay leaves and olive oil, followed by ham cooked in a red wine and fennel juice. Poppaoe lit the lamps. Claudia watched her uncle finish off the last of what he called his 'Special Vintage'. He leaned forward, elbows on the table, and grinned at her.

'Well, Claudia, what news do you have for us?'

Claudia looked over her shoulder. Poppaoe, Januaria and the rest were back in the tavern entertaining Burrus, who was telling frightening stories about the monsters, giants and trolls that prowled his northern forests. She turned back. Now was the time.

'The young woman whose corpse was found here, she was certainly not a saint. Presbyter Sylvester has told me that.'

In any other circumstances Claudia would have burst out laughing at the effect of her words. Polybius gaped. Apuleius put his face in his hands. Oceanus nervously thumbed the pickled ear hanging on the cord round his neck. Narcissus the Neat stretched out for his wine cup.

'I don't want to hear any more lies,' Claudia declared. 'I will tell you exactly what Presbyter Sylvester and I have discovered. This morning he gave me a copy of Celsus' *De Medicina*.' She ignored Apuleius' loud groan. 'Now Celsus talks of many poisons. In fact he made me reflect on a number of things, but one of the subjects he mentions is arsenic, and he describes, in great detail, the death and embalmment of Alexander the Great at Babylon some six hundred years ago. Alexander's body was marvellously preserved, probably due to the arsenic which someone had used to poison him. I am sure the same thing happened to Fulgentia, or whatever her name was. So I want the truth, and I want it now!'

Polybius recovered his wits and opened his mouth, but Claudia looked at him warningly.

'You deserve the truth,' Apuleius began, raising his hands, gesturing at his companions to remain silent, 'and I will tell you the truth. The name of that young woman was Fulvia and she killed herself. Let me give you the details. Years ago my wife and I were sheltering Christians fleeing from the persecutions of Diocletian and Maxentius. Now we all know what happened: families broke up, people wandered

231

the roads, entire families disappeared, children would return home to find parents gone, parents would return to find sons and daughters taken up in the middle of the night. Fulvia was a refugee, an exile from Tarentum. She was passed on by various local Christian churches until she reached Rome.' He sighed. 'To cut a long story short, four years ago we took Fulvia in. She may have proclaimed herself a Christian but she was a thoroughgoing nuisance. She was hysterical, hot-tempered, bitter and constantly critical; her real vocation was to be an actress or a dancer. Everything was a drama for Fulvia. She used to threaten my wife and me with going to the authorities, denouncing Christianity, becoming an apostate. At other times she threatened to kill herself.' Apuleius drew in a deep breath before continuing.

'Now I am an apothecary, a physician. One day I had a confrontation with her, and she became hysterical, screaming and shouting at me. She threatened that she would take some powders, kill herself, and I would be to blame. Of course, I didn't believe her. That same night, in the early hours, I heard sounds from downstairs. I came down. I have a special chamber where I keep potions under lock and key. Fulvia had managed to break in and open one of the coffers. She thought she'd taken some relatively innocuous powder; in fact, she'd mixed too much arsenic with her wine and there was nothing I could do to save her. She eventually slipped into a coma, then death. The marks on her neck and shoulders are due to when I tried to make her vomit or to dilute the poison she'd taken with salted water, even some milk. But as you know,' he smiled bleakly at Claudia, 'if you've read

Celsus, the antidotes for powerful poisons are fairly futile. Fulvia died. I knew what would happen. Already I was under suspicion of being a leading Christian in the local community. If Fulvia's corpse was found in my shop, the Vigiles would come, then the soldiers. I had Christian manuscripts, sacred vessels concealed there. I couldn't afford to risk anything. So I came to my old friend Polybius, who had just taken over the She Asses, and told him what had happened. At the dead of night I moved the corpse here. We washed and cleaned it. I anointed it with a wax-like substance to close the pores of the skin, sealing the powder within, and wrapped the corpse in linen.'

'Arsenic gives off a powder,' Claudia declared. 'I saw traces of it when I first viewed the corpse.'

'True,' Apuleius conceded. 'I told people that was from the wood; it's the one effect of arsenic which is difficult to conceal. We thought no one would notice. I also had some denarii from Diocletian's reign. I thought I'd put them over the eyes – this would help date her death to years earlier.'

'And then what?' Claudia asked.

'I went to a local embalmer and bought the coffin. I carved the Christian symbols on it. We put Fulvia in it and buried her out here in the garden. We always intended to move her. The rest you know. The morning Venutus discovered her, Polybius naturally panicked and so did I. I was truly astonished at how well the corpse had been preserved.' Apuleius gestured at Oceanus and Narcissus. 'We took them into our confidence and they swore to help us.

Anyway,' he sighed, 'we took her out, washed her, resealed the skin and cleaned the inside of the coffer. We then peddled the story that it might be a Great Miracle, the work of God. On reflection,' he added ruefully, 'it was. If Fulvia's corpse had been discovered the night she'd died, my wife and I, well, we could have been crucified or sent to the amphitheatre.'

'You still could be,' Claudia declared. 'They would certainly accuse you of murdering her, of hiding her body, and you, Oceanus, Polybius and Narcissus, would be cast as accomplices.' She pointed at Narcissus. 'The story about the old porter in the gatehouse?'

'A story,' he mumbled. 'He'd remember anything if you gave him a coin for a cup of wine.'

'There is one thing you must all do,' Claudia whispered fiercely. 'Presbyter Sylvester will never mention this, and neither must you. You must keep your mouths firmly shut, and take an oath on anything you hold sacred that you will never, ever discuss this again. Let Helena have her Blessed Fulgentia. We know the truth. Polybius, you have made a great deal of money out of this trickery. I suggest you have the most to lose. Now you've repaid Torquatus' loan, I have one thing to demand of you.'

'Which is?'

'No more business ventures.' Claudia jabbed her finger. 'No more spices from Punt or precious sandalwood from Arabia or gum and resin from Lebanon, nothing! Do I have your promise?'

They all held their hands up like consuls taking the oath. Claudia had to suppress a smile.

'Tell me, Apuleius,' she did not wish to deepen their embarrassment, 'is arsenic that effective?'

'It's a true killer,' the apothecary replied, 'and its effects can rarely be traced. The patient suffers from stomach cramps and nausea as if he has eaten something bad or his blood is tainted. You've helped me, mistress.' He leaned across the table. 'I and the rest have already been thinking of how to help you. I mean, over that actor Theodore.'

'And,' Claudia asked, 'you've remembered something?'

'We've remembered nothing,' Apuleius declared, gesturing at the others to remain silent. 'But do you recall, Claudia, when Theodore came here he was suffering from cramps? He claimed he didn't feel well?'

Claudia felt the cold night breeze about her shoulders.

'What are you saying, Apuleius?'

'I am always intrigued by a man who dies in such circumstances. Naturally Fulvia's death weighed heavily on me. I thought of poison again. Mistress, in this tavern that night, no one entered whom Polybius didn't know. Remember, it was by ticket only; everybody was queuing up to see the Great Miracle.'

'And?'

'Which one of Polybius' customers would want to poison an actor they'd never met before?'

'What are you implying?' Claudia asked.

'If Theodore was murdered, and I think he was; if he was poisoned, and I suspect he was,' Apuleius half laughed, 'then that happened long before he came here. Mistress, did you stop at any wine shop?'

Claudia tried to recall all the details. 'We did visit the Temple of Hathor near the Coelian Hill and met its high priest, Sesothenes, but I cannot remember Theodore eating or drinking anything. Thank you, Apuleius. Now, gentlemen,' she smiled, 'unless you are going to make another great discovery . . .'

They all took the hint, thanked her and left. Claudia heard them laughing as they went back up the garden path and into the tavern, to be greeted by roars of welcome by Burrus and his ruffians. She sat in the dark, watching the lamps flicker out. She preferred the dark to think. Moreover, it was such a beautiful evening, the sky completely cloud-free, the stars seeming to hang low, the full moon riding in all its glorious golden majesty across the dark blue heavens. She wondered how Murranus was doing, her mind going back to those macabre murders at General Aurelian's villa. Was there a loose thread? And Theodore's mysterious death? She'd found the Celsus manuscript fascinating, and recalled what Apuleius had said. If that was true, she thought, if Theodore was murdered, where did he eat or drink last? And why had he insisted on visiting that temple and that strange high priest?

Claudia felt her stomach tingle with excitement. Of course! She nipped her arm in self-punishment. She'd forgotten that! She'd passed it off as Theodore wanting to thank his favourite goddess before he joined the company at the She Asses, but that could have waited. So why did he go to the Temple of Hathor? She glanced up at the sky. It had been a long day, but she still felt fresh, not ready for sleep, whilst Burrus and his ruffians needed to work. They'd been sent into Rome to watch her, so watch her they could!

A short while later, Claudia left the tavern escorted by five German mercenaries. Burrus shuffled behind like one of the great trolls from his dark forests, grumbling under his breath at being snatched away from the coy glances of Januaria, the delicious food of Celades and the strong-bodied wine offered by Polybius. He and two of his companions carried torches taken from Polybius' stock; these, together with the clink of their weapons, made the street shadows shift away. Tinkers, counterfeit men, wizards and conjurors, the sellers of cheap stolen goods, the pimps and prostitutes all fled before what they recognised as a true menace. Claudia was absorbed in her own thoughts. She wished she'd concentrated more on Theodore. He was the key and she had forgotten that. Something else pricked her memory, something she'd read in Celsus' book and learned at the villa, but at the moment she could make no sense of it. She must first visit the Temple of Hathor. They went deeper and deeper into the slums, heading down a needle-thin street to where the temple stood in its own grounds. The denizens of the slums warned each other of the approach of strangers at night. Claudia could hear their shouts echoing eerily.

'Woman coming! Woman coming! Soldiers with her! Soldiers with her!' The message was passed along by these disembodied voices. Claudia felt she was walking down a path in Hades, with some dark-winged herald going before her.

When they reached the open square before the Temple of Hathor, the building looked deserted and boarded up. The doors were locked, bolted and barred. A beggar squatted on the top step. Claudia, escorted by Burrus, hurried across.

'The priests are here?' she asked. 'They've closed the temple, but are they here, in their house at the back?'

The beggar, milky-eyed, skin all sore, blinked and wetted his lips.

'Hungry I am,' he said, 'and I heard the shouts! Woman coming! You are a plump, delicious little morsel. If you hadn't these with you . . .'

Burrus half drew his sword. The man's voice turned wheedling.

'I am only a beggar,' he whined. 'I need something to eat and to drink. I'll tell the pretty lady everything she wants to know.'

Claudia pressed a coin into his hand; his skin felt rough and serrated, and his middle finger was missing.

'Soldier I was,' the man whined, following her gaze. 'Lost it in a battle far to the north fighting warriors like these.'

'The priests?' Claudia asked. 'Sesothenes and his followers, are they in the house at the back?'

'Go see, go and search,' the old man replied, 'but you'll find no one, they've gone they have, all gone.'

Claudia stared up at the carved images of Hathor, the Egyptian Goddess of Happiness, on either side of the door; these didn't look so pleasant or alluring, but rather grotesque and sinister in the half-light. Followed by Burrus, she walked down the side of the temple, looking up at the boarded and shuttered windows. They reached the garden wall; its gate was locked, so Burrus kicked it open. They entered the tangled, dark-shrouded garden, stumbling about, and eventually Claudia found a path which led into the centre. She stopped before another statue to some Egyptian god she didn't recognise and glanced around. At one end stood the house, cloaked in darkness, its windows also boarded; from somewhere close echoed the blood-chilling howl of a dog. She walked to the rear of the temple; there was a small door, padlocked and studded with iron nails, that not even Burrus could move. Further up, on either side of the door, were windows. Claudia found some empty crates, piled them together and climbed up. She pulled at the shutters; they held fast, so she got down. Burrus clambered up and, with the hilt of his sword, broke his way through.

Helped by Burrus, Claudia climbed the temple wall, grasped the sill, pulled herself over, then dropped into the darkness within, bruising her leg and stubbing her toe. After a hoarse conversation with Burrus outside, the German managed to pass a torch through. It fell in a shower of sparks. Claudia picked it up, pointing it downwards so that the flame regained its strength, then held it out. The temple had a row of pillars down each side, and an altar near where she stood with steps leading up to it; on this perched an empty cupboard, the naos or tabernacle, its doors flung open. Claudia walked the full length of the temple and back. It smelt dank. She heard the mastiff howling again and wondered if there was some underground chamber beneath the temple, though the barking came from outside, from the direction of the house rather than the temple itself. She walked along the wall, the flickering torch bringing to vivid life the scenes carved there. Suddenly she stopped and gasped. The walls of the temple were covered in crude paintings depicting the various stories about the gods of Egypt. Most of the paintings were about Hathor, Lady of Happiness, the Lady of Jubilees, the Woman of Drunkenness, the Bringer of Glee. As Claudia studied these, her mouth went dry. It had been years since she'd attended a temple or watched any votive offering being made, be it pagan or Christian, but now she recalled how Egyptian priests, whatever cult they followed, always wore masks. Was it possible? she thought. Was that why Theodore had come back here? The actor hadn't recognised anyone's face, but he had recognised the masks from the Temple of Hathor.

Claudia ran across and shouted at Burrus. After a great deal of cursing and muttering, torches being flung through and filthy oaths uttered, the Germans also climbed into the temple. Two torches were extinguished and had to be relit, whilst Burrus and his men bruised legs and arms. Claudia quietened them and organised a thorough search. They found a door to a small recess; Burrus kicked this open and they stepped down into the smelly, cold darkness. Claudia went first, moving carefully, holding the torch before her. When she reached the bottom of the crumbling steps, she looked round. Nothing but an empty cellar, damp earth and stone walls, oil lamps in one niche, a candle in the other. She crouched down, peering through the darkness, while Burrus and the rest fanned out holding the wall, their heads almost touching the ceiling.

'Nothing,' Burrus declared, coming back, 'nothing but this.' He threw what looked like a piece of leather at Claudia's feet.

She picked it up and turned it over. It was a leather sack; on one side she recognised, etched in silver, the abbreviation for Senator Carinus. She got to her feet, stomach pitching, her heart beating fast.

'What is it, little one?'

'Quickly,' Claudia urged, pointing towards the front door of the temple, 'seize that beggar.'

Burrus and his companions hurried back up the steps into the temple. Claudia heard the beam being lifted, bolts being drawn, the doors creaking open. She sighed in relief when she heard a yelp; the beggar hadn't moved! Burrus dragged him back inside. When Claudia went back up the steps, the beggar was kneeling in a pool of torchlight, gazing fearfully up at the great shaggy beasts staring down at him. Burrus drew his sword and laid the flat of its blade on the man's shoulder. The beggar whimpered, head going down to the floor.

'Please,' he begged, 'I know nothing.'

'What do you know?' Claudia crouched down, tipping back his head. She opened her wallet and took out a silver coin. The man stared greedily. 'See,' Claudia urged, 'I don't wish to harm you. Tell us what you know. Where are Sesothenes and his priests?'

'They've gone,' the beggar replied. 'Those mastiffs you

hear howling, they belong to them. They left them here as guards, but they've gone.'

'Where to?' Claudia urged.

'Back to Egypt, that's what I heard, making pilgrimage they were, taking statues to the Lady Hathor's temple at a city called—'

'Memphis,' Claudia declared. 'From which port?'

'The only port,' the beggar grinned, chewing on his black teeth. 'Ostia! They've gone there, all singing and happy.'

Claudia tossed a coin to the beggar and rose to her feet.

'Burrus, which one of your lovely lads is the best rider? I need him to take an urgent message to the Emperor. Another must ride to Ostia and tell the harbourmaster to use his authority. Sesothenes and his priests must not be allowed to leave. They are to be arrested and brought back here to Rome.'

Late the following evening, Claudia was satisfied that she had made the right decision. Burrus had dispatched his riders and Sesothenes and four of his companions had been arrested at the port of Ostia, just as they entered the harbour to take ship to Egypt. They'd been placed under arrest and were now on their way back to Rome. At the same time, soldiers sent by Helena from General Aurelian's villa had ransacked the Temple of Hathor and the house standing behind it. They'd found the dogs wandering inside, savage, cruel brutes, and had had no choice but to kill them. Everything else in the house, they reported, had either been burned or taken away. They could find nothing to substantiate Claudia's suspicions, but that sack was enough to convince her. Sesothenes and his gang of priests had organised the kidnappings, she was certain of that. She remembered Chaerea, how Burrus had said that he had been savaged by dogs before he'd been killed and his corpse burned. Sesothenes had used those dogs. He had also used the information he'd gathered amongst the rich and wealthy who made offerings at the temple, to discover who went where, and so plan his abductions. Nevertheless, Claudia was also certain that the hunt was not finished. She would have to wait until she confronted Sesothenes herself.

The following morning an imperial messenger arrived at the She Asses tavern. Claudia was to accompany him back to the Palatine. Helena had decided not to wait on ceremony. She had set up her own court in the Peacock Chamber, a gloriously lavish building at the heart of the palace. Constantine sat enthroned, Helena to his right, the priest Sylvester to his left, a public sign of the growing power of the Christian Church in Rome. Claudia and Murranus sat on stools to the left of the throne. Across the tiled floor were five more stools for Sesothenes and his companions. The five priests had been arrested but not harmed. They looked smug, arrogant, ready to defend themselves and insist on their rights. They were ushered into the imperial presence dressed in white gauffered robes, their shaven heads and faces gleaming with oil, precious bracelets and rings winking on wrists and fingers. They bowed, genuflected and took their seats. Sesothenes glared across at Claudia, lips moving in some wordless curse.

'We are here,' Constantine trumpeted, 'in an imperial consistory where I am Pontifex Maximus et Judex, Supreme Pontiff and Judge.' He pointed at Sesothenes and his companions. 'Serious charges, the gravest allegations, have been levelled at you: kidnap, extortion, murder and treason. What say you?'

'Innocent, Your Excellency.' Sesothenes' voice was strong and carrying. 'We are priests, citizens of Rome, former soldiers of the Empire. According to the law we must know our accuser.'

Constantine glanced at Claudia.

'I am she,' Claudia retorted.

'I thought as much.'

'Why?' Claudia mocked.

Sesothenes smirked and looked away. Claudia tried to keep calm. The only real proof she had was a leather sack lying on the floor between them, and the beggar, now held by the guards in an antechamber. She did not wish to bring him in; just his presence was threat enough. She could not trust him; he might say anything, change his mind or even revoke his testimony. She stared round the chamber, Sesothenes was conferring with a colleague on his left. The Emperor and Empress remained impassive. Murranus too, strangely enough, was distant, lost in his own thoughts. He had kept well away from her and now sat, hands on knees, studying her out of the corner of his eye. The colour had returned to his face, whilst a quick examination of the side of his head showed the bruise was healing beautifully.

Claudia wondered what was about to happen. She shuffled her feet to hide her unease; something was very wrong, even though Helena was openly delighted at the arrest of Sesothenes and the others. The news had already been proclaimed around Rome, and this consistory court was part of that proclamation, yet it wasn't really necessary. An imperial judge could have tried the case in the halls of judgement. Constantine, by referring the matter to himself, was advertising this confrontation even more, whilst the presence of the enigmatic Sylvester ensured that the powerful Christian community was being involved in what was happening. But why was the Presbyter sitting next to the Emperor? What had Helena planned? Why was the Augusta so quietly confident? She had not granted Claudia an audience to discuss the matter, or even allowed Murranus to speak to her.

'What proof do you have?' Sesothenes' question cut the silence like a lash.

'There.' Claudia pointed at the leather sack lying on the ground. 'It bears the inscription of Senator Carinus; he has been shown it. He recognises it as a sack used for part of the ransom paid for the release of his daughter.'

'And?'

'It was found in the cellar of your temple.'

'What proof is that?' Sesothenes turned to the imperial thrones. 'Excellencies, anyone could have placed that in our temple. Our shrine is open; many pilgrims come with votive offerings. Someone could have left it there deliberately.'

Constantine nodded slightly as if in agreement.

'Excellencies,' Sesothenes pressed the point, 'we have all heard about these abductions. A great deal of gold and silver was delivered; these sacks could lie all over Rome.'

'Four days ago,' Claudia tried to keep the desperation out of her voice, 'Murranus here was attacked, assaulted on a lonely country road outside General Aurelian's villa – you know what happened. Outside I have a witness, a beggar man who plies his trade in the portals of your temple. He claims that on the night before the attack, you and your companions loaded a cart, pulled by two horses, and left the temple.'

'And I have witnesses,' Sesothenes retorted, 'that four days ago wagon took me and my companions to visit the Sacred Groves of Diana, which, as you may know, also contain a shrine to our goddess and patroness, Hathor, Lady of Gleefulness.'

Claudia decided not to reply to that. Sesothenes was cunning; undoubtedly others would be ready to come forward and take an oath that what he said was the truth.

'But why did you leave your temple?' she accused. 'Stripping both it and your house of all possessions, burning what you could not take with you?'

'This is Rome.' Sesothenes half laughed. 'We were going on a long journey, a sacred pilgrimage to Egypt to worship before Hathor in her white-walled city of Memphis. We intended to stay there some time. Our temple and our house contained our possessions; those we wanted to take with us, we loaded on to carts and took down to the port of Ostia; the rest was rubbish, so we burned it. We did not wish to return to find both our house and our temple pillaged.'

'And the dogs?' Claudia asked, clenching her fist in annoyance. Sesothenes seized on this weakness.

'We have guard dogs, as do many temples in Rome,' he replied, smirking at her. 'The very fact that we left them there is sure proof that we would eventually return. We paid someone to go in to feed and tend to them. What crime is that? What proof is there that we are guilty of abduction, kidnap, murder and treason?'

'And your masks?' Claudia asked. 'I have studied the rites of Hathor; those who serve her wear masks at the sacred dance and sacrificial offerings.'

'Our masks were cumbersome and old; we burned them as well. We planned to buy new ones when we reached Memphis.'

'And Theodore,' Claudia persisted, 'the actor who was murdered at the She Asses tavern; he visited your temple?'

'Precisely,' Sesothenes broke in, glancing sly-eyed at the Emperor. 'He died in your care, at your tavern. None of our company visited the She Asses that night; we had nothing to do with his death.'

'But why did he visit you?' Claudia repeated the question. 'Why should an actor who had recently witnessed the abduction of the Lady Antonia wish to visit you before coming to the She Asses tavern?'

'The answer is logical enough,' Sesothenes answered. 'He wished to render thanks; you witnessed what happened. I met him in the temple porch, remember? We went inside. Theodore walked forward and stood before the altar. He sprinkled some incense on the sacred flame, then left. What are you implying?'

'Why should he do that?'

'To give thanks for his escape, I suppose.' Sesothenes shrugged. 'I had a few words with him and wished him well, that was all. He returned to your care.' Sesothenes pressed the point. 'He went to your tavern, where according to rumour he was poisoned. When he visited our temple, we gave him no food or drink, nothing!' Sesothenes flung out a hand. 'You have laid serious allegations against us, yet the proof you offer is paltry! A sack, a visitor to the temple, the fact that we took care of our own possessions, that we visited a shrine outside Rome and prepared to journey to our mother shrine in Egypt. The cult of Lady Hathor has as many devotees,' he glanced quickly at Presbyter Sylvester, 'as that of the Christian Church.'

Claudia decided not to reply, but glanced at the Empress. Constantine, sitting beside her, looked as if he was asleep; he sat slouched, eyes half closed. Helena was staring at the far wall as if totally engrossed by the painting describing Aeneas' escape from burning Troy.

'You talk of our Church.' Sylvester stirred as if waking from a sleep. 'You are a priest,' he continued conversationally, 'like me. You must, therefore, keep a Liber Diurnalis, a Journal of the Feasts, the dates of sacrifices and rituals. On the days the other abductions took place, can you prove precisely where you and your companions were, and who saw you there?'

Sylvester's question was unexpected and caused anxiety. Sesothenes blinked and glanced quickly at his companions.

'We could account,' the high priest replied slowly, 'but it would take time.' He stumbled over his words. 'We would have to contact certain devotees of our temple.'

Claudia noticed that Sesothenes was impatient to dismiss this point.

'Claudia,' Sesothenes turned back to her, 'you said that Murranus was attacked four days ago. He is well known as a champion gladiator, a warrior. According to what we know, many of those who attacked him were either killed or injured, but look,' he gestured at himself and his companions, 'not a cut, not a scar, no injury.'

'That is no proof of innocence,' Claudia declared. 'You sent others to do the deed, ruffians you hired from the slums of Rome; you wanted them killed, silenced, that's why you attacked Murranus. I'll return to Presbyter Sylvester's question,' she added quickly. 'If you were given the precise dates and times, could you account for your whereabouts?' She forced a smile to hide her own unease. If she wasn't careful, this case would descend into a mere wrangling match of accusation and counter-accusation.

'I am being accused,' Sesothenes shouted, 'I and my fellow priests, former soldiers, citizens of Rome, by this—'

'And by me!' Murranus declared. 'I too am a citizen of Rome, Excellencies.' Murranus turned towards the Emperor. 'We could sit and argue like children squatting in the streets. The evidence against Sesothenes is compelling; there is a case to answer. He was preparing to flee Rome, he was absent from the city on the morning that I was attacked and Alexander was murdered. He was visited by Theodore for some strange reason, a man who was later mysteriously

murdered. Sesothenes has yet to account for his movements and those of his followers on the other occasions
young men and women were abducted. A sack used by
Senator Carinus to pay the ransom was found in the cellar
of his temple. Sesothenes owned mastiffs. The Lady Antonia
talked of dogs while the imperial agent Chaerea was savaged
before his body was burned.'

Claudia glanced sharply at Murranus. She could not recall
if she had told him such details, but he was talking as if
well versed in all that had happened. Something was very
wrong. The case was about to take an abrupt turn. Sylvester
was leaning forward, tense. Constantine was watchful,
Helena smiling to herself.

'Caesar has the right to bring any case before him,'
Murranus continued in a loud, carrying voice. 'All citizens
of Rome have the right to appeal to Caesar, and there is
no further appeal from Caesar except to God.' He sprang
to his feet. 'I appeal to my God, the Lord Jesus Christ. I
also appeal to the customs of ancient Rome and the Ius
Gladii, the Power of the Sword. Excellency, I challenge
Sesothenes and his companions to put their trust and faith
in their goddess Hathor, as I do in the Lord Christ. Let the
truth be decided by the sword in the arena!'

Claudia froze, horrified. The room swayed, and a roaring
like that of a mob dinned her ears. Sesothenes and his
companions were arguing fiercely amongst themselves.
The Egyptian sprang to his feet, looking confident. He
was accepting the challenge. He had realised there was
no other way out, that to refuse might confirm the allegations against him, whilst five men against one in the

arena meant the odds were strongly in his favour. Presbyter Sylvester was staring at the floor. Constantine was beaming. Burrus, alerted by the excitement, was coming forward from the door. Helena sat, a look of triumph in her stare. Claudia just bowed her head and mouthed the word 'bitch'.

'Murranus, are you so stupid, so full of your own—'

'Shut up!' Murranus bit into the piece of chicken before grasping a morsel of barley bread and dipping it into the mushroom and onion sauce. 'Shut up!' he repeated.

Claudia, face flushed, eyes glaring, pushed away her platter.

'Why say that?' she screamed back, ignoring the curious stares of the other customers at the She Asses tavern.

'You must hear what I have to say,' Murranus continued, making matters worse by winking at her.

Claudia could not control herself. She sprang to her feet, knocking the platter and cup from the table, and stormed out into the garden. She walked to the very end, next to the crumbling wall, and slipped behind the luxuriant undergrowth, a place she always visited whenever she wished to hide from everyone else. She sat down with her back to the wall and yielded to the tantrum seething within her, beating her fists against her knees, drumming her heels on the ground and mounting a litany of curses against Constantine, his mother, Presbyter Sylvester and anyone else responsible for this débâcle.

At last breathless, Claudia closed her eyes and breathed

in deeply. Helena was a cunning bitch! She had achieved the result she wanted. The suspects, innocent or guilty, had been named and proclaimed throughout Rome. Helena had kept her public promise: justice was being seen to be done, whilst she had turned her vindication of imperial authority into a public display of the righteousness of the Lord Christ, who would deal out justice to the gods of Egypt. Claudia opened her eyes. She dared not think of the alternative. She glared through the tangled bramble growth and glimpsed the pinpricks of light from the She Asses. The only thing Murranus had promised her was that he would keep it quiet, at least for this evening, and make the announcement the following morning. Once that happened, Claudia knew, the She Asses would be visited by the crowds, whom Polybius would welcome with open arms.

Claudia had attempted to seek an interview with the Empress, but Burrus himself had refused her and escorted her from the palace precincts. She had tried to go back to visit Murranus, but again entrance was denied. Furious, she had stormed home and locked herself in her own chamber, only coming out when Murranus returned for the evening meal. Polybius and the others suspected some-thing was very wrong, but they'd have to wait. Claudia ground her teeth. On reflection, it was little wonder that Murranus had been kept from her, or that Helena had refused to meet her. Murranus must have been encour-aged to appeal to that ancient right of the sword! Claudia pulled a face. Not that he needed much encouragement! Murranus was deeply aggrieved that young Alexander had died in his care, whilst he himself had been beaten and humiliated. A cleverly woven trap, Claudia reflected, for Sesothenes and his coven. She had little doubt they were guilty; that sack had been a hideous mistake. If the imperial prosecutors did a thorough search, drew up a list of dates and times, the evidence against the priests would accumulate, but there was more, Claudia was sure of that. A tangle of lies and deceit still lay about her. Helena could posture and turn justice into a public spectacle, but the real truth . . .

'Claudia, Claudia.' Murranus' voice echoed through the dark. 'Claudia, I know you are in there, please come out.'

She sighed, got to her feet and walked out on to the lawn. Murranus, muffled in a cloak against the night breeze, was standing holding a lantern. He went to put an arm round her shoulder, but she shrugged it away.

'Murranus, how could you?' she muttered.

'Quite easily.' Murranus had drunk deeply and swayed on his feet. 'The Augusta confided in me, as did Presbyter Sylvester; the rest was simple. They are guilty, Claudia.'

'They are not the only ones!'

'What do you mean?'

'Murranus, there are still many questions about those abductions, not to mention the murder of the veterans, but let's not change the subject.'

'I am not.'

'Why did you agree?'

'It was necessary. The evidence against Sesothenes was compelling, but not convincing.' Murranus groaned and squatted down on the grass, placing the lantern beside him.

'Claudia, I recognise Helena's trickery, but I am a warrior. A young man was committed to my care. He was murdered, along with four other good men, no different from your uncle Polybius, Oceanus and the rest. Their shades demand vengeance. There is something else.' He leaned forward. 'Rumours are out. The betting has begun. The Empress has pledged me a purse of gold, as has Urbana, now that she is a very wealthy woman.'

'We don't need their money!'

'Yes we do, Claudia.'

'Murranus,' Claudia knelt before him and took his face between her hands, 'a warrior you are, but once again you are going into the arena. You will face five men, former soldiers, ruthless killers, all trained in arms. Has Helena considered, has Sylvester thought, has Urbana reflected, that you could lose!'

Murranus gently prised her hands loose. 'Claudia,' his voice filled with passion, 'I swear this to you, I may not win – that is the roll of the dice – but Sesothenes and his companions will certainly lose.'

Claudia stared at a point behind Murranus' head. Helena had definitely persuaded Murranus to fight, but what about Sesothenes? What had she done to convince that evil priest to respond? Claudia recognised the Empress as a gambler, but a very crooked one. How had she loaded the dice?

By the following morning, the impending contest was known throughout Rome, Mercury the Messenger spreading more details through the entire slum area around the Flavian Gate. Claudia, furious, still had to admire Helena's cunning. The abductions, as well as the murder of Alexander, were now forgotten. The suspects had been caught; imperial justice had been vindicated. If Sesothenes and the others were innocent, if they did escape judgement, what did the mob care? They were to be entertained, free of charge. The entire proceedings were given an extra spice by Murranus' open declaration for the Lord Christ. The gladiator was known to be sympathetic to the new religion, but many viewed his declaration as the work of Helena. According to Mercury the Messenger, the marketplaces, schools and taverns were speculating about why the Christians, who openly avowed non-violence, had allowed themselves to be named in a bloody fight to the death in the arena. Was it a sign of further change, an accommodation between Christianity and the state? Mercury also informed Claudia of how placards and graffiti were appearing around the city championing one or other of the combatants, the gamblers were placing their bets, whilst public opinion was swaying against Murranus. After all, wasn't he getting older? Hadn't he been severely injured in the recent attack? And his five opponents, were they not former soldiers whose drill was just as hard and ferocious as that of the gladiator school?

Claudia, sick with worry, closed her ears to all this and tried not to think. Murranus sensed her mood and absented himself, keeping well away from the She Asses and the delicacies served by Celades. He fasted, eating only sparingly, whilst undergoing the iron-hard discipline of training. Unlike last time, however, when he had prepared for his fight against Meleager the Marvel of a Million Cities, Murranus now trained in public and the reports were not good. He was slow, sluggish, some said even slightly frightened of his sparring partners. Claudia truly felt like a mouse, one cruelly trapped by ugly rumours, whispered comments; even Polybius, rejoicing in his new-found wealth, looked worried. Now and again her uncle would slip away to see Murranus for himself. On his return he always looked glum.

During those first few days Claudia only experienced spiralling terror as she squirmed and cursed Helena. She wondered if she should go down on her knees and beg Murranus to withdraw his challenge, but she conceded that would be fruitless. After a while her own hard discipline exerted itself. She had to forget, to concentrate on the problem in hand; there was a task to be finished. She excused herself from the She Asses and, whenever possible, went back to her little spot in the garden close to the curtain wall, where she moved a stool, a table and her writing tray. She would sit in the dappled shade and reflect on everything that had happened.

Her thoughts turned to one vexatious problem: Theodore's death. He'd definitely been poisoned, but according to Polybius and Apuleius, he hadn't eaten or drunk anything at the tavern. Claudia wrote down everything she knew about Theodore, from the first time he impinged on her life to his sudden and unexpected death at the She Asses. She concentrated on this. The only time she returned to mingle with the customers was to satisfy her own hunger, as well as to establish what the murdered actor did on that fateful evening. She swiftly drew one conclusion. Theodore had taken a goblet of wine just before he retired, but complaining of queasiness, he had not eaten or drunk anything else. The wine spilled in his chamber meant the cup was still full when it was knocked over. She compared all this to what she had written, and suspicions no bigger than a prick on her memory began to surface. She spent an entire day reflecting on everything she had seen and heard, yet impassable obstacles hindered the path she was trying to follow. She sent for Sallust the Searcher. He met her full of apologies that he had made no progress on the identity of the young woman whose corpse had been unearthed in the very garden in which they were meeting. Claudia dismissed this even as Sallust, sad-eyed and down at the mouth, grasped her hand.

'Claudia, Claudia, the games take place in three days. I've heard the news. Is Murranus mad? Rumours seep from the gladiator school; his friends are concerned about him, stories about injuries, of him being too slow. They say the odds against him are mounting. The Egyptian and his company are training in the Field of Mars.'

Claudia pressed the tips of her fingers against Sallust's lips.

'Enough,' she whispered. 'I want you, Sallust,' she moved her fingers and touched the tip of his nose, 'to use that,' she forced a smile, 'to ferret out gossip and chatter.' She handed over two small scrolls. 'This is a letter for the Augusta, the other is for Murranus. I will await their replies and whatever you learn.'

In the end Helena responded immediately, or rather

Chrysis the Chamberlain did so on her behalf, confirming everything Claudia had asked. Murranus dictated his reply to a city scribe but then added in his own rough hand: *I miss you, I love you, I never stop thinking of you.*

Claudia wept quietly and touched the scroll with her hand before launching into a silent litany of new curses against Helena, the Emperor and the mob. The customers at the She Asses caught her mood and kept well away. She refused to mix with them, even when Petronius the Pimp held a special evening to give a mock lecture on Priapus and popular devotion to the cult of the penis. This was well attended and the raucous laughter echoed across the garden where Claudia sat staring down at her scraps of parchment. Celades tried to tempt her with filleted beef cooked in a rich pepper sauce. The Pict was now a transformed man, cheery-faced, full of schemes for the future. He, Polybius and Narcissus the Neat dreamed of a marvellous partnership: Polybius and Celades would look after the body and all its pampering before death, while Narcissus, with his embalming skills, would set up shop in the same insula and offer a service second to none for life after death. However, everyone knew that such matters would have to wait. Murranus was about to fight for his life, and Claudia realised that, instead of blaming him, she must accept that she had played her own part in what was happening. She berated herself, cursing her own self-absorption, and vowed not to act the victim. She sent Murranus a love note. He replied by slipping into the She Asses for a brief while, going out into the garden with her, holding her tenderly yet passionately, whispering that he would not die and she must trust him.

'We'll save the day,' he whispered. 'We will sit here with our own children's children, play the fife and dance the dance. Trust me, Claudia, I am a warrior. My death does not call me, not yet.' He kissed her gently and left.

Chapter 10

Ita feri ut se mori sentiat.
Strike him so that he may feel he is dying.
Suetonius, *Lives of the Caesars, Caligula*

The following morning, the day of the games, Burrus and
a company of German guards stormed into the She Asses.
They occupied the eating hall, spilling out into the garden.
Claudia had hoped to go with Polybius and Poppaoe.
Burrus soon changed that. After she'd washed, dressed
and come down to meet them, he and his rough-faced
rogues surrounded her. Blue eyes glaring in his wine-
flushed face, Burrus knelt before her, one great paw on
her shoulder.

'Little one, Freya's child, you must come with us. The
Augusta has ordered it. We knelt before her this morning.
We have taken the oath. You must come with us, you
are to be her guest in the imperial box. You are not to
meet Murranus. Little one,' he pleaded, noting Claudia's

angry expression, 'Murranus has to fight. He must not be weakened or distracted. You are to come with us and stay with us until . . .' Burrus shrugged, 'until the end . . .'

'Salve! Salve! Salve Imperator!' The crowd packing the Flavian amphitheatre rose as a man to greet their Emperor as he entered the imperial box, which was draped in purple, cloth of gold, painted ivy and silver-coated laurel leaves. Constantine, at least three cups of wine down him, was in a jovial mood, resplendent in his purple-edged snow-white toga, a gold-encrusted victory wreath around his head. He lifted his hand and returned the salute of his devoted people.

'Ave atque salve!' he roared back before lowering himself into the gorgeous peacock throne overlooking the red-gold sand of the amphitheatre. On each side of him stood the imperial standard-bearers, heads and shoulders covered with wolf pelts, bearskins and the hides of other animals. They raised their standards, each boasting the glorious golden eagle with outstretched wings, the sacred emblem of Rome's power. Constantine abruptly remembered himself, and rose to gesture to the throne beside him, as his mother, the Empress Helena, took her seat. Again the crowd roared. Helena acknowledged this with a flick of her hand. Others filed in: the Vestal Virgins in their old-fashioned robes and Greek hairstyles, the officers and flunkies of the court, together with personal guests, Senator Carinus, his daughter Antonia, and other parents whose children had been abducted. The imperial

box had been extended and lavishly furnished with imitation walls, its high ceiling festooned with all the signs and symbols of victory: carvings of champions, victorious athletes, gladiators with raised swords, laurel crowns and palms of victory. The corners were draped in purple and silver cloths. Along the sides stood a range of tables from which slaves served tasty morsels of fish, spiced meats, honey cakes, iced fruits, as well as cups of chilled wine and crushed fruit juice. Despite the fan-bearers with their pink ostrich flabella drenched in perfume, the air was hot and close.

Claudia, sitting at the far end near the door, where Burrus could keep an eye on her, fanned herself and sipped at a cup of juice. She was drenched in sweat and just wished the tension would break. She felt as if she'd been listening for ever to the blare of the trumpets, the clash of cymbals, the eerie tunes of the pipes, all the rites, ceremonies and music surrounding the games: the procession across the arena, the display of weapons, the mock fights, the drollery of the tumblers, clowns and dwarves. Every so often she would rise, stand on the top step and peer down at that oval of golden sand, then stare longingly at the great yawning gateways which led into the pitch-black tunnels lit by flickering torches. Murranus would be standing there. She stepped down and glanced at where Urbana sat close to Lady Cassia, with Leartus standing behind them. All three still displayed the signs of mourning, though Urbana had eagerly accepted the Emperor's invitation to see divine justice, as well as his own, carried out. Claudia was about to approach them when Constantine abruptly gestured to the trumpeters; the Emperor had waited long enough. Claudia sat transfixed. A long, piercing blast silenced the clamour of the mob packing the narrow tiers of the amphitheatre. Above them flapped the great woollen awning the engineers had managed to extend so that its billowing folds, soaked in perfumed water, would afford some protection against the fly-infested dust and the fierce glare of the sun.

The trumpet blare was repeated. The games were about to begin. The white-robed patricians in the lower tiers forgot about their hampers, their chilled wine, honey cakes and sugared plums and figs. They bellowed at the slaves to bring their parasols closer. Men, women and children dabbed the sweat on their necks and faces with cold scented cloths, all eyes on that cavernous gateway leading into the arena. Above these, the wealthy ones of Rome, swarmed the plebeians in multicoloured tunics. These grasped their tickets, carved shards of bone, and fought to regain their seats, no longer caring for the traders selling hot spiced sausages, balls of meat, slices of fruit and pannikins of allegedly fresh water. Even the whores and pimps, ready to take advantage of the frenetic excitement, stopped touting for custom. The killing was about to begin!

The Gate to the Underworld, as it was called, opened, and figures from Hades, grotesque in their horrid masks, entered the arena to the roar of the crowd. Charon, Lord of Hell, and all his associates, garbed in black, paraded to a cacophony of trumpets and cymbals around the arena, brandishing their instruments of torture: spikes and

mallets, fire-hot blades and iron-tipped whips, implements they would use to spur on laggards who didn't
want to fight, as well as to test whether a fallen man
could stand to fight again.

Once they had processed out of the arena, the combatants entered. The Egyptians were led by a standard-bearer,
the green banner he carried displaying the likeness of the
Lady Hathor. Lean, muscled and oiled, the five men were
all dressed in leather kilts and stiffened leg wrappings
under embossed greaves; on their heads were broad-
brimmed helmets sporting horsehair plumes with visors
covering their faces; their sword arms were sheathed in
thick quilted coverings whilst their shields were small
squares of dark blue with a shiny metal boss in the centre,
their swords rather long and slightly curved. They paraded
insolently, lifting their visors, and paused in front of the
imperial box. Claudia stared down at them. She could
not really understand why they had accepted the challenge. True, it would have been foolish to refuse, but it
was an insolent response to a challenge from a champion
gladiator. Did they put their trust in their own training,
background and numbers? Or was it something else? They
acted confidently, yet Murranus too was so certain of
victory. What other mischief had Helena plotted?

Another blast of trumpets and Murranus came out of
the gateway to be greeted by acclamations which suddenly
faded as the gladiator stumbled and limped forward.
Claudia stared horrified. Murranus was garbed in his usual
arena armour, a thick loincloth, knotted at the front,
with a broad gold braided belt, quilted leg and arm

paddings but no metal greaves to protect either leg or arm. What, Claudia wondered, did he intend? Surely he'd left himself exposed? Moreover, he carried the old-fashioned short stabbing sword and an oblong shield with a silver boss in the middle. Would this be protection enough? Murranus' head and face were hidden by a rimmed, visored helmet with a pouncing panther on top displaying a blueish-black horsehair crest. He too stopped before the imperial box and stared up. Claudia was sure he had glimpsed her; she could only stand frozen with fear.

The Emperor raised his hand, the trumpets brayed again. The gladiators lifted their swords and shouted their salutations; once more the trumpets shrilled to the clash of cymbals. Constantine lifted a piece of white cloth and let it flutter to the sand. The crowd cheered as the fighters separated. Claudia stared round the box. Everyone was absorbed. Urbana, Cassia, Leartus, Carinus, the slaves, the standard-bearers sweating under their animal pelts, the guests and their families, all stared down at the macabre dance about to begin in the arena below.

Claudia hated such spectacles. She recalled the lines of the poet Juvenal: *Today our rulers stage shows and win applause by the turn of a thumb against those whom the mob order them to kill*. Murranus, her beloved, was down there, his life at the whim of the mob, not to mention the savagery and skill of his opponents. She watched as the gladiators drew slowly apart. Murranus called it the ritual of recognition, as adversaries assessed each other's strength and weaknesses. Sesothenes and his companions formed an arc, closing in on Murranus, who stood in an attitude almost of defeat, shield down, sword half raised. He seemed to be uncertain, fumbling with the straps of his shield. The Egyptians edged closer. Murranus faced forward, only to hastily retreat. The crowd hissed. Murranus kept backing away. The Egyptians edged forward. Murranus broke into a run, fleeing towards the far end of the arena. The mob rose, yelling and booing. The Egyptians, caught off guard, hesitated, then two of them broke into furious pursuit, running close together like hunting wolves. The mocking cheering turned into an ominous chant.

Abruptly Murranus stopped and turned. He'd loosed his shield and now hurled it directly into the path of his two pursuers. Both stumbled, one went down. Murranus, famous for his speed and being lightly armed, closed in swiftly, leaping between them, dealing a savage blow to the face and neck of the Egyptian on his left. The other, about to pick himself up, found his own shield had become tangled with the fallen one. He hesitated too long. Murranus danced behind him, delivered a swift slash to the side of his neck and the man collapsed. The silence in the amphitheatre was almost tangible. Murranus' speed and sudden ambush had astonished everyone; his flight, the abrupt stop, the thrown shield, using the impetus of his opponents against themselves. The other three Egyptians were confused by this ferocious surprise. They stopped, one hanging well back. Claudia couldn't distinguish which was Sesothenes; she only had eyes for Murranus.

By now the mob had recovered, and fickle as ever broke into thunderous cheering and applause, but Murranus was already moving. He swiftly dispatched one of the fallen Egyptians who was still moving, dragging his body closer to the shield and the other corpse, then picked up one of his opponent's shields and danced to the right and left, using the tangle of corpses and fallen weaponry as a line of defence. Claudia swayed unsteadily on her feet. Her throat was so dry she could not speak; all she could see was that black-crested figure dancing to the left and right as his three opponents closed in. They were indecisive, confused. If they broke up and tried to outflank the makeshift defence, it left them exposed. If they advanced in a line they would have to clear that tangled obstacle where one slip could be fatal. They paused and drew together. Claudia realised that Sesothenes must be the one in the centre, his head turning to the left and right as he whispered to his companions.

The crowd grew impatient. Murranus seemed to be mocking his opponents. He put aside his shield, drove his sword into the sand and crouched as if resting, hands hanging downwards. The three Egyptians moved forward. They decided to separate, one going to Murranus' left, the other two to his right. They advanced cautiously. Claudia wondered if Murranus would leap forward over the corpses and drive a wedge between them. However, still crouching, he turned as if to face the threat from his right, only to spring to his feet, holding the dagger taken stealthily from one of his dead adversaries. He hurled this at the man approaching from his left. The dagger missed

268

its intended mark – the right side of the man's stomach – but caught the Egyptian's thigh a glancing blow; he stumbled, pulling back his shield even more. Murranus, picking up his weapons, streaked forward like a hunting dog, using his shield as a battering ram, and forced his enemy back. The Egyptian, wounded and confused, panicked; more concerned at the shield constantly ramming him, he left himself exposed and fell onto Murranus' sword. Murranus held him skewered, then twisted him round and, withdrawing the sword, pushed the dying man towards his remaining two opponents. The mob bayed with pleasure. The hum of excited conversation in the imperial box rose like the song of a beehive.

Claudia wasn't paying attention. She only had eyes for that figure dancing away from his defeated opponent still writhing on the sand. The man was trying to loosen his helmet straps so he could gasp more air. Murranus did not close to give him the mercy blow. He had reached the climax of the contest. He had used surprise, savagery and speed; he might not be able to use them again. He was now sweat-soaked, heavy-limbed. However, his opponents were no longer arrogant. Indecisive, they kept close together, slowly edging forward.

Murranus peered at them through the grille of his visor. He recognised Sesothenes; he must concentrate. He must not think of Claudia, the mob, the heat, the sand or the pain in his own left side. He had sprung his trap, one which always worked. More gladiators were slain by sudden ambush than sword play. He edged back, blinking away the sweat, watching his opponents. Was there further room for trickery? He noticed Sesothenes' comrade holding back; was he frightened, too cautious, an opponent who'd panic? Was that why he had stayed with Sesothenes? Murranus recalled his flight and abrupt turn. Yes, the gladiator with the yellow-feathered plume had hung back. He was weak, a man who probably depended on his sword when he should use his shield. He was the one!

Murranus danced forward, shield up, sword out, driving Sesothenes away before edging towards his comrade. The man lashed out with his sword. Murranus sank to one knee and, shifting his sword to his shield hand, scooped up sand. Yellow-plume rushed in; Murranus flung the sand straight at his enemy's visor and swiftly retreated. Sesothenes was moving in now. Murranus met him, sword and shield clashing in a furious fight. He kept his position. He must not lose sight of the gladiator he'd blinded. The man was now removing his helmet. Murranus concentrated on Sesothenes, driving him back in a whirl of steel, using all his skill and speed. Sesothenes had a weakness, a tendency to lurch forward with his head, exposing the side of his neck. Murranus waited, feinted and then struck, the edge of his sword biting so deep the blood spurted out of the neck wound like wine from a cracked jug. Murranus did not hesitate; he drew away to confront Yellow-plume. He was not aware of the roaring crowd, the sea of faces, the fluttering cloths, the flowers being hurled. The contest was over. The last Egyptian was no real opponent; Murranus killed him after a brief furious clash, driving his sword deep into the man's belly before knocking him away. The mob were on their feet, screaming their delight. Murranus moved back to Sesothenes. He kicked away his sword and, leaning down, undid the buckles of the dying man's helmet, staring into eyes already clouding in death.

'For Alexander!' Murranus whispered. 'An offering to Claudia, to all of us and to all of them.'

The crowds were already shouting: 'Kill him! Kill him! Let him have it!'

Murranus rested the tip of his sword on Sesothenes' throat and, still watching those eyes, pressed down with all his strength.

In the imperial box, Constantine and Helena, all propriety forgotten, were on their feet, hands extended. Urbana was clapping with joy. Cassia was hugging her. People pressed forward, shouting and cheering. Claudia, transfixed, heard one shout, one refrain and abruptly broke from her reverie. She had discovered another key to the mysteries confronting her!

'I told you not to worry!' Murranus, his head crowned with a laurel wreath, swayed dangerously on his makeshift throne in the garden of the She Asses tavern.

'You're drunk!' Claudia teased.

'I am not, I am just happy. I fought and won!'

'Charon's balls!' Claudia muttered. She stared round at Polybius' guests. They were all drunk as sots. Some were fast asleep. Petronius the Pimp had declared Simon the Stoic was his long-lost brother and they'd fallen asleep in each other's arms. Narcissus the Neat was now not so neat but sat embracing a flask of embalming fluid as if it was his true love. Polybius and Poppaoe were staring into each other's eyes as they drifted off to sleep. Oceanus was trying to stick on his severed ear with some honey.

'May all the gods, Murranus . . .'

A loud snore greeted her words. The gladiator was gone. The wreath had slipped and he sat, a smile on his face, fast asleep. Claudia wondered if, come the morning, he'd still remember his promise to marry her immediately.

She stared into the darkness. Murranus' victory in the arena seemed aeons away. She had attempted to go down and see him, but the crowds had pressed so close it had been impossible. Moreover, Burrus had returned to say that Sallust the Searcher was waiting for her at the foot of the back steps to the imperial box, so she'd hurried down to meet him. What the searcher had told her was not surprising; it simply confirmed all her suspicions. She'd returned to the tavern late in the afternoon and drawn up her own indictment, going through it step by step. She'd become so convinced, she'd sent the pot boy Sorry to Presbyter Sylvester asking him to visit; so far he had not replied. Claudia ground her teeth. She was glad it was all over! Helena had vindicated herself, but Claudia wanted to seal the door on this matter. She stuck her tongue out at the sleeping Murranus.

'I'll deal with you tomorrow,' she whispered.

Claudia sipped some wine, dozed and was shaken awake by a wide-eyed Sorry.

'Mistress,' he pleaded, 'someone important.' He pointed back at the tavern.

It was Sylvester, cloaked and hooded, escorted by two of Helena's Germans.

'Excuse the late hour.'

Claudia brushed this aside and took the Presbyter into the far corner. She asked if he wanted to eat or drink. He smiled and said he was fasting, part of his vow to the Christ Lord for Murranus to win.

'And he did!' he added, eyes all merry. 'A great victory. You've heard the news?'

Claudia shook her head.

'They discovered another house the Egyptians owned and found more evidence, some clothing taken from one of their hostages.' He shrugged. 'They were lucky not to be crucified.'

'Murranus was fortunate not to have been killed.'

'But he wasn't, was he?' Sylvester murmured. 'Murranus' victory has brought him wealth and the Empress' favour. She'll never forget it. It also purges any guilt he may have felt over young Alexander's death.'

'As well as vindicating the power of your Christ.'

'His power does not need vindication,' Sylvester replied. 'But there again, it did no harm.'

Claudia was tempted to tease the Presbyter with quotations from his own scriptures about the use of the sword. In the past he had quoted the same to her. Sylvester pushed back his hood and watched Sorry pull across the bolts on the main door. He waited until the boy scampered away.

'Well, what do you want, Claudia?'

She told him in a clear, logical sequence, testing her hypothesis against Sylvester's questions and defending it in the face of his criticism. The more she spoke, the more concerned Sylvester became, lapsing into silence, plucking his lower lip, shaking his head. An hour passed; outside the sounds of laughter echoed as members of Polybius' party awoke to revel again. Once Claudia had finished, her voice hoarse with arguing, Sylvester rose to his feet.

'This is, as you say, Claudia, a matter for the Empress. She will decide.' He glared down at her. 'But it is very, very serious.'

The next morning Claudia was the first to rise. She found Celades fast asleep in the kitchen, a wineskin in one hand, a piece of roast pork in the other. She broke her fast, slept again and woke much refreshed. She washed, changed and went down into the tavern. Celades, bleary-eyed, was now in the kitchen, grilling strips of beef. He was still full of the previous day's exploits and the banquet he had prepared.

'Cook what you have to, Celades,' Claudia declared, 'but be ready to prepare something else.'

'What do you mean?'

'Just wait and see,' Claudia retorted.

The rest, including Murranus, were nursing sore heads, moaning to themselves, only too eager to escape to a chamber upstairs or back into the garden. At last, late in the afternoon, Polybius came down to greet the usual regulars. He announced that Murranus was fast asleep, but once darkness fell, the festivities would recommence, this time in Claudia's honour. She was protesting at this, only to be interrupted by a thunderous knocking at the door before it was flung open. Burrus, hand on the hilt of his sword, almost charged into the eating hall, followed by three of his companions and a host of servants wearing imperial livery, all carrying linen bundles, wine flagons and other pots and jars.

'Where is the warrior?' Burrus thundered.

'Upstairs!' Claudia shouted back. 'Drunk, hungover, tired, but like the rest of you, ready for the next piece of mischief.'

'Good!' Burrus beamed. 'The Empress sends this.' Two bulging leather purses were thrown on to a table. 'And this.' A third followed. Polybius scooped them up in the twinkling of an eye.

'The Augustus and his mother will dine here tonight just after sunset.' Burrus gestured at more servants filing in with their burdens. 'They have sent what they intend to eat and drink, and look forward to tasting the recipes of your new chef.'

Celades, standing in the kitchen doorway, clasped his hands and moaned with pleasure. Polybius chewed his lip as he weighed the sacks, quickly scrutinising what was being brought in.

'No one else.' Burrus' left hand descended on the thin shoulder of Simon the Stoic. 'The Excellencies and their guests will celebrate the victory of their champion.' He glanced fierce-eyed around the eating hall. 'A great honour! So be prepared.' The German waited until the imperial servants had delivered all their burdens, gave Polybius a mock salute, winked at Claudia, then left slamming the door behind him.

At first silence reigned, then Poppaoe began to wail. Polybius stood disconcerted but Celades rose to the occasion. He quickly inspected the contents of the linen bundles and bustled back, leather apron on, to announce he would prepare a banquet fit for the gods.

'Braised cucumbers, mushrooms in honey,' he proclaimed, 'baked plaice, fried liver, ham in red wine and fennel sauce.'

The die was cast. Polybius decided he'd turn his favourite part of the orchard into a dining area: lamp-stands were brought out, more were begged and borrowed, lanterns hung from trees, tables, couches and stools loaned by the likes of Apuleius and other friends and neighbours. Polybius wondered how many guests there would be. Claudia, who suspected what was about to happen, replied about ten in all. The garden of the She Asses was transformed into a veritable paradise, the air sweet with the fragrant smells from the kitchen. Polybius turned away his usual coven of rogues as he became aware of the great honour being bestowed on him, declaring that by tomorrow evening all Rome would know that the She Asses was a tavern frequented by their Excellencies.

Murranus eventually came down. Claudia dispatched him up the alleyway so Torquatus could cut his hair, shave his face and take him to the nearest baths.

'And don't drink a drop!' Claudia shouted after him. 'You must be stone-cold sober.'

Murranus bowed mockingly to her and sauntered off. Claudia slipped into the kitchen and drew Polybius and Celades aside. She told them what would happen and what they were to do. Polybius shrugged in resignation. He knew better than to question his iron-willed niece. Celades was astonished, but readily agreed to carefully follow her instructions.

Darkness was falling as the imperial entourage arrived in a clash of arms and the fiery glare of torches. The imperial litters, curtains drawn, massed in the small square before the tavern, which was immediately ringed and sealed off by rank after rank of the imperial guard. Burrus and his contingent filed into the eating hall then out into the garden to patrol the walls and guard the gates. Polybius' household, Claudia included, knelt to receive the distinguished guests. Claudia sighed with relief when she saw the party: Constantine, Helena, Sylvester, Urbana, Cassia and Leartus. The Emperor, clad in purple-edged snow-white robes, waggled his fingers at them and immediately went into the kitchen, emerging with a slice of ham which he ate noisily, slurping wine from Polybius' favourite goblet.

'Mother,' he spluttered, 'this is marvellous.' He glanced quickly at Claudia, a calculated, cold-eyed stare, a sign that the Emperor, as usual, was acting the buffoon.

Helena graciously greeted them all and, hugging Claudia close, kissed her on both cheeks. Claudia sensed the Augusta's excitement; her unpainted face was tense, her dark eyes watchful.

'Be careful, little mouse,' she whispered, 'but the stage is now yours.'

She drew away, hitching the silk-tasselled purple mantle around her shoulders, fingering the amethyst on its gold chain around her neck. She glanced around and, in mock anger, asked where the champion was. Constantine demanded the same. Polybius blustered that Murranus wanted to be well prepared and would their Excellencies like to go out into the garden? Constantine replied that their Excellencies would like nothing better. Claudia exchanged cool courtesies with the rest of the guests and followed them out. She was relieved when Murranus joined them. Constantine, seated at the centre of the couches arranged in a horseshoe, immediately began to question the gladiator about his victory in the arena.

'There'll be more rewards for you, my boy!' he shouted, and promised the gladiator the cup he was drinking from, immediately apologising when Helena whispered loudly that it wasn't his to give.

While the first courses were served and the wine cups filled, Murranus held the guests spellbound as he described his tactics.

'I wanted them overconfident,' he declared, 'but above all I wanted them to separate. I guessed that some would not be as brave or as skilled as others. Once that happened, my chances improved.'

Constantine, of course, interrupted with a spate of questions. The wine flowed, the guests were drinking copiously, and, judging the moment was ready, Claudia nodded to Polybius and held up her hand to speak.

'Excellencies.' Claudia swung her feet off the makeshift couch. 'Let us sit in silence in the Frisian custom,' she ignored Murranus' questioning look, 'until our cups are filled, then let us toast our champion.'

Constantine thought it was a splendid idea. Polybius, Poppaoe and Narcissus circled, filling goblets. Celades approached Leartus to serve him.

'*Larg na maith?*' Celades asked in a loud voice.

'*Larg na maith malan,*' Leartus replied without thinking – then froze.

'What's that?' Constantine asked. 'I thought you said this should be done in silence?'

Leartus stared owl-eyed across at Claudia.

'Celades is a Pict,' Claudia declared. 'He just asked Leartus in his own tongue if his goblet should be filled with red or white wine. Leartus is supposed to be a Parthian, yet he understands the Pictish tongue, an astonishing achievement. What was his reply, Celades?'

'I want red, please!' declared Celades, standing behind Leartus.

'Celades,' Claudia continued conversationally, 'you told me earlier how the son of a Pictish chieftain has a sacred circle, a tattoo on his right thigh imprinted there just after his twelfth year.'

'Yes, mistress.'

'Leartus, modesty aside, show us the sacred mark.'

'What is this?' Urbana shrilled. Cassia too became agitated, her hand going out to grasp Urbana's arm.

I was correct, Claudia thought – you are both terrified because your guilt will soon be known.

'Burrus,' Helena called into the darkness. The German stepped forward.

'There is no need.' Leartus rose to his feet. He shrugged, undid his belt and opened his tunic.

'Amongst our tribes,' Celades declared, 'the circle would be coloured in sacred paint.'

Burrus brought across a torch and held it as close as he could. Claudia studied the tattoo engraved on Leartus' thigh.

'Slightly faded, the skin puckered, but still clear to see.' She gestured dismissively with her hand. Leartus picked up his belt, wrapped it round himself and sat on the edge of the couch staring coolly across at her.

'You are no Parthian!' Claudia accused. 'You made a mistake during the recent games; carried away by excitement, you shouted "*narifa*", the Pictish word for victory – you repeated it twice. You, Leartus, are a Pict, a warrior, the son of a chieftain. Eighteen years ago your father included you as part of his war band. I will not repeat the details, everyone knows them. The band were massacred by a wing of Roman cavalry led by Stathylus. He captured your father and cruelly tortured him to death. Stathylus and his companions thought your father was the only survivor, but you also survived. You left your jewellery on another corpse and hid in the heather. Your father survived for hours; his only consolation was that he knew what you had done. He realised the corpse they'd brought was not you. You wanted vengeance for him. In the full light of day you saw what happened to your father. More importantly, you also had time to study the faces of his torturers: Roman cavalrymen who, now the fight was over, took off their helmets and pushed back their coifs. Later you followed that cavalry troop south to Colchester. You caught one of them, probably when he was drunk, killed him and abused his corpse.

'I don't truly know what happened then, but I suspect you were captured, enslaved and made a eunuch. The legions were withdrawing to Rome and you were taken with them. Once in the city, you entered the service of Cassia. Celades told me how the Picts are skilled in sign language; you became proficient, her companion as she moved from courtesan to Christian. I suspect you had a pleasant life until General Aurelian decided to hold one of his reunion parties. You saw Petilius; more importantly, Petilius saw you. He probably recognised your father in you. He hadn't forgotten that hideous death out along that lonely wall in northern Britain.

'Leartus, you have some effeminate ways; you also have access to your mistress' wardrobe and perfumes. Do you know,' Claudia stared up at the star-strewn sky, 'I wondered about those gruesome murders committed in the fetid side streets of Rome. No woman would go down there on her own, but of course, you are still a warrior, Leartus, whatever has happened to you. You would have no fear, particularly when you are intent on revenge. So let us imagine how it happened! Slipping through the side streets and the alleyways with a leather sack containing a veil, a woman's cloak, perfumes and paints for your face, you would stalk your victim, hunt him as your father did Romans in the heather so many years ago. At the appropriate time you'd attack. Your victims thought they were meeting a whore; in fact, they were facing vengeance. Of course, with Crispus and Secundus it was very easy. General Aurelian brought them back to his villa so it was just a matter of watching and waiting. Once again you acted the woman; you carried a jug into those baths, enticed one then the other inside, stabbing both with swift thrusts to the belly, cutting their throats and abusing their corpses, an offering to the shades of your father, his second wife and all those who died so many years ago.'

'We did not know this.' Urbana spoke.

'Oh yes you did,' Claudia replied coolly. 'You knew he was a Pict.' She spoke slowly so Cassia could follow her lips. 'You knew about the murders; you must have noticed certain items going missing. At the time these men were killed, Leartus was absent. But there again, what did you care? After all, I suspect Leartus was accustomed to such a disguise: he used the same when he met Sesothenes and gave him your instructions. You see, Cassia,' Claudia leaned forward, 'I used Sallust the Searcher. He discovered a little about your past. You are a Christian convert but before that you were a courtesan and, like all leading courtesans of Rome, devoted to the goddesses of Egypt, Isis and the Lady Hathor. You knew Sesothenes; you knew about his nefarious ways.'

'If that's true,' Urbana retorted, 'if Sesothenes knew that Cassia was involved, why didn't he confess it?'

'Why, of course he wouldn't,' Claudia retorted. 'He might suspect, but he had no firm evidence against you. Moreover, to accuse you he would have had to incriminate himself. Accordingly, Murranus' challenge seemed the safest path for everyone. If Sesothenes won, there'd be no further problem. If he was killed, he and his companions would be silent for ever. I can understand your joy in the imperial box when Murranus was victorious; a problem had been cleared away. Hence Leartus' scream of triumph, so excited he lapsed back into his Pictish tongue.'

'Whom are you accusing?' Urbana declared. 'Cassia, Leartus, even me?'

'Of course I am.' Claudia glanced round the ring of couches. They were all watching intently; even Constantine had forgotten to drink. Sylvester sat, head bowed, hands in his lap. Helena was staring into the darkness. Murranus shook his head in disbelief.

'I will present my indictment. Urbana, you are certainly a wealthy woman; well, you are now,' Claudia added, 'though not before. Religion is a powerful mix. You, Urbana, and Cassia embraced Christianity. No real conversion, you were just exchanging one cult for another. You both became obsessed with the story of Mary Magdalene, Christ's woman friend who, according to Presbyter Sylvester, fled Judaea after the resurrection of Christ and landed in Marseilles with her sister Martha and brother Lazarus. You dreamed of finding her tomb, but that costs money.'

'My husband was wealthy.'

'Aurelian was wealthy but he did not indulge you, Urbana, because he did not really love you. He resented your conversion, your absorption with relics. I read his memoir. Do you realise that in the last few years he hardly mentions you? Of course you still had influence with him. When Petilius recognised Leartus, you were probably instrumental in making sure that the veteran never met your husband to discuss what he had seen. Did you urge Leartus to strike swiftly and decisively to end the matter?'

Urbana glanced away.

'Of course,' Claudia continued, 'if Petilius had met your husband and talked to him, you would have supported Leartus. After all, there is no crime in being a survivor of a massacre, especially when Petilius would have had to tell the truth about what really happened to his commander in that lonely mile fort in the north of Britain so many years ago.'

'What has this got to do with the kidnappings?' Constantine broke in, ignoring his mother's angry gesture.

'Oh, everything,' Claudia replied. 'Urbana needed money.'

'She's wealthy!' Constantine slurred.

'No,' Claudia replied, 'I suspect she simply had an allowance, an income which she spent on her costly searches. Sallust soon discovered the terms of your husband's financial support of you, not to mention the clauses of his will. Before Aurelian died, you depended totally on your husband's allowance. You desperately needed money, so what did you do? You're a high-ranking lady of Rome, Urbana, you listen to all the gossip. It was so easy to discover about parties and expeditions, their times and places, even Antonia's secret spot in her own garden. You decided to organise the abduction of the children of wealthy Romans, demand a ransom, free them and have your own source of income. Well, that was the first part of your plan. You and Cassia are . . .' Claudia paused; she was tempted to say 'lovers', but she had no real proof of that. 'You are allies. Through her and Leartus disguised as a woman, you opened negotiations with Sesothenes, who had a reputation for nefarious dealings, something Cassia remembered from her past when she was a courtesan. Your scheme was perfect. As I've said, you learned all the details of the patrician families of the city. You are also a leading Christian, able to discover all there is about the catacombs. No real harm was done: the children were returned safe, their wealthy parents lost some gold, Sesothenes received his share and you were able to continue to finance your search for sacred relics. You and Cassia became immersed in that. Religion was no longer important to you. The Magdalene became an obsession, your world centred on it. You'd spend anything to realise your ambition. Of course your husband might wonder where your wealth came from, but you were so friendly with Cassia, it would be easy to obfuscate, to lie, to deceive.'

'But Alexander?' Murranus asked. 'He was killed.'

'Ah – that was different, the second part of Urbana's plan. As I've said, I sent Sallust the Searcher out to Aurelian's villa. The General's will is now public knowledge. According to that, once he died, all his wealth would go to Alexander. Only if Alexander died without issue would his wealth go to you, Lady Urbana. I reflected on that when Murranus was talking about you.

He emphasised how you were *now* a wealthy woman. You and Cassia realised that the kidnappings could not go on. Alexander was too much of an obstacle, so you decided that he had to die, both he and his father, that was to be Sesothenes' final piece of villainy.

'Murranus was hired as a bodyguard, chosen specifically. First, it was a good way of showing how much you cared for your stepson, but that was a lie. Second, it was an excellent way of getting rid of the other rogues Sesothenes had hired. On the day of attack, he sent them in. They were wounded or killed. If any did survive they were shown no mercy. Now Murranus had told you that he was taking Alexander into Rome, but he is certain that the only people who knew the exact time of his departure, were you and General Aurelian. He didn't even tell Alexander, so as not to get the boy too excited. Finally, I could understand Aurelian being proud of Murranus' decision to take his son to Rome, but you, Lady Urbana, with all these terrible kidnappings in Rome, didn't you object? Especially since you'd come to the palace to complain about the abductions to the Empress herself.'

'You encouraged it.' Murranus pointed at Urbana. 'Yes, you did. At no time did you counsel against my taking Alexander into the city.'

'If this is all true,' Helena asked, 'why did Urbana actually come and see me after Senator Carinus' daughter was abducted? What was the logic in that?'

'Ah,' Claudia replied. 'At the time, I thought they were just busybodies, but we now come to a further proof, the actor Theodore. He was present when Antonia was abducted. Theodore's story was a mixture of fact and fiction. He saw no face but, being a devotee of the Temple of Hathor, he certainly recognised those masks. If Sesothenes had not been so eager to escape, he would have killed Theodore, but he was under strict instruction that there was to be no violence, no hurt. Instead he swiftly communicated to Urbana the danger Theodore posed.'

'I'll ask it again!' Constantine interrupted. 'Did Sesothenes know Urbana? Are you sure of that?'

'I believe,' Claudia replied, 'that Urbana worked solely through her intermediary Leartus, disguised as a woman. Sesothenes would be informed of the details; he and his associates would gather their gang and strike. Leartus would later collect the ransom money and give Sesothenes his portion. The high priest wouldn't care; he was being enriched, provided with a safe place in the catacombs, and, as he may have suspected, patronised by someone very powerful.'

'Wouldn't he be suspicious,' the Emperor asked, 'at the change in instructions: to kill young Alexander?'

'No,' Claudia retorted. 'Why should he? It might even divert suspicion from Urbana, her beloved son being killed. No!' Claudia moved a hair from her face. 'Sesothenes would be informed that it was revenge on the Empress for sending Chaerea into the catacombs to spy on them. At the same time it was an expeditious way of getting rid of the ruffians Sesothenes had secretly hired. I doubt very much if they were told about Murranus; he'd have been described as an ordinary guard.' Claudia smiled at her beloved. 'They soon learned differently. Murranus

287

couldn't save Alexander, but he fought so well, it became highly dangerous to continue the struggle and so they retreated. Sesothenes and his companions took care of any survivors.' Claudia paused. 'Your Excellencies,' she pointed at the accused, 'imagine two women obsessed with an idea, redoubtable women who'd clawed their way upwards. Urbana is full of resentment at her husband, the terms of his will, his lack of support for what she holds important! She draws Cassia in, and, of course, Leartus; the eunuch is a perfect foil. He has no love for Rome, certainly not for its generals and senators. And then,' Claudia shrugged, 'the past catches up.'

'And Theodore?' the Empress asked sharply.

'Ah, our actor was being very crafty. He wanted to make sure that those masks were from the Temple of Hathor. He wanted to think and plot, he probably planned blackmail, that was why he insisted on visiting the temple before he went to the She Asses. He'd also been frightened. If he recognised the masks he could be implicated; after all, he was with Lady Antonia when she was kidnapped. Anyway, Sesothenes passed the information on. Lady Urbana, the caring lady of Rome, acted swiftly. She visited Senator Carinus, collected Theodore and went to the palace. Later that same day, Theodore died of poison.'

'Yes,' Urbana shrilled, 'but he died here.'

'No.' Claudia shook her head. 'Theodore did not drink poison here. I have checked most scrupulously. He was hungover. He complained of stomach pains, which began after he visited the Palatine Palace, the one occasion when you three, Urbana, Cassia and Leartus, were closeted with him. I was with the Empress, you had to wait; the imperial chamberlain served you wine and honey cakes. I have established that. At the time it was three against one. Cassia distracted Theodore, whilst you, Urbana, served the poison, pouring it into his wine, some slow-acting potion which would start like indigestion. The writer Celsus lists such poisons and their effects. Lady Urbana, you are proficient in poisons, aren't you? Leartus claimed you were an expert on herbs, yet there's nothing about poisonous plants in the library at Aurelian's villa. I suppose such texts are kept separately in your own chamber, along with your powders. You are an assassin! Alexander's blood is on your hands, as is your husband's. If Alexander died and General Aurelian survived that would not advance your plans; both had to die together. You are cold-hearted and scheming. You knew the effect Alexander's death would have on his father, and you helped Aurelian into the dark. A secret potion, a deadly powder mixed with his wine, and his death would be viewed merely as a result of terrible shock. I am sure,' Claudia added with a smile, 'the imperial searchers who are now ransacking the villa will find more evidence of your knowledge of herbs.'

'How dare you!' Urbana shouted.

'The imperial chamberlain Chrysis,' Helena sweetly declared, 'has been dispatched to your villa. He will search it from the cellars to the farthest part of your garden. If you have nothing to fear, then it will serve no harm. If damage is done, the imperial treasury will compensate you. That is,' Helena's voice changed, 'if you ever return there.'

Claudia was watching Leartus, who sat, shoulders slumped, lost in his own thoughts.

'Leartus?'

He looked up. Claudia's heart leapt. If he conceded . . .

'You are a warrior,' Claudia declared, 'and the son of a warrior. You bear the mark of a chieftain. You invoked the blood feud. Some might say you carried out true judgement against men who murdered their own officer, tortured your father and were directly responsible for the deaths of all of your comrades, not to mention your father's second wife. You could have appealed to the Emperor for justice. General Aurelian would have listened, but instead you took the warrior's path. You are still a Pict, Leartus. Here is your chance to die like a warrior. You are undoubtedly guilty of the crimes I have listed against you. Two paths open up before you. Slow, excruciating torture at the hands of the imperial interrogators, followed by crucifixion outside the city gates; or a warrior's death here tonight, at the hands of another warrior, Burrus. The choice is yours, to confess or not.'

Leartus kicked off his sandals, stood up, took the chain from his neck, the bracelets from his wrists, the rings from his fingers and threw them to the ground. He undid his belt and shrugged off his tunic so he stood naked in his loincloth. Tilting back his head, he began to chant in a strange language, staring up at the sky, stretching out his hands. Cassia tried to claw his arm but he shrugged her off. Urbana screamed, clear proof of her own guilt, but Leartus continued to chant, his voice growing stronger. He paused and squatted, hands on his thighs, and stared across at Claudia.

'You are fortunate, mistress,' he began. 'Your man is a warrior. I watched him fight in the arena. My heart went out to him. What you say is true. I am the son of a Pictish chieftain, a former slave, castrated by my captors, sold in Rome, employed by the Lady Cassia. I never, how could I, forget that night. I became separated from my father. I hid beneath a corpse out in the heather. I took my torque and bracelets and put them on another body. The night passed. Dawn came. The Romani were drunk. They thought we were all dead. I watched them take off their armour so they could enjoy my father being tortured.' He clawed the side of his face. 'I always prayed,' he whispered, 'that the time of blood would come.' He smiled. 'General Aurelian's parties! One after another, year in and year out, then it was the turn of the Fretenses. I saw them! The time of blood had arrived. The ghosts of the past had caught up with my soul. Petilius recognised me. I certainly recognised him and the rest. I invoked the blood feud. My father's shade and those of his followers demanded their deaths. I was still a warrior. I enjoyed killing them. I do not regret it.

'For the rest,' he sighed, 'you are correct.' He gestured round the garden. 'Rome! Do you like it, Claudia?' He pointed at Urbana and Cassia. 'They don't. They are the daughters of British tribesmen. They enjoy Christianity because it's still special, not truly Roman. They once worshipped Egyptian goddesses, whom they replaced with the Magdalena. I thought it was amusing. Aurelian would not do what Urbana wanted. He underestimated the dark rages, the pride seething in her. She hated Aurelian and all he stood for. It was so easy. I dealt with Sesothnes, meeting him disguised in the dark, giving him instructions, distributing his share of the spoils. As you said, no one was hurt, no real harm was done. Why should I object if a few fat, wealthy Romans lost their children for a few days for a small portion of their wealth? Especially compared with what I had lost. I never really overcame my hatred for Romans or their city.' He turned his head. 'I had no objections to their games or their stupid pursuit of dusty knowledge. When Alexander was killed, I began to wonder, then General Aurelian died and I suspected. The gods know that I had no hand in that. I watched your man in the arena and I knew what it was to be a warrior, to fight in the sunlight, to be honest and true. If you had not confronted me, perhaps I would have left Rome, taken my secrets to the grave, but why should I die on a cross? For what? No, I'll take the warrior's way.'

'And what Claudia has accused Lady Urbana and Cassia of is the truth?' Helena asked sharply.

'It is the truth.' Leartus got to his feet. 'I wish to be gone.'

'Burrus!' Helena called into the darkness. The German came forward, his sword already drawn. 'Not here,' the Empress declared, 'not here, where we are being entertained. Find some lonely spot. Let it be done quickly.'

Leartus bowed towards Claudia and, ignoring the rest,

allowed the German to take him away. Helena was now sitting up on the edge of her couch; Constantine no longer acted the drunk.

'You should be crucified!' he shouted. 'For the evil you have done.'

'No, no,' Helena interrupted. 'You, Cassia, I believe, once called yourself the Queen of the Night. You are correct. Both of you are Queens of the Night, ladies of the dark. You plotted kidnappings, abductions, murder and treason. You, Urbana, killed your own husband, a general of Rome, and his lovely young son Alexander, for what? For money? And you, Cassia, as always, you followed. You were hers,' Helena spat the words out and pointed at Urbana, 'body and soul!' The Empress straightened up. 'Claudia's accusations are proven. Leartus' confession simply confirms it. I am sure my searchers at the villa will seal your fate. However, you will not die on the cross.'

Urbana began to sob.

'Silence,' the Empress ordered. 'Murranus here appealed to the ancient rites of Rome. So do I. Both of you will be taken out to the Polluted Fields and sealed in an underground chamber. You will stay there without food or drink for forty days. If you are still protesting your innocence at the end of that period, I will think again, but I believe you are truly guilty. The Empire demands justice and so does God.' Helena raised a hand and snapped her fingers. 'Take them away.'

*   *   *

The trumpets brayed, sending the birds whirling up to the sky to cry raucously at being disturbed. The Polluted Fields had been prepared for the entombment of two leading ladies of Rome. Urbana and Cassia had been paraded in a cart throughout the city, squatting in dirty, ash-strewn clothes, their heads shorn, their faces branded, exposed to the fury of the mob. They left the city by the Coelian Gate. By then the mob had grown tired of the catcalling, throwing stones and refuse. Behind the cart marched a squad of the imperial guard, and alongside it a troop of auxiliary cavalry. Both women were broken, and by the time they reached the Polluted Fields they crouched heads down, not even touching each other.

Helena had ordered Claudia and Murranus to witness the women's end. The summons had been delivered by Burrus, who was now helping the prisoners, wrists and ankles chained, out of the cart, dragging them along the pebbled path towards the grey stone steps which led down to the execution chamber built beneath the earth. Claudia, at the Empress' command, had already visited it to ensure all was prepared. She had never experienced such an eerie, sombre, godforsaken place. Grey walls, grey paving stones, grey roof, no aperture, no window, nothing but a bench and a table and, on that, a pewter tray with two earthenware cups of water and chunks of dry rye bread, the last they would ever be given. The door was of heavy oak reinforced with steel bands and metal studs. Once it was closed, there would be no light, no air, nothing but a yawning darkness. Claudia had felt a pang of sorrow for both women, but Murranus reminded her of Alexander coughing out his blood, Aurelian dying heartbroken, as well as the terror and squalor experienced by the children who'd been kidnapped.

The executioner, a jolly-faced man without his hideous dog mask, had followed them around asking if all was in order. Claudia had replied that it was. Now she and Murranus stood at the top of those sombre steps watching the two women being hustled towards their deaths. She hardly recognised them. They now clung to each other, sobbing quietly, faces streaked, clothing nothing more than stained rags. At the top of the steps the chains were loosened, their ropes cut and both women were thrust down into the darkness. Neither one looked at Claudia, who had brought them to this place of justice. Claudia closed her eyes as she heard a shriek, then the executioner pushed them into the chamber, slamming the door behind them, padlocking the chain, nailing up the notice of death.

Claudia opened her eyes and stared across the execution ground. Nearby rose five crosses, gibbets for the corpses of the Egyptians Murranus had killed. She averted her gaze; the bodies were drained of blood, smeared with dung and dirt after being dragged through the city. She truly hated this horrid place with its sparse grass, grey stone chambers jutting above the earth and wooden gibbets stark against the sky. She pinched Murranus on the wrist.

'Follow me.'

They left the execution ground and walked across the heathland to where they had once sat sharing bread and wine. Claudia stretched, sat down under the shade of a holm oak and stared back at the guards. Most of them were being dismissed, except for the four who would spend the first quarter of the day on guard. Claudia picked at a tuft of grass, smelled its freshness and rubbed it between her hands.

'Ye gods,' she muttered, 'Helena has had her vengeance.'

'Justice!' Murranus replied, sitting down beside her. 'Justice, Claudia, think of the dead.'

'I am,' she retorted, staring down at the gibbets stark against the sky. 'But I have one question for you, Murranus.' She turned to face him squarely. 'Why were you so certain, I mean about winning?'

'Because I'm the best.'

'Arrogance!' she snapped and jabbed a finger in his face. 'Tell me the truth.'

'They were guilty,' Murranus declared. 'You know that. The house owned by the Egyptians provided the evidence; more was found in the catacombs.'

'Tell me,' Claudia shouted. 'Tell me now or I'll get up and walk away. I watched you in the arena, Murranus, I cried for you. I deserve to know.'

Murranus blew out his cheeks. 'Helena,' he spoke softly, 'she told me to challenge them and then we plotted.'

'What?'

'She encouraged Sesothenes and his followers to accept my challenge by telling them I was injured, that the blow to my head had been very serious. She did this through others, time and again the same message, how I was slow, disconcerted. I joined in the pretence, deliberately acting so at the gladiatorial school. She helped matters along by secretly placing considerable silver on the wager that the Egyptians would win.'

'Bitch!' Claudia retorted.

'She did more than that. She sent her spies back into the training ground. I was informed of all the preparations by Sesothenes and his gang. Who was the most dangerous, who was slow, what tactics they were deploying. Helena even offered to drug them, but that would have been too obvious.' He smiled at Claudia, who was glaring furiously at him. 'In the end they were killed. They were not gladiators.'

'No,' Claudia declared softly. 'They certainly were not, and neither are you, Murranus.' She seized his face between her hands. 'That was your last fight!'

Author's Note

Many of the strands of this historical novel are based on fact. The historian Eusebius of Caesarea gives a graphic description of the conversion of Constantine before the battle of the Milvian Bridge. The same historian also details the deep psychological hold Helena exerted over Constantine, who conferred on her the title of 'The Most Noble Lady'. The Empress' search throughout the Roman Empire for relics of the Saviour is also well documented, particularly her desire to find the True Cross.

The persecutions of Diocletian and Maxentius were a brutal purge of the Christian faith. During this pogrom it was common practice for women accused of being members of the new faith to be carried off, threatened, sexually harassed and eventually executed. One of the best-known examples of this was Catherine of Alexandria, who was martyred in Rome shortly before the date in which this novel is set.

The remains of Christian martyrs were collected secretly and given sacred burial. The most famous example was that of St Peter, whose remains were always thought to lie beneath St Peter's Church in Rome, though this was not scientifically established until late in the 1960s. Once the persecutions were over, the Christian Church emerged from the catacombs and, through men like Sylvester, began to exert its political muscle, quickly winning favour with the Empress and her son. They also gained possession of notable temples in Rome such as the Pantheon. The Christian era had begun, the Church, within a lifetime, moving from a persecuted sect to becoming the state religion.

The preservation of a saint's body was regarded as a sign of God's favour. It is one of those phenomena science cannot explain. One of the most recent instances is the corpse of the visionary St Bernadette Soubirous, to whom the Virgin Mary appeared at Lourdes. Of course, arsenic also has the power to slow down, or even halt, the process of decomposition. Until the advent of scientific pathology, it was very difficult to detect except by the exhumation of the corpse. There are many types of arsenic and their effects vary, but it is quite probable that a character like Theodore was killed by such a potion. It is also worth pointing out that when the Gare du Nord in Paris was built in the nineteenth century and cemeteries were dug up and corpses removed, it became common knowledge just how many corpses had not decomposed; perhaps they, too, were the victims of murder. Certainly the historians Plutarch and Quintus Curtius comment on Alexander's corpse being marvellously preserved, even though he died at the height of summer in Babylon.

One of the most thorough guides to arsenic and its effects

is the ponderous but very detailed study by A. W. Blythe, *Poisons: their effects and detection* (London, 1920). Blythe's description of the potency of arsenic in corpses after death is worth quotation.

A remarkable preservation of the body is commonly observed, when it does occur it may have great significance particularly when the body is placed in conditions in which it might be expected to decompose rapidly. In the celebrated continental case of the apothecary Speichert [1876] the body of Speichert's wife was exhumed eleven months after her death. The coffin stood partly in water, the corpse was mollified, the organs contained arsenic, the Church yard earth yielded no arsenic. R. Koch [the defence lawyer] was unable to explain the preservation of the body under these conditions in any other way than from the effect of arsenic, and this circumstance, with others, was an important element which led to the conviction of Speichert.

Finally, the legends of Mary Magdalene have appeared in many recent books, the most notable being *The Da Vinci Code*. According to local legends, Mary Magdalene and her associates landed near Marseilles and moved out into the countryside to found their own settlement, and around this story a rich and detailed folklore has emerged.

Paul C. Doherty
November 2005
www.paulcdoherty.com